OBJECTS IN LAKES

RACHAEL RAMAS

RISING ACTION

Distributed by Simon & Schuster

ISBN: 978-1-998672-38-7
Ebook: 978-1-998672-39-4

FIC031100 FICTION / Thrillers / Domestic
FIC030000 FICTION / Thrillers / Suspense

#ObjectsInLakes

Follow Rising Action on our socials!
Twitter: @RAPubCollective
Instagram: @risingactionpublishingco
Tiktok: @risingactionpublishingco

To my daughter,
who gave me the courage to believe
in childhood dreams again

AUTHOR WARNING:
PROCEED WITH EXTREME CAUTION

Dear Reader,

This book is not for the faint of heart. Within these pages lie stories soaked in grief, secrets, and bad choices. If you have ever:

- Lost sleep over a tragedy you couldn't stop,
- Wondered what really happens behind closed doors,
- Trusted a neighbor only to realize you never truly knew them,
- Or been haunted by the what-ifs of one reckless night…

then consider this your warning.

Here you will find a child's drowning that will break your heart, infidelity that cuts deep, alcohol and drug use that spirals, and neighbors who wear smiles in the daylight but hide shadows in the dark. This is not a comfort read. It's a confrontation. A reminder that the people we wave to across the street, toast glasses with at 4th of July parties, or lean on in fragile moments may hold the heaviest secrets of all.

If any of this feels too close, too raw, or too real, this is your chance to step away.
If not? Breathe deep. The water's colder than you think, and the truth is murkier than it seems.

With dark honesty and no apologies,
RACHAEL RAMAS

OBJECTS IN LAKES

PROLOGUE

MONDAY 9 P.M.
JULY 4, 2016

THEN

She's lying near the dock. I'm waiting for the exhale. A dark thought flickers through my head, something sinister. I know the difference between right and wrong, but sometimes I can find a grey area. A rush of energy surges through me. I have only moments to make a decision. Moments that will determine the rest of my life.

She appears asleep. She looks classically pretty, like a Disney princess. People cheer from up the hill as fireworks start shooting off from the small island in the middle of the lake. The vibrant colors illuminate her body–making her look like something out of a fairytale.

When nothing's good enough, we tend to hurt the ones around us. I've never lashed out before, but I've felt it creeping up for quite some time. And oddly, this is an escape from pain for me. Her chest appears to be moving, but I can't be certain. I also can't risk it. With a final, measured breath, I commit to the choice before me. Gently but firmly, I guide her into the embrace of the water, where she slips beneath the surface, her slight silhouette swallowed by the depths.

It's easy to label someone as bad, but it's harder to ask *why*. A summer storm approaches overhead, violent dark clouds appearing vividly over the water, blocking out the moon. The incoming rain will wash away my summer's sin. I hear the wind whisper, "I'll save you." Everyone has their own bent version of the truth. My secret truth rests with her now, at the bottom of the lake.

PART ONE

"The alternative to tragedy, or at least to the risk of tragedy, is damnation. The only place outside of Heaven where you can be perfectly safe from all the dangers and perturbations of love is Hell."

—C.S. Lewis, *The Four Loves*

CHAPTER 1

FRIDAY 3 A.M.
JUNE 23, 2023

It was trash day on the lake. Dawn had yet to break, but Olive Wentworth awoke in pure panic at her usual time: 3:03 a.m. She found herself drenched in sweat, heart hammering in her chest, a paradox of exhaustion and alertness. She stayed motionless for some time, a high-pitched buzz lingering in her ears. She was her very own sleep saboteur. Since the incident, for seven years, as dawn crept through the curtains, the same vision entwined itself into her slumber—a bitter reel of memories. It was a dream that began with the innocence of her daughter's laughter, the sweetness of her tiny hands reaching out, and kisses as light and fresh as strawberries. But these images, so full of life, would cruelly morph into the harrowing sight of her daughter's motionless figure abandoned at the water's edge.

Only in Michigan can you travel from Paradise to Hell, two local destinations, in a mere five-hour drive, much like the five hours of sleep Olive was able to obtain, transitioning from something so beautiful to so dark. As the calendar pages fluttered closer towards the dual milestones of July Fourth's festivity and her own forty-second birthday on the third, they fanned the embers of her anxiety rather than quenching the fire of her turmoil.

Despite the internal ferment of these looming dates, the morning outside was ordinary: a mid-June Friday in Bloomfield Township. It was trash and recycling pickup, the weekly ritual. Olive found solace in these simple routines; her long Friday strolls through the subdivision offered quiet glimpses into the lives of her neighbors. Since the onset of the pandemic and her only son's recent entrance into college life, solitude had become her prevailing companion. But the discarded items on Fridays kept her going, telling tales of their own—*clues* about what her neighbors were up to.

Michiganders, polite by nature, weren't exempt from the whispers that cloak even the affluent suburbs of Detroit. Olive observed that the courtesy here only refined the gossip that simmered beneath the polished veneer.

Just last Friday, she spotted a telling tableau right outside her window. There, Mrs. Schmidt was a silhouette against the morning light, unceremoniously laying out her husband's prized possessions at the curb. A kayak and a bicycle, one of each tagged with a forlorn "FREE" sign. In that silent giveaway was an unspoken declaration, a subtle yet definitive echo of the rumors that had been caressing the neighborhood's curiosity, whispering of the Schmidts' fractured vows.

Terrance Wilson, a once-celebrated defensive end for the Detroit Lions and now a self-assured bachelor, resided adjacent to her home. Olive occasionally caught glimpses of top-shelf, aged whisky bottles mingled with containers from gourmet meal prep kits in his recycling, the remnants of his solitary, yet seemingly refined, lifestyle.

Then there was the Baker residence; their recyclable bin was once a reservoir of wine bottles. Malbec to be exact. Lately, however, it had been showcasing a healthier palette of empty bottles of water and diet pop. Rumors swirled that Julie Baker had checked herself into rehab. Olive seldom observed Colin Baker nursing a drink, but his wife Julie turned into a spitfire under the influence. At a past July Fourth gathering, she drank so fervently that her lips bore a shade of maroon. The scene had prompted Olive to coin a playful nickname for her, "PAM" —Purple-Ass Mouth. Olive even felt the moniker suited her more, given her towering stature. Olive had yet to encounter a tall "Julie." That occasion marked Olive's final dance with alcohol, seven years ago in retrospect; she had grown older, yet not necessarily wiser. Because while seven was synonymous with luck and completeness, Olive felt deprived of both.

Shifting her focus to the present, Olive rested her eyes on her husband of seventeen years. He was immersed in a deep, untroubled sleep, seemingly devoid of any worldly concerns. How effortlessly serene it would be to live as a man. She takes a breath as the cooing of a mourning dove resonates through the room from the ajar window. Inhale; *coo, coo*; exhale. The remnants of her dream linger, its presence hovering right at the surface of her awareness, proposing a sanctuary she could almost inhabit. Because at the beginning of that dream, her daughter was still very much alive. However, the time has come to embrace reality.

She extends a tentative hand, coaxing her phone awake. The screen now glows 5:43 a.m., a silent testament to the hours lost to her restless mind's meanderings. As she shifts her body from bed to bathroom, she stubs her toe against the door. "*Gosh darn it*" is a typical midwestern phrase, but in this moment, Olive yearns to utter something more potent. Clamping her hand over her mouth, she stifles the pain curdling inside, careful not to disrupt her husband's peaceful slumber. Richie needs his rest. After all, as Dr. Richard Wentworth, he was obligated to save lives once he woke up.

She momentarily confronts her reflection in the bathroom mirror, a sight she no longer has fondness for. She exchanges no daily affirmations or self-appreciations, only touches the small scar residing on her right cheek. Then, with a limp, she proceeds to the kitchen and activates the coffee maker. It's her most cherished moment of the day, when she can observe the sunlight gradually illuminate and dance on the lake's surface. Duck Lake, it seems, has ironically lost the ducks it is named after in the past few years. In hopes of drawing some ducks up the challenging ascent of her hillside home, Olive procured a bird feeder the previous summer. Yet, it mostly attracted the sporadic robin or curious squirrel.

Her quiet rumination and the calm of dawn are soon abruptly shattered by the sound of an object colliding with the hardwood floor. Investigating the noise, she rounds the corner to discover their family photo, once enclosed in a frame, now broken into countless pieces. She should have known better than to rely on those adhesive wall frames. Her eyes pause on the photograph with a tenderness that feels like a caress, her gaze absorbing the sunlit smiles that beam back from what seems like another lifetime. Each face is an echo of joy, captured in the permanence of print, a visual whisper from a past drenched in the laughter of when she had two children, instead of only one.

"Hon, is the coffee ready?" Her husband is awake and today holds importance for him. Olive opts to abandon the failed frame for now and inspects the brewing coffee. For a fleeting moment, she envisions herself seizing the piping hot handle and pouring it onto her left hand. It's a searing, misguided yearning for something palpable, a cry for attention that could manifest in a physical form—a burn that her husband would have to acknowledge, something to break his constant cycle of work. A reason significant enough to make him stay, instead of them continuing as two separate vessels, drifting past each other's harbors in the night with little more than a handful of words exchanged. Perhaps then, she might let a single tear finally slip free. She's aware these are just intrusive thoughts, as Dr. Eisenberg would say. However, she's also acutely aware that the past seven years have felt like a vague, indistinct haze, akin to the sensation one experiences when driving to a well-known location and arriving with no memory of the journey.

As the initial sip of coffee caresses her husband's lips, an assertive knock at the front door causes them both to jolt. They rise, still clad in their matching His & Her bathrobes. The microwave clock displays 6:06. Olive looks at her husband, then the door. In the seventeen years they lived on Duck Lake, no one has ever knocked on their door this early. As he meets her emerald eyes, her petite frame makes Richie seem taller than he actually is. "Stay here," he directs, striding towards the front door.

From her vantage in the kitchen, Olive strains her ears, attempting to discern who could be visiting at this early hour. However, all she can catch are muted exchanges, punctuated by the occasional heated undertone. The door rapidly clatters to a close. Richie rushes past her towards the bedroom. Olive holds her breath for a moment, treading on metaphorical eggshells as the look on Richie's face is no longer inviting.

He then reenters the kitchen. "Don't forget, the award ceremony is tonight. How about you wear that green dress?"

"Who was that?" Olive asks, disregarding Richie's question.

"What?"

"At the door?" she whispers.

"Nobody," Richie murmurs before disappearing into the bathroom, where the sound of the shower begins to fill the space between them.

After their daughter's tragic passing, Olive felt as if she wore an invisible "N" over her heart, her own personal scarlet letter. But unlike Hester Prynne's, this one didn't mark shame so much as negligence, a quiet guilt she bore. Richie's warmth had cooled into indifference, and hers followed suit. Because female nature, she believed, is like an echo—an emotional reflection. And in the lingering stillness of a world still reeling from the pandemic's aftershocks, Olive felt her isolation thickening, her solitude deepening into something harder to put a name to. Yet, she refrains from burdening her husband with the turbulence that lies lurking within her. This evening is to be dedicated to celebrating his achievements; she is resolved not to taint the occasion for him. She must regain her composure and focus. It's time to take her pills.

The air grows thick as she opens her tacklebox of medications and finds the "Friday AM" slot empty. There will be no time for her neighborhood trash walk today.

"Well, honey, doctors are sadists who like to play God and watch lesser people scream," Dr. Eisenberg says while chuckling and leaning back in his chair. The light peering through the window reflects off his balding head that still holds a few strands of grey. Olive stares back at him with no expression. Ironically, for someone who once wanted to become a doctor, she hates doctors' offices. She also hates the way Dr. Eisenberg speaks, not because he's long-winded and loves quoting movies, but because his mouth makes a whistling sound that irritates her. If only she hadn't just discovered this morning that one of her medicines needed a refill. She didn't even remember taking the last pill, and she was not going to bother her husband to write the refill on today of all days.

"Name the movie," he commands.

"Dr. Eisenberg, I really appreciate you sliding me in today, but I'm kind of in a hurry. If you can refill the prescription, that would be great," she answers back, refusing to engage in his trivia. He stares at her with a concerned look and responds to her, *Juno.*

"I'm sorry? Juno, Alaska?"

"No, *Juno* the movie. Where that young girl gets pregnant ..."

"Dr. Eisenberg, I just really need my refill," Olive interrupts. "I have a big event tonight for Richie, and I have to be with it and alert." The familiar grip of anxiety tightened within her at the prospect of facing the day unaided by her medicinal ritual. After her daughter's funeral, once the stream of bundt cakes and sympathy cards had trickled to nothing, her husband buried himself further into work, leaving her alone with nothing but her own ways of coping. Her son was her only reason to stay on earth, but she needed strength and found it at the bottom of pill bottles. The small, prescribed salvations kept her treading water in a sea of loneliness. Now, they were her only companions, the quiet supporters in her silent struggle.

"Have, want, and need are all different requests." He was back at it with his banter and staring at her more intently now, as if studying her face for any sign of life. "Olive, I've got to be honest, I'm worried about you. You've been on so many different medications over the past several years. You, of all people, with your medical background, have to know it's not great for your body. I really think it's time to give some of this stuff a break."

Olive presses her frail hands against her temples. It is glaringly obvious that Dr. Eisenberg lacks any real understanding of motherhood. His ignorance is blatant. Had he any insight, he would comprehend that a mother's body can take up to seven years to recuperate from childbirth completely. But what is the recovery period for losing a child? Particularly when it occurred due to her own inadvertence? The answer is simple: it's forever.

"James, you of all people know how upset my husband can get. I don't think he would like to know that you are refusing a request that will allow me to joyfully attend his big medical event tonight." Olive hated name-dropping, but she also loved the way people respected her husband. He was one of the top oncologists in the state, prominent in the community for saving lives, having very elite connections, making money for charities, fundraising for their church, St. Thomas, and sponsoring all the Little League teams. Because he was respected by the community, so was she. She had come a long way from being thirteen years old, left outside a 7-Eleven to wait while her dad bought twenty-four-oz Labatt Blues and scratch-off tickets.

Dr. Eisenberg pulls out his prescription pad and starts writing with a black ballpoint pen. "I believe in the power of medication. I also believe you no longer need this stuff." He pauses and stops writing. "Did I ever tell you about the time I almost got abducted by the Oakland County Child Killer?" The doctor loved to tell this story. No one truly knew who the Oakland County Child Killer was, as the killer was never caught, and his last abduction was in 1976. But Dr. Eisenberg seemed to understand.

"Timmy asked me to go up to the corner store with him on our bikes. I said no, I had to finish my homework. Next thing we know, Timmy is found dead in a ditch six days later. The last victim. That could have been me with him, don't you know it? And soon thereafter, the sketchy elder gentleman who lived down the road moved out. I know it was that guy. It's never a boogeyman. It's always someone you know." Dr. Eisenberg grabs a tissue, tears forming in his eyes. He had started to become more sentimental in his old age. Olive figured that meant it was time for him to retire.

"Boy, I was so sad for Timmy and even more so for his poor mother. I prayed for her every night until she passed. She was never the same. I do know she started going to some meetings, maybe a grief meeting or some therapy. Hey, I bet you could find something like that? Try something new?" He finishes his speech, the whistle sound of his mouth still burning in her ears.

Therapy.

Her father used to tell her therapy was for weak people, but then again, some people have a therapist, while her father had a bottle of bourbon.

For Olive, the online grief forum she had turned to in the raw aftermath of the drowning became a cacophony of platitudes that rang hollow in her ears. "She's in a better place," they said, or "Time heals all wounds," and the ever-echoing "You can't change the past." The multitude of voices, each one crooning a different tune of supposed solace, eventually drove her to silence them all. In a decisive click, she erased her presence from social media, shutting out the relentless noise that could not fill the voice of her loss.

Olive stands up and bends down to grab the script. "The difference between me and Timmy's mom is that I found my four-year-old daughter floating dead a couple of feet from my own home, Doctor. No serial killer took her from me, only God Himself." Olive remembers praying for a miracle, but it didn't happen. Richie did everything he could to bring her back. But she was gone.

Olive grabs her designer purse and tucks her dark, long, wavy hair behind her ears. She pauses. Maybe she was being too hard on the old doctor. "I appreciate your help. I do. Have a good day." Now she just needed to get through this impending evening.

CHAPTER 2

FRIDAY 6 P.M.
JUNE 23, 2023

Olive enters the ballroom of The Townsend Hotel arm in arm with her husband. The theme is fire and water. A massive fire dancer demonstrates the concept of heat, the flames licking the air as the dancer's moves seem to crackle with intensity. The underwater theme came from the live jellyfish tanks with fish that resembled coral. Little stations set up around the room offered some of the best food Detroit has to offer.

Olive wears her most expensive one-carat emerald earrings and a matching vibrant silk dress. Both bring out the green in her eyes. She knows she is an extension of Richie with the things she is wearing. He'd given her the earrings a year after Kate was born, the following May. It wasn't a Mother's Day gift from Richie, but more of a *sorry we found out our baby girl has cancer* gift. It was a rare genetic blood disease, but she was expected to beat it. Olive had been hopeful back then.

The event was black tie, so Richie is, of course, in his freshly steamed Armani tux, his jet-black hair slicked back. He had always been dangerously handsome, and when combined with his intelligence, it was lethal in a James Bond way. His handsome face is accentuated by a strong jawline and a charming smile, making him all the more alluring. And his eyes. Olive could never exactly pinpoint the color. She supposed they were brown, but they were mesmerizing, captivating orbs—sometimes brownish hazel, other times a greyish green framed by long, feathery lashes that seemed to draw you in. It was his eyes that first caught Olive's attention during their initial encounter in a chemistry class at the start of her first year of medical school. Back in those early days, his eyes seemed to see only her.

Now, everyone is looking at Richie. He is the focal point of the evening. She is to sit there, smile, and look pretty. Her dress is revealing but not *too* revealing. Her rib cage silhouette peers through. She wears her hair in a glam updo, the picture of sophistication.

Richie kisses her collarbone while entering the ballroom, mouthing the words *beautiful*, his way of apologizing for being short with her earlier that morning. Olive is then quickly left unattended at their assigned table. She stands, waiting to greet her husband's co-workers, who are to be seated soon. She watches from afar as Richie gets hugs and high-fives. His star is on the rise. He's a big name now; nobody can doubt that.

The year Kate was born, Olive was elated to attend a similar award ceremony. It was her first opportunity in years to socialize with adults, leaving their six-year-old son, Landon, and newborn Kate in the care of her mother-in-law. She'd put on a sexy dress for the occasion, one Richie had chosen. He told her it made her look skinny, and she thrived on the little compliments he gave her. The dress fit snugly, and the milk made her chest look full. That evening was all glitter—champagne flutes clinking, music pulsing past midnight. But by morning, Olive sat on the couch in worn pajamas, cradling baby Kate, sipping lukewarm coffee, cartoons flickering in the background. She never minded supporting Richie's ambitions, but a small part of her still wondered what might've become of her own. Would her career have taken root if Richie hadn't pushed her to leave med school by her second year after getting pregnant with Landon? Richie had insisted there was no need for her to take on more student loan debt; he'd take care of everything. He was traditional in that way, preferring her to be at home. Within nine months, he'd used his inheritance to buy the lake house. And while it was beautiful, Olive remembered how lonely those early days were, just her and two little kids, the silence louder than she expected.

Now, surrounded by hundreds of people dressed to the nines, she feels even more profoundly, deeply alone.

The sound of someone suckling water next to her shifts her

attention. It's Mrs. Satchel, Dr. Satchel's wife. "He's such a catch; you're a lucky lady," she says with a wink. She's older, probably in her early sixties, but still looks magnificent. Fillers and a facelift can do wonders.

Olive nods with a shy smile.

"Where did your son decide to attend college? Please tell me he's a fellow Wolverine?"

Olive shakes her head. "Landon received early admission to CCS."

Mrs. Satchel sits there, her brow knitting in confusion.

"The College for Creative Studies in Detroit. He's actually working with a professor there this summer on an internship project. Only two students were selected."

"How wonderful. Richie made it seem like he was maybe going to be pre-med or pre-law. There's always time for him to change his mind, honey."

Olive nods politely. To Richie's dismay, she knew their son inherited his creative genes from her. She, too, enjoyed painting and the arts but was determined to go to medical school after her mother passed from ALS when she was in her early teens. She tried to think of the last time she had painted something. It had been years. What Richie didn't know was that their son was, in fact, doing medical work, making 3D imaging for amputee victims. Landon didn't want her to tell his father, didn't want to give him the satisfaction. He had slowly pulled away from Richie over the years, most likely because he was now the sole offspring left to carry on the family name in a good light. But she was proud of Landon and told him often. She missed him terribly since he left, but she knew it was his time.

As Landon grew more independent, Olive hoped fragments of her old self might return. But the emptiness only deepened. With the seventh anniversary approaching, something stirred—a quiet awareness. It hinted at a life beyond survival, a pull toward something greater, like a beacon flickering past the waves where she still felt lost.

The lights dim quickly as more people approach their tables and take their seats. Olive finds herself still waiting on Richie, and it feels excruciating because she hates small talk. She had a habit of going inwards and disconnecting from others when anxiety takes over, locking herself away like Rapunzel in a castle, cut off from real human connection. But there was nowhere to hide here. The air around her begins to feel hot, causing her to sweat profusely. She scans the room until she finds the guest of honor. Richie is still in his element, leaning in, shaking hands, and patting backs. She opens an Altoids container in her clutch, discreetly swallowing the orange contents.

A loud echo booms from the stage as Dr. Satchel knocks his Scotch against the podium microphone. Richie quickly beelines to his seat next to Olive. He fumbles with his phone as he slides it back into his jacket pocket. He puts his arm around her and smiles. But it isn't his normal smile. He usually has a commanding presence, always leading and never being led, but tonight he seems on edge.

"Tonight, we gather here to honor Dr. Richard Wentworth, head of oncology, and his team, for their achievements and another milestone in cancer research." He pauses to take a swig of his drink. "Richie, get up here, old boy."

The audience applauds and Richie heads to the stage. "Thank you, Dr. Satchel, but I believe you are the oldest boy in the room tonight." His co-workers all chuckle. "But really. This is quite the honor. This is such a special award to receive." He takes a moment and looks around the room. "This cure would have saved my daughter, Kate, if she hadn't drowned many, many years ago. I was working on this cure with her as we didn't have many candidates at the time who qualified. We lost her tragically in an accident before it could be finished and have been waiting to complete it until now."

Olive's face flushes. She knows people are staring at her. She was not aware that Richie was going to bring up Kate. She didn't even actually know why he was getting this award. There were too many to keep track of. She did know, however, that she preferred to be known as Dr. Richard Wentworth's wife, not the mom of the girl who drowned in Duck Lake. She hears people whispering behind her as her heart hammers in her chest.

Richie clears his throat. "Many people have the idea that a doctor is just one person who finds an antidote and makes money from it and hopefully saves lives along the way. However, they often overlook the fact that behind every doctor, there's a whole team. So, I am but one man among many trying to make a difference. I'm so grateful every day for all my successes. And sometimes I wish that I could go back to being that little boy named Richard serving up ice cream at Darby's with my dad, dreaming of becoming a doctor one day."

All eyes are back on Richie and Olive chuckles in her head. She knows he hated working at his family's famous ice cream store. He thought it was beneath him. She also knew he despised his late father. He was verbally abusive and treated Richie like garbage. He'd been even more cruel to Richie's mother, reducing her to little more than a prisoner in their home, never allowed to leave or live a life of her own. Outwardly, Mr. Wentworth Sr. exuded charm. A textbook Midwesterner: courteous, dependable, the kind of man others admired for his grit and quiet integrity. He was the neighbor you waved to, the man you trusted without question. No one would have guessed what he kept hidden behind closed doors.

"Lastly, I want to thank my amazing wife, Olive. Without her, I wouldn't be standing up here today. Her grace and compassion allow me to pour everything into these research projects and my patients. This one was for Kate, honey." Richie steps back from the podium. The audience sits back in amazement, then stands up and applauds. Dr. Richard Wentworth smiles as he steps down off the stage.

Now standing, Mrs. Satchel nudges Olive's elbow and winks again. Olive then feels the extra dose of medication hit her with an overwhelming force, blurring the vibrant dance of fire and water into a disconcerting haze. The jellyfish, once clear in her vision, now seems to be swallowed by the flickering inferno at the periphery, and Richie's figure approaches her through this distorted tableau, moving as if through a thick, resistant atmosphere, while the audience's applause persists.

Olive sits in a bathroom stall at The Townsend, eyes fixed on the ceiling as the lights seem to flicker overhead. She knows it's not the fixtures—they're far too elegant, too expensive for that. The flickering is happening inside her, a symptom of the disorienting haze she's been slipping in and out of. Outside the stall, the sharp cackling of two women echoes through the tiled space, punctuated by the click of high heels on marble.

"You know Lisa Hernandez was the original one who found it, right? Men always snatch the credit," one of them says.

"Lisa freaking Hernandez. She was noticeably absent tonight," the other states.

The sound of water running and paper towel ripping etches in Olive's ears.

"Well, it doesn't hurt he's hot as hell. I'd gladly trade my health for a chance to get some one-on-one time with McDreamy," the other responds, then both women erupt in laughter.

"You're so bad."

CHAPTER 3

MONDAY 9 A.M.
JULY 4, 2016
THEN

Olive watched from the deck as Kate and Landon ran down towards the dock, where a nearby wakeboard boat's velocity pushes the waves hard against their human-made beach. They had at least 110 feet of prime lakefront footage as they chased a duck they'd named Lulu. She was the closest thing to a pet they could have, and she visited often. In fact, ten-year-old Landon was convinced Lulu lived under their dock. He'd been a quiet and serious child since birth, but very sweet with Kate, and especially Olive. Richie was tough on him. Newly four, Kate, on the other hand, was a spitfire. For dealing with a life-altering disease since essentially birth, she wouldn't sit down for a minute. Her joy was infectious. She especially enjoyed the Michigan summers that turned into beautiful fall evenings. She hated winter and spring because that's when her father brought her to the hospital for testing the most. Olive knew she didn't like the poking and prying and experimenting.

The children continued to observe in awe as Lulu's little body swished through the cresting miniature mountains of the lake; each time she flew from in front of the children, they had to run to regain their view.

"I have her," Kate said to her brother. She ran down the shoreline by the dock, catching her breath.

"No, you didn't, you scared her!"

"No, I had her and then *you* scared her."

"You didn't have her," he said back sternly. He tried to peek under the dock to see if she was hiding there. He pulled out a frog to show Kate. She looked disgusted. "Here, let's play with Mr. Frog." He held out one hand to walk Kate back towards the grass, the other gripping the amphibian.

Olive smiled at them from up on the dock as she painted a beautiful willow tree that was on an easement between their property and the Bakers'. It was the same tree she had painted at least a dozen times. She had always been fascinated with it, but this time, she felt like she was seeing it for the very first time. Its whimsical branches dangled in the wind, almost touching the clear water.

Her serene thoughts were interrupted by the sound of Richie on the phone inside. She could see him pacing back and forth while biting his fingernails. He only bit his nails when he was stressed. She assumed it was about their annual Fourth of July party, which they hosted every year. Richie would always combine her birthday, which was the day before, with it into one big party. He liked to go over the top with catering the food and renting out a bartender, a Slip 'N Slide, and volleyball nets. He was even considering attempting his own firework show next year because he thought the town's fireworks were starting to become subpar.

She dropped her brush and walked down by the children who were now picking strawberries in their little garden. The decorative garden pinwheels spun with the wind, activating their chimes. In the distance, one of their neighbors played loud children's music from their boat speakers. "*Down by the Bay, where the watermelons grow, back to my home, I dare not go.*"

"Mommy, can we plant watermelon next summer?" Kate asked, her mouth full of plump strawberries.

"Of course, my love." Olive laid down in the old hammock next to them. She rocked back and forth, listening to the children continue to eat up all of her fresh produce like little bunnies.

"Mom, can I tell you something?" Landon continued to talk, without waiting for a reply. "Did you know that there are over 11,000 lakes in Michigan? And the Great Lakes are the largest freshwater system in the world?" Olive continued to rock back and forth as Landon kept talking. He had a photographic memory, so he could recite everything he learned from the books he read. The fresh air was starting to get to her and she struggled to keep her eyes open. "And did you know we also have the world's largest collection of freshwater sand dunes?"

"You don't even know all the Great Lakes, Landon," Kate replied, her hands on her little hips.

"Yes, I do, it's easy to remember. It spells HOMES. Huron, Ontario, Michigan, Erie, Superior."

A subtle weight shifted onto Olive's lap, tiny and familiar—it was Kate. Olive feigned sleep, a smile playing on her lips. Then came the added weight of Landon, making the hammock sway precariously.

"Four hugs a day—that's the secret to getting by," Landon whispered, sharing one of his wisdom-beyond-his-years phrases as he held her in a protective embrace. Kate wriggled, vying for more space, inching closer to Olive's face, until her small hands cradled her sun-kissed cheeks.

"Mommy, time to wake up. Wake up …"

CHAPTER 4

SATURDAY 3 A.M.
JUNE 24, 2023

Olive jolts upright, her skin prickling with the chill of an unseen lake, shivering as though she'd been swimming in the cool embrace of autumnal water. The phantom sensation of Kate's small hands on her face lingers. Her dream had been severed prematurely by her daughter's delicate voice, earnest and lucid, pulling her from sleep's grasp—and rescuing her from the dream's inevitable haunting finale that always waited in the shadows.

Her mind flashes to a moment of seeing her daughter's lifeless body face down, floating in the water, dazzling fireworks going off above her. Red fireworks. And red lights *now* fill her bedroom. Walking over to the window, she sees that there is a cop car and an ambulance parked out front, lights flashing, illuminating the street. It looks like they're parked in front of Terrance's house. Terrance and Richie were close back in the day. They used to banter back and forth in a verbal swordplay about who had the bigger ego and the bigger dick size.

Since his knee injury ended his football career, Terrance Wilson had invested heavily in real estate, while also purchasing rare sports cars and dating high-profile women. He was also a huge sports gambler and had lost a lot of money to it. He was still rich enough, however, for Terrance to stay in Richie's good graces. Yet Olive hadn't seen him around in quite some time, not that she had been seeking him out.

She mostly kept to herself unless it was something she needed to do for her son. The first three years after Kate passed, she only left the house to drive Landon to school and pick him up.

Last she heard, Terrance was on vacation in Sarasota visiting his daughter, Hannah, but he must have returned. Although, she hadn't noticed his trash cans out this past week.

From across the room, Richie groans loudly, then jerks a pillow over his head. She drops her gaze to the floor beside the bed, revealing her clutch, heels, and dress lying in a pile. Olive gradually reconstructs the events of last night. Her last memory was in the restroom—or was it driving home? Her focus shifts across the street, drawn by sudden movement at Terrance's house. The paramedics aren't coming from the front door, but from around the side, emerging from the backyard. That part of the subdivision curves around an inlet near the canal entrance, and like her own, Terrance's house backs up to the lake. They both share that shimmering view, the kind realtors highlight with bold font. Now, that same peaceful lake glints under the flicker of flashlight beams cutting through the darkness. Two figures trail behind a lead paramedic, maneuvering a stretcher up the slight slope of Terrance's yard. The person on it is heavyset—likely Terrance—strapped in tight, the wheels clicking softly beneath the weight. An officer steps forward to meet them, guiding the stretcher toward the open ambulance at the curb.

The sight jars something loose in Olive's memory. That hill. That same incline. She'd been carried up it once, too—her own backyard, her own blood trailing down her cheek as the world tilted off its axis. She'd felt no physical pain at the time. She only felt like the world was being pulled out from underneath her.

"What is going on?" Richie mumbles. He starts to pull the sheets down, tossing his pillow to the floor.

"It's Terrance. Something happened."

"What do you mean?" Richie gets up and heads toward Olive, peering out the window.

"Is that … Hannah?" he asks while squinting.

Olive nods yes, unable to speak. It sure is. Terrance's daughter is also at the side of the house, her hands clutching her mouth, as the officers speak to her. Hannah Wilson is not an eleven-year-old anymore. She's eighteen now, fully grown. But Olive could recognize her beautiful, naturally curly hair anywhere. She used to be best friends with Landon and would stay over most weeknights in the summer. Terrance only had custody of her over summer break, and she resided in Sarasota the rest of the year with her mother. All of that changed after the drowning, though.

"Why is Hannah here?" Richie enquires in a hush tone. "She hasn't been here since …" he stops himself. It had been since the night Kate passed away. In fact, there was speculation Hannah may have been one of the first to find her since she called 911 on the cellphone her mom gave her for emergencies. Olive couldn't blame her for not wanting to visit anymore. Landon took her leaving hard, but they continued to write to each other for years afterwards.

"I'm going to make a couple of calls and find out what's going on," Richie says in his stern doctor voice.

What is going on? Olive wonders, still mesmerized by the sudden reappearance of Hannah Wilson.

CHAPTER 5

SATURDAY 3 P.M.
JUNE 24, 2023

That afternoon, Olive sits quietly on the deck, the breeze teasing at the edges of her thoughts. She decides to skip her afternoon medications. Maybe Dr. Eisenberg was right; maybe it's time to ease up on them after all these years. They've done their job, perhaps too well. For too long, they've dulled her pain, her feelings, leaving her with just one mask to wear. And what good has it done? Not to mention, she can hardly recall leaving the event the night before—in the same way, the details of the night her daughter drowned remain a blurred void in her memory. And now, yet another tragedy has struck her neighborhood—another story of a life lost beneath the inviting surface of Duck Lake. Because there's the surface, which always looks safe and welcoming, and then there's what lies just beneath it.

And Olive can't shake the thought of how much longer she can stay afloat before she, too, is pulled under—grappling desperately at the rocks on the lake's bottom, searching for the truth hidden in the depths. Two bodies found in the same lake doesn't sit right with her.

To keep her mind from racing, she decides to pull out the old paint and easel kit. Richie has been gone since five a.m., when he received an update that Terrance had been rushed to the hospital with a slight pulse and left quickly after that. The cops had left as well. The neighborhood is now oddly quiet for a Saturday. Only one fishing boat floats out on the lake.

She paints the last bit of green onto the same old weeping willow tree when a mix of emotions swirls in her mind. Some parts are still hazy, but the ache in her heart is sharp and clear.

She wonders if she will have to paint the same tree for the rest of her life. That same tree that Richie and Terrance were in front of, trying to bring Kate back with CPR. She knew in her heart it was her fault. She knew because she couldn't fully remember the night. She'd had way too much to drink, and Richie often reminded her of that whenever they went at it after the drowning. She was irresponsible like her father. It was her job to watch over their daughter; she said she would before the party even started.

"Clearly, the mom was too inebriated to watch after the little one," the neighborhood whispered in hushed tones that nonetheless managed to pierce her being. How could she, in a moment marred forever by a lapse in judgment, expect a bunch of ten-year-olds to keep an eye on little firecracker Kate? Olive only went up the hill for more sparklers and a drink refill. Then she awoke with a shard of glass embedded in her cheek and a dead daughter.

They say time heals all, but her wounds were still open, raw and weeping, just like that old tree on the easement. After seven long years, one would expect a scar to form over such wounds. Instead, hers remained a profound lesion, occasionally crusting over, only for her to inevitably tear it open again, denying it the chance to mend fully. Perhaps this unresolved agony was why they never left. Many would be reluctant to reside in a place marked by such a tragic loss, but for Olive, relinquishing the sight of the beloved willow tree and the lake, both adored by her lost daughter, felt like a forfeit. If she lost the house, she would lose Kate entirely.

In this sacred place, she still felt a lingering closeness to her, as if she could still feel her presence, even though she was no longer physically there—much like how one of Landon's amputee clients might experience the phantom sensations of a missing limb. She insisted they stay put. Maybe that's where the resentment started to grow for Richie. He would much rather have sold the old thing and bought something bigger and better on a different nearby lake.

Olive lowers her brush into the crimson hue and touches

it to the weeping willow on her canvas, intending to dot the sky with a dash of color. However, another sudden intrusive thought overwhelms her concentration, and the brushstrokes stray, staining the whole cottonwood with the deep tint of wine.

"That's quite the painting," a man's voice rings out from behind her, startling her. She turns to find her next-door neighbor, Colin Baker. Communication between them has been minimal in recent years, restricted to the cursory Michigan head nod. Half the willow tree was technically his; the easement made it too hard to know the owner truly.

"I'm sorry, I didn't mean to scare you. My wife, Julie, she ..." He pauses. "She recently left. I mean she'll be back. She will." Colin says this in a hopeful tone that leaves much to Olive's imagination. Colin had always been one to keep to himself, much like her. And *Pam*, or technically Julie Baker, was presumably still safely tucked away in a rehab center as far as she knew, given the whispers around town. "And I just dropped my daughter off at sleepaway camp. I have no idea what to do with my time, and I don't mean to be a gossip. But I was up early this morning because I couldn't sleep. I noticed an ambulance at Terrance's house. I know Richie and he were close, and again I don't mean to pry ..." Colin lets out an exhale, then buries his hands in his Wrangler Jeans. His deep blue eyes reflect off the crystal-clear lake. He is a full decade younger than Richie, but he's aged like fine wine. He appears to have grown up since she last saw him. He has gained some weight, but in a healthy way.

Olive brushes her hair back, accidentally rubbing some red paint on her cheek.

"You don't mean to pry, huh?" She questions. Colin looks a little disheveled and puts his ringless hand through his thick, strawberry blond hair. He clearly didn't get the sarcasm in her tone, which may not have been appropriately timed considering Terrance's precarious state.

"I'm sorry, I'm just giving you a hard time. Sometimes I forget how to talk to people, I'm a bit of a hermit," Olive adds.

"No worries," Colin says, though his hands sink deeper into his jeans' pockets and his eyes flick briefly toward the lake.

"I don't know anything. Richie left for the hospital this morning; a co-worker called him and said Terrance was taken there after his body was discovered in the lake by his daughter, Hannah. Do you remember little Hannah Wilson? She used to run around your backyard when you guys moved in. Before your daughter was born, I believe."

Colin nods, then looks at her intently. "Um, are you okay?" He points to her face. Olive looks at him, dumbfounded. Without hesitation, he leans in and uses his bare hand to wipe away a line of acrylic that has dripped down into her ear. For reasons she can't quite pinpoint—like the eerie tug of déjà vu—the sight of his hand reaching toward her, coupled with the smear of maroon paint, pulls her back to the Fourth of July party. Or maybe it's the lingering image of him, his purple-lipped wife, and her own blurred recollections of drinking on the deck. Her memory, always fickle, provides no answers, only fragments that refuse to fit together.

"Oh my gosh, I'm so embarrassed." She quickly grabs a rag lying by her paint set and wipes it off. She then hands it over to Colin to wash his hands. They're both speckled with red paint, just enough to make the scene vaguely resemble a low-budget crime drama.

The sound of a quintessential duck call then grabs their attention. A small brown duck with an orange bill and a distinct dark marking on its right wing floats near the dock. *Is it Lulu?* Olive wonders. Both of them venture down to the dock to get a better look. "I haven't seen a duck here in ages," Colin murmurs. He takes a moment to catch his breath from the steep hill.

"I know!" Olive replies, tears almost forming in her eyes.

Both stand there watching the little duck.

"She's beautiful," Colin says.

"How do you know it's a girl?" Olive asks.

"Because that quack is the sound of a female mallard. Only females quack, usually two to ten times for courting purposes."

Olive looks at Colin, surprised.

"I was a Boy Scout," he explains.

Olive hesitates, trying to discern her neighbor's intentions.

Few approach her voluntarily, unless they seek medical advice, which they hope she'll relay to Richie. But Olive recognizes that her reclusiveness is, in many ways, a cocoon of her own making. And while she knows a butterfly can't stay in a cocoon forever, she's still unsure how to tear through the silk without falling apart.

Their duck watching is cut short when the screen door slams open. Olive turns to find that Richie is home and making his presence known. His chest puffs out as he stares directly at Colin. Olive waves up to him.

"Is everything okay?" she yells up to him.

"Of course not. Get up here." He turns with a huff and heads back inside.

Olive begins her climb back up the hill, but she can feel Colin's gaze fixed on her. He clears his throat to get her attention.

"Hey … is everything okay with *you*? I'm sorry I haven't really checked in since, you know, everything. Sometimes I'm just in my own world."

Olive contemplates the question. She can't remember the last time anyone asked if she was okay. It was probably Landon when he left for college. Or her mother-in-law, but in a condescending way.

"Yeah, I mean, yeah. I'm good," she responds, starting back up the hill. Behind her, Colin mutters under his breath, "What are the chances of two drownings on the same lake?"

Olive halts mid-step, a dull ache forming in her forehead, no doubt a consequence of skipping her noon medication. The weight of his question hangs heavily in the air. Slowly, she turns back to meet his deep blue eyes, now more piercing and intent.

"This may be a little forward," he calls out, his voice carrying up the hill, "but I'm going to a meeting tonight, if you want to join?"

She squints at him, a faint smirk playing on her lips. "A Boy Scout meeting?" she quips.

Colin doesn't reply, and after a moment, Olive smiles to herself and resumes her climb up the hill, leaving his offer—and his question—behind her.

CHAPTER 6

MONDAY 10 A.M.
JUNE 26, 2023

It's the morning of Terrance Wilson's funeral. Dead at fifty-one. Although his body had been discovered drifting by his dock at the canal entrance of the lake, the prevailing belief was that he had accidentally overdosed. Richie, having received the toxicology report from the hospital where Terrance was briefly responsive before succumbing, explained that he had inadvertently combined a lethal mixture of opioids, benzos, and alcohol.

Despite the lack of apparent injuries or indications of a struggle, and with only a modest amount of water discovered in his lungs, the mere fact that Terrance's body was found in the lake plunged the community into a whirlwind of unanswered questions and swirling rumors.

The police had yet to openly disclose all their findings, which left everyone more tense than usual in the lead-up to the funeral. Olive could practically hear the chatter all around her: *Another drowning on Duck Lake? How odd.* And it was.

Richie had also conveyed to Olive, through tears, that he had spoken with Hannah about the funeral arrangements. Apparently, she had stumbled upon her father unconscious near his dock on the water's edge. Terrance was supposed to pick her up at the airport, but he didn't show up. Olive found herself wondering what brought Hannah back after all these years. The funeral arrangements had been taken over by Terrance's mother, a die-hard Catholic, and had been expedited due to Hannah's need to return to Florida promptly.

As Olive sits in the pew, staring up at the large wooden cross in the center of the room, the atmosphere feels heavy.

A wreath of white roses with a photograph of Terrance is in a plain wooden frame on one side of the cross. People start to fill in the pews around her. Richie stands next to Hannah and her grandmother, comforting them, while Olive recognizes a few professional football players in attendance as well as a well-known ESPN broadcaster.

Several familiar neighbors stroll past her, their eyes briefly meeting hers. Discomfort nudges her eyeline downward to her open-toed shoes. Shoes last worn to Kate's funeral. Hushed murmurs dance around her as more attendees pass by to take their seats, "Wasn't he the one who found the little girl?" The approaching anniversary of Kate's drowning looms in the whispers. Olive's heart quickens, her palms dampening. Her eyes remain stubbornly fixed on those black shoes, even as the sight of them teeters her on the precipice of madness. It feels as though she's attending Kate's funeral all over again, only this time, the casket before her is substantially larger.

Hearing the sound of a woman silently weeping behind her brings Olive back to the surface of her pit. She turns around to find her mother-in-law, Trudy. Trudance Wentworth was not a sight for sore eyes. Her nearly eighty years have been etched with deepening scowls for each passing birthday. Every year, she seems to cultivate a fiercer temper, often leaving Olive feeling like an unwelcome third party in her marriage to Richie—a far cry from the warm mother-daughter bond Olive yearned for.

"Hi, Trudy," Olive says. She rests her hand on Trudy's as she clutches a white tissue. Trudy quickly withdraws her hand.

"This is just devastating. He was still so young. You know I just *loved* Terrance," she states. Her vein-ridden hands clutch her Prada bag tightly. She is donning a vintage Chanel dress and elegant pearl earrings. It's funny that she used the word 'love,' as she had never told Olive or Richie that she loves *them*.

Mrs. Schmidt pushes into the pew next to Trudy, leaning in to whisper, "Ope, let me just squeeze past ya, dear." She's the neighbor infamous for recently tossing her husband's prized possessions to the curb, and by all accounts, securing the house in their ongoing divorce. She is one of the original owners in the neighborhood and is closer to Trudy's age than Olive's, but seems pleasant enough. She is famous for the annual neighborhood bake sale and is in charge of the local farmers' market.

"I haven't been to one of these since little Kate's," Mrs. Schmidt says. She knows how to break the ice. Her heavyset body barely fits in the pew. Trudy doesn't seem too pleased to be sitting next to her. Or the comment about her late granddaughter. Olive looks back down again at her open-toed shoes. Mrs. Schmidt leans over to Olive, nudging some Bibles out of the way. "It was so nice of Richie to cover the expenses for this funeral."

This comes as a surprise to Olive, but in a community as intertwined as this, news propagates quickly. Hadn't Terrance been well-to-do?

"A little birdy told me," she continues, pointing over to Hannah, who is greeting more people at the big church doors. Landon walks in and gives Hannah a big hug. He's a spitting image of his father: jet black hair with the most beautiful long eyelashes surrounding his dark brown eyes. Why is it that boys always get long, natural eyelashes? He is taller and leaner than Richie, but much more empathetic, which Olive tried to instill.

Landon avoids eye contact with his dad and walks over to Olive, kissing her cheek and sitting down. He turns and hugs his grandmother as well. Olive smirks at his tie, which isn't tied correctly, and his blazer, which he has clearly outgrown.

"I always get chills in big old churches like this one. I can feel the holy spirit in here, I tell ya." Mrs. Schmidt did not like moments of silence.

Trudy pulls out the in-memory pamphlet that all attendees were given and pretends to read it. "

"I swear I had these same chills on the fourth, Trudy." Mrs. Schmidt nudges Trudy's arm, knocking the pamphlet to the ground. "Olive, we found you a bloody mess and then you said something happened to Kate before any of us knew a thing. Trudy and I thought you'd lost it from the fall. It's all coming back to me as I sit here, I tell you. Cannot believe that was what? Seven years ago? Seems like just yesterday. And now another neighbor found in the same damn lake." Mrs. Schmidt makes the sign of the cross.

Olive quickly looks over at Trudy, who continues to stare down at the pamphlet. Was it possible *she* found her own daughter before Richie and Terrance? Before the other children? Her mind is flooded with questions, but this isn't the time or place.

A priest walks up to the chancel and the choir stands behind him. Richie quickly pushes in next to Olive, putting his arm around her. He gives Landon a glance and a nod, then leans back and gestures a hello to his mother and Mrs. Schmidt before the service starts. Under different circumstances, it would have been a nice family reunion.

CHAPTER 7

MONDAY 3 P.M.
JUNE 26, 2023

As Olive gets ready to head home from the funeral lunch at a local restaurant on the water, she notices Richie and his mother arguing in a corner. There was nothing unusual about that. Typically, Trudy would pick a fight about finances or his not inviting her over more often. Mrs. Schmidt is eating her body weight in the tiny sandwiches laid out next to the lemonade while talking casserole recipes with Terrance's aunt. Terrance's mother, Bernice, is weeping now, her shoulders shaking as a friend pulls her close, whispering something Olive can't hear. But Olive doesn't need to listen to it. She knows that kind of grief: the kind that hollows you out from the inside. In her mind, there's only one thing more unbearable than burying your parents, which she's done twice. It's burying your own child.

Hannah stumbles in, her curls frizzed and tangled, cheeks flushed and puffy from crying. Her eyes barely register Olive as she grabs a red raincoat from the hook by the door and slips out the side exit. Landon follows without hesitation, his brow drawn with quiet concern, falling into step behind her the way he used to when they were little. Olive gives them a moment, then steps out after them.

She finds the two huddled closely, holding hands, and barely speaking above a whisper. "Hey, stranger," she says, approaching Hannah with her arms out, offering a hug. She isn't sure why. She is not a touchy-feely person, but seeing Hannah visibly upset pulls at her mom heartstrings. Hannah gives a side hug and pulls out a vape pen from her raincoat pocket. She takes a long inhale and then lets it all out. Vapor dances off Olive's skin.

"Hey," she replies. She holds the vape pen out towards Landon.

"I'm good. We'll chat soon. It was good to see you, Hannah." Landon extends his hand, gently tucking a stray curl behind Hannah's ear. Their eyes interlock before he pivots towards Olive. "I'll see you soon, Mom. Love you."

A weight settles in Olive's chest, a mingling of heaviness and unspoken longing, her hope for more time with Landon unfulfilled, though she knows today isn't about mother-son bonding. "Are you sure you don't want to have dinner at home before heading back?"

Regret colors Landon's voice. "I wish I could, but I'm already behind on my summer credits and lab stuff as it is. Getting today off was a stretch. I'll be back next weekend for your birthday. Promise."

He gives her a big hug. Olive smiles, reminiscing on the "fun fact" he had learned as a child in school, or maybe it was therapy, but he's held onto it ever since: everyone needs four hugs a day for survival. And when the only person who called her lately was from the Rite Aid pharmacy to let her know your prescription was ready, the hug was everything she needed and more.

Landon quickly runs off towards his car as raindrops start to fall gently. Both women stare into the distance as a flash of lightning darts through the unsettling clouds encroaching over the water. Hannah takes another drag, then stares into Olive's eyes. "It wasn't an accident." She takes another drag. Olive isn't sure what she's implying. That her dad killed himself?

"What do you think happened?"

Hannah shakes her head, her wild curly hair falling heavier as the rain picks up. "I don't mean my dad. I knew that was coming. That's why I flew in. He wasn't right in the head the week leading up to this. He would call me in the middle of the night and be talking all kinds of crazy. I knew I needed to check on him after he met with a freaking hypnotist. I didn't expect to find him like that. Then again, I never knew what to expect from Dad. It's not like he ever followed the rules."

Olive stands in silence. Hannah was right; Terrance tended

to wiggle his way around the rules. He'd almost killed a man in a bad bar fight when he was playing college football for the Florida Gators. He somehow got out of that one. He'd also been issued DUIs on numerous occasions during his years with the Lions, yet somehow kept playing with no repercussions. His defense lawyer claimed that being put on a concussion protocol had something to do with it.

"All this just stirred up a lot for me. From the past. Especially finding him in that lake. That's when I realized it wasn't an accident with Kate. The Fourth of July party. My dad ..."

They are interrupted by Hannah's grandmother, "Get in here, child, there's a storm brewing!" She's right. A storm is brewing out on the lake, as well as in Olive's mind. Whatever Terrance knew about that night was now buried with him. But what had Hannah uncovered to deem Kate's death not an accident? And in a community filled with honest, trustworthy people, who would want her four-year-old daughter dead?

They walked back into the dining room. Richie approaches them, hugging Hannah, then Terrance's mother, Bernice.

"Thank you so much again, Richard. It just means the world to us that you were able to help. Terrance thought of you as a brother," Bernice says.

Richie wraps his arm around Olive's waist. "Anything we can do to help."

Olive stares down at her wet shoes, then back up at Hannah, who's crumbled up her father's memorial pamphlet and thrown it in the trash. What *did* she know?

CHAPTER 8

MONDAY 7 P.M.
JUNE 26, 2023

Olive watches from the front living room window as Hannah stands on the driveway of Terrance's house and hugs her grandmother and great aunt as they prepare to leave. A return flight to Florida awaits Hannah tonight, meaning Olive has limited time to uncover the meaning behind Hannah's assertion that Kate's death was not accidental. She had considered discussing it with Richie but hesitated—not wanting to disturb him right after losing a good friend.

Olive swiftly puts on a sweatshirt and running sneakers, grabs her phone, and heads out the door as Terrance's mother and aunt drive away. Her heart drums rapidly in her chest. Are there possible cardiac side effects of having recently eliminated the latest medication from her regimen?

She tries to avoid eye contact with Colin, who is fiddling around with some golf equipment in his garage.

"Olive, wait. Hold up."

She doesn't stop, but she slows down and turns her head slightly. "I'm in a rush to catch Hannah before she leaves. What's up?"

"Uh, yes. The funeral was today. Give her my condolences. I just wanted to extend an open invite again to that meeting." He pauses.

Olive blinks, still unsure what meeting he's referencing.

"It's an Al-Anon meeting, to be frank with you, for friends and families of alcoholics. I don't really like going alone. I remembered you mentioning a few stories about your dad, and I thought it might be helpful for you, too," Colin explains. Olive racks her memory, trying to recall when she shared this with Colin. Before Kate passed, they used to host many parties in the summertime. She used to drink then and probably divulged more than she should have.

Olive's attention is quickly drawn to the headlights of a white Honda pulling up into Terrance's driveway in her peripheral view. "Listen, let's chat about this later, okay?"

She slips away from Colin, leaving him ensconced in the suburban twilight cast by the streetlights. She reaches Terrance's place just in time to witness Hannah stepping out the front door, luggage in hand. She turns to fasten the lock on the door with her key.

"Hey again," Olive says.

"Hey, I'm sorry, this is my ride to the airport." Olive turns to find the rideshare driver behind her, reaching for Hannah's suitcase.

"I could have driven you."

"It's okay. It's been a long couple of days. I really need to decompress and head back for my summer midterm, it's half my grade. Sorry for bringing up Kate. Funerals can stir up a lot."

Olive nods, waiting for Hannah to expand her thoughts.

"It's funny how, as a kid, you believe all the adults have it figured out, but then you grow up and realize no one does. They were all lying. My dad included." She looks down at the front door key and hands it over to Olive. "Can you hold on to this? A realtor's supposed to reach out soon. My aunt said she might stop by and check on the place, but she's always busy, so I'm not really counting on it."

"Yes, of course," Olive replies, clutching the key.

"The odd part is he didn't even have a prescription for some of the stuff found in his system." She reaches for her pocket, retrieving her vape and taking a long draw.

"Do you think someone did something to him?" Olive questions, concerned.

"No, he was an addict. If there was a will, there was a way to find some. He kept telling me he was going to get off them. I knew once he checked himself out of rehab in Tampa that he would never do it. He spent almost all he had on those stupid pills *and* gambling."

Olive starts to piece together why they had to step up for the funeral expenses.

The sound of a basketball hitting the hard cement echoes throughout the neighborhood, catching the attention of both women. It's Colin, still attempting to organize his garage. "And you better watch out for that one." Hannah points over to Colin.

"Colin? He's like a Boy Scout."

"He didn't seem so harmless when I was here last. I had a layover during Christmas break, went to check on my dad, get my one-day winter fix, you know the deal. Anyway, I saw this dude coming at Dr. Wentworth. Shouting at him. I realized when I saw *him* that he was the same guy I'd been scared of the night of the party."

The rideshare driver, now in the driver's seat, honks his horn. Hannah reaches down for her other bag.

"Wait, what party?" Olive questions softly, her ears pulsing loudly.

"The Fourth of July party. I've tried to push this stuff out of my mind, man, but I've been seeing a therapist. He's helping me address my childhood trauma." Hannah gestures air quotes when saying *childhood trauma*. She pauses to take another drag of her pen.

"This therapist … did they help you remember anything further about that night?"

"Landon, another neighborhood kid, and I were playing hide and seek with Kate. You had just walked up the hill. You said you felt dizzy and needed a drink, I think. Anyway, Landon and I had the best hiding spot on the side of the house, behind the Jacuzzi. Kate was counting down by that big old willow tree, and I pulled a tubing raft in front of us to block anyone from finding our spot. Then, out of nowhere, we heard shouting. Landon ran off, but I saw that guy, Colin, and Dr. Wentworth arguing. At one point, Colin had his hand around *your* husband's neck. My dad then walked over, and he let go. Most men became cowards when my dad walked into a room, ya know. But the look in Colin's eyes was crazy."

The rideshare driver honks again.

"Listen, your rating just dropped to three stars now, bucko," Olive quips at him before returning her attention to Hannah. "Why do you think your dad was bringing up what happened to Kate recently?"

"Well, right before the overdose, my dad wouldn't stop talking about that night. He'd seen a hypnotist a few days prior—said it was to enhance his past memories through hypnotherapy. He called me one night, late, insisting he'd found Kate and was going to help her, talking about salvation and shit. I don't know … maybe that's why that night has been on my mind again," Hannah finishes, sliding her vape pen into her jean pocket, her hands slightly trembling.

Olive pulls her close. "I'm truly sorry for what you've been through," she whispers, her breath a warm whisper against Hannah's hair. Olive's suspicions regarding Colin stir anew. In her heart, Terrance had always been a gentle giant, possibly carrying the weight of regret for his failed rescue. Colin, however, remains an enigma, a puzzle she has yet to solve. She might have to take him up on his open invitation to that meeting.

CHAPTER 9
RICHIE

TUESDAY 7 P.M.
JUNE 26, 2023

"Richie, my apologies for the late call. It's Dean," one of my esteemed colleagues begins on the other end of the line. It always amuses me when people state their names during calls; I recognize Dean's number and have it saved. I ease into the plush leather chair in my home office, gazing through the bay view window at my wife as she embraces the daughter of our late friend. I'm acutely aware that his passing will set off a ripple effect, with my wife's unpredictable behavior being just one facet of the larger picture. Personally, I'm already drained from the emotional and financial toll of today's funeral, and from losing a dear friend. Nonetheless, I must set those thoughts aside as I prepare for the significance of Dean's call.

"You got the interview," Dean shares enthusiastically. "The board rallied behind you, and thanks to your recent award, *The New England Journal of Medicine* has agreed to feature you as Oncologist of the Year. Well, technically in the top ten, but you'll be on the cover. Can you believe it?" His excitement is palpable, and rightfully so, as this recognition will bring more attention to our hospital.

"That's fantastic news, Dean. I truly appreciate your support," I respond, my eyes remaining locked on my wife, who has paused to converse with Colin Baker on her walk back home. My lips curl and I stiffen, spine snapping straight as a rod. The longer they linger, the tighter my grip on the phone becomes. If they're still talking in another minute, I'll give them a reason to stop.

"Absolutely. They'll contact you in the next couple of days to set up the initial interview. It's a spotlight feature, so I anticipate they might schedule multiple sessions."

I nod, although Dean can't see my response. My attention is still fixed on Colin, his infuriatingly smug smile directed at my wife.

"Richie, there's one more matter to discuss. It's concerning the Lisa situation. We're addressing it as effectively as possible, and the board is firmly in your corner, of course. However, she's indicating a potential legal course of action," Dean remarks, his unease evident through the phone.

"Don't concern yourself with Dr. Hernandez. We anticipated nothing less from that scheming woman. I've got it under control," I assure Dean. He refrains from further inquiries, understanding that I'm a man of my word. After we end the call, I observe my wife heading around the back, with Colin's unwavering gaze dead set on her. The doorbell rings, causing my heart rate to spike further, if that's even possible.

I open the door and discover a grey-haired man holding a bouquet of two dozen exquisite long-stemmed red roses. Without a word, he hands them to me. Colin and I exchange a glance before I shut the door and proceed to read the card:

Lavish flowers for lavish secrets.
Stay the fuck away from my family
or I will continue to be a thorn in your side.

The card doesn't reveal who sent the flowers, though I can think of a few candidates. There are things I'd prefer to keep buried deep in the ground, but the trouble with dirt is that whatever grows from these salt-of-the-earth people and their endless gossip never stays hidden for long. Still, one name stands out more prominently than the rest. When the devil doesn't pay you any mind, it's said you might be on the wrong path. Conversely, when the devil engages with you, it could signify that you're attempting to pursue a righteous cause. I can't definitively judge whether my actions are morally sound, but one thing is unmistakable: Lisa Hernandez embodies evil in the flesh.

CHAPTER 10

TUESDAY 6 A.M.
JUNE 27, 2023

Olive stirs awake on the family room sofa, greeted by the morning light filtering through the glass sliders. The last thing she remembers from the night prior, following her conversation with Hannah, was accepting Colin's invitation on her walk back home. Once home, she had only intended to unwind with a single episode of her latest reality TV indulgence before taking a shower and going to bed. Still, exhaustion or withdrawals, apparently had other plans. And she somehow managed to sleep straight through the night—the worries of the previous day momentarily forgotten.

As her senses return, the scent of fresh roses engulfs her, her sight falling upon a new bouquet gracing the kitchen table. She inhales deeply, the smell awakening her a little more until the peaceful moment is interrupted by an abrupt crashing noise. The microwave clock reads 6:06. Now fully alert, Olive springs up and follows the clammer to find the fallen picture frame once again. It seems Richie had rehung a new frame without using the proper adhesives. Venturing into his study, she retrieves the replacement adhesive from the office junk drawer. As she closes it, a glimmer on the carpet near the leather study chair catches her eye.

She bends down to take a closer look and finds a woman's bracelet, made of delicate silver and adorned with intricate designs. Two opals sit in the middle of the band. She has never seen it before, and it definitely does not belong to her. She examines it closely, trying to shake off the feeling of doubt. After all, her husband has never given her any reason to question his devotion. She can't ignore the feeling of uncertainty in the pit of her stomach. Olive hears the garage door open, but doesn't move. Moments later, Richie enters, his eyes fixated on the bracelet she holds.

"There goes the surprise. Were you snooping?" he asks bluntly.

"No, I was grabbing something. What surprise?"

Approaching her, Richie places the bracelet on her wrist. "Guess I wasn't as discreet as I thought. Must've slipped from my desk. I know opals are your favorite. Happy early birthday."

Olive pauses for a moment to ask herself if opals are her favorite. If she is being honest, she isn't really a fan of jewelry to begin with. "I'm … I'm sorry. I didn't mean to find it. I was trying to fix the frame." She gestures toward the fallen picture. She then takes in Richie's appearance—sweaty, wearing dirty sweatpants, and with messy hair. "Where were you? Why didn't you wake me to come to bed last night?"

"Grabbed a quick morning run. You looked so peaceful on the couch. I didn't want to disturb your sleep," Richie explains, his breath still catching from exertion. But he hasn't met her eyes even once.

"And the roses?"

Before Richie can elaborate further, his phone rings, he puts his finger up and gestures that it's important as he walks outside onto the deck. Meanwhile, an early morning commotion across the street grabs Olive's attention. It seems Mrs. Schmidt is receiving a scolding from Terrance's aunt for handling their mail. Olive decides she'd have a better vantage point from Landon's bedroom.

Through Landon's front window, she watches as Mrs. Schmidt now slowly heads back to her own house. She must have missed most of the scene, her morning entertainment disappearing from view.

Moving to Landon's sideview window, she spots Richie down by the dock, still engrossed in his phone conversation.

The room feels empty and eerily quiet now that it's devoid of her son playing video games or listening to music. When he left a semester early for college, it had taken a piece of her heart. Possibly the one piece that was left. She looks around at the trophies, science awards, and the many, many books. Pride swells in her. He has always been adaptable to whatever environment he is placed in. He has been her one success.

She glances over at his desk, and a small picture of them fishing on the dock many years ago catches her eye. Richie is noticeably absent. She remembers he had promised to take Landon fishing that day after work and an emergency happened at the hospital. Landon has held on to all those tiny, hurtful moments. In Richie's mind, he was providing everything that a son could ever want and need: a lakeside home, a new car for his sixteenth birthday, an excellent education, and connections galore. The relationship between Kate and Richie, however, had been noticeably different. He adored her. He'd called her his research assistant and would take her on special trips to the toy store and out on the boat to look for Lulu most nights. She was his.

After Kate passed, Richie had been devastated but had gone back to work. Olive was left to pick up the pieces and be there for her son. Landon never judged her. She couldn't imagine what he had gone through with Kate's death. Oftentimes, kids think the world orbits around them and that everything that happens—good or bad—is because of them. Olive had sought therapy for him when Kate was initially diagnosed, but cancelled it when she started to recover, then reinstated it to help him navigate his grief. Yet she had neglected her own needs—she put the proverbial oxygen mask on her son before herself.

She's brought back to the moment by a glint from the afternoon sun dancing on her hand, reflected by the bracelet. Dizziness overwhelms her, and she lies her head down on her son's bed. As her eyes close, she can almost feel Kate's tiny hands cupping her cheeks, that tender memory cradling her as she drifts off.

CHAPTER 11

MONDAY 6 P.M.
JULY 4, 2016

THEN

"Mommy, time to wake up. Mommy, wake up. People are here, the party is starting!"

Olive opened her eyes, still swaying back and forth in the hammock, realizing she had fallen asleep. She peered up the large hill to see Mr. and Mrs. Schmidt approaching Richie on the deck, handing over their farmers market prize-winning cherry pie. A loud noise came from the home of the young, newlywed neighbors, the Bakers. They likely couldn't have afforded their lakeside home if Colin Baker's dad hadn't left it to him, or so the small-town rumor went. His wife, Julie, had slammed their sliding glass door hard, exiting quickly as Colin trailed behind her. His face looked flushed, angry even. He pulled a bottle of wine out of his wife's hands, replacing it with his grasp as they approached Richie and the Schmidts, who were smiling warmly.

Olive walked up the hill, hand in hand with her redheaded daughter, her smile beaming ear to ear. She rushed toward Landon and Hannah, who were trying to get the Slip 'N Slide set up and running.

"Landon, wait for your father to help with that," Olive said sternly as her son lifted a mallet and some pegs. He forced a grin and gave a curt tilt of his head, clearly unamused by her insistence on patience.

"I can help!" Terrance proclaimed loudly, one hand holding a cocktail, the other gripping Hannah as he spun her around in the air. Her laughter filled the sunny sky, a sound that would soon give way to the magical glow of nightfall and fireworks.

Olive left the kids in Terrance's care and slipped inside through the walk-out basement entrance, sneaking past the early guests to freshen up. As she exited her bathroom, the home phone rang in Richie's office. Glancing outside, she saw her husband animatedly pretending to swing a bat—no doubt retelling the story of his home-run hit during this summer's "Everybody vs. Cancer" charity events. He glanced at her from outside and gave her a playful wink.

Ring. Ring. Ring.

The phone kept blaring, the sound screeching in Olive's ears.

"Hello?" she answered.

"Hi, is Richard there? He wasn't answering his cellphone," a woman's voice asked urgently.

"He's outside right now; we're hosting a little Fourth of July get-together. Can I leave him a message and have him call you back?"

"Sure. Tell him it's Lisa Hernandez from the hospital. Tell him it's … timely."

"Will do. Have a wonderful holiday."

Lisa Hernandez abruptly hung up. *Odd*, Olive thought to herself just as the doorbell rang. She spotted two tiny handprints pressed against the glass of the front door and immediately recognized them, those of her friend Audrey's son, Joey, Landon's best friend. Olive opened the door and let them in.

"Who's ready to party?" Audrey squealed, throwing her red, white, and blue-painted hands around Olive's waist. Behind her, Big Joe, Audrey's husband, rolled his eyes and asked, "Where should I put the tuna casserole?"

"Under the deck would be great. We have some banquet tables set up by the volleyball net," Olive replied as Joey pushed past her and slid the back glass door open, darting onto the deck.

"Is Laura coming?" Audrey asked, a hiccup escaping her.

"I'm not sure," Olive replied. "She mentioned they might be heading up north to Petoskey."

"Oh my gosh, do you remember those matching Petoskey stone necklaces we made with the boys last summer? They were so cute! Anyhoo, where's the drinks?"

Olive couldn't help but smile at Audrey's larger-than-life personality. "Downstairs under the deck. Blue cooler is for alcohol; white one is non-alcoholic."

Audrey grinned and headed outside, with Olive following closely behind her.

Landon bumped into them both, little Joey now by his side. Olive cupped her son's face and said, "Hey, can you go tell Daddy that a Lisa Hernandez from the hospital just called? She said it's urgent."

Landon rolled his eyes. "It's always urgent."

Audrey looped an arm through Olive's and leaned down toward Landon. "It's also urgent that your mom and I get a drink. Go tell your dad about the phone call, then you boys can play hide-and-seek or something. I've also got sparklers and devil bangers to keep you guys busy."

Olive turned to Audrey, whose blonde hair swayed in the hibiscus-scented air. "Thank you."

"Of course. What are mom friends for?"

Olive grinned and asked, "But seriously, what the hell is a devil banger?"

"Those little popper things. Sorry in advance, it's going to make a mess in your yard, but it'll keep the kids entertained." Olive gave her a thumbs up as Audrey scanned the food spread, her expression growing annoyed. "Shoot. I'd better check on Joe real quick. I don't see where he put our casserole. Lord knows he'd lose his head if it weren't attached." Audrey bent down, grabbed a cold Molson from the blue cooler, and trotted off toward the garage, tugging at the hem of her denim skirt as she went, to where Big Joe was puffing on a cigarette.

The sudden blast from a loud boombox hit Olive like a slap in the face back near the coolers. She noticed Harold Schmidt humming along with the old tune, clearly his song choice. "The Wreck of the Edmund Fitzgerald," a 1976 hit, and the same year the Oakland County Killer reared his ugly head.

"You know what this song is about?" Mr. Schmidt quizzed Colin Baker, both of them now biting into hot dogs. Olive continued to eavesdrop while noticing from a distance that Terrance had finally gotten the Slip 'N Slide working and the girls were gleefully sliding down it.

"'The lake, it is said, never gives up her dead,'' Colin sang along with the tune before adding, "Of course. My dad always used to play this one...the sinking of that ship in Lake Superior, the one that killed every last crew member."

"Twenty-nine to be exact. Old Gitche Gumee," Mr. Schmidt replied.

"Gitche what?" Olive finally chimed in. She had been eavesdropping, but this was *her* party.

"Gitche Gumee," Mr. Schmidt repeated. "It's another name for Lake Superior. A Native American phrase meaning 'big lake.'" Olive took his word for it—Harold Schmidt was a Park Ranger, after all.

"And a little morbid fun fact ..." Colin stammered, his scrawny shoulders pushing up a bit, as if bracing himself for the weight of what he was about to say. "Lake Superior's water is so cold that a dead body would never float to the surface because the water is never warm enough to grow the bacteria needed to make it rise."

He grinned, seemingly unfazed by the grim revelation. The image of a dead body suspended in the icy grip of Lake Superior sent an involuntary shiver through Olive. It also brought Richie's brother sharply to her mind.

"Sorry if that was weird. I'm a biology teacher. Well, technically, going to be a biology professor as soon as I finish my PhD," Colin added. By that point, Olive's eyes were no longer on Colin, who was still rambling on about science, but instead on Harold Schmidt, who was glaring at Terrance, laughing exuberantly on the upper part of the deck.

"Prick," Mr. Schmidt mumbled under his breath.

"Who? The big guy?" Colin asked, his curiosity apparent.

"Yeah, he turned the neighborhood against my banning of wakeboards. It erodes the lake, don't you know it," old Mr. Schmidt grumbled.

"That I do. Only have a Jet Ski, personally," Colin replied

with a slight shrug.

"Mrs. Wentworth! Mrs. Wentworth! Can Kate and I have more sparklers? We're going down by the lake!" Hannah called out, her voice ringing across the yard and catching Olive's attention. The sky had dimmed, and the last light of the sun was slipping behind the horizon, casting long shadows over the yard.

"Sure thing, honey," Olive replied, glancing toward the cluster of neighbors who had just arrived. "Give me a few minutes to greet people and offer them a drink. Remember, you and Landon are in charge of Kate." She winked at little Hannah Wilson, who nodded with a beaming smile.

Olive turned her attention back to Colin and Mr. Schmidt, but only Colin remained standing there now, his gaze fixed on her as Julie approached from behind.

"Speaking of drinks," Julie slurred, her voice thick and unsteady as her glassy eyes peered into Olive's soul. "Why don't you and I get to know each other a little better? Share a drink upstairs with me, yeah?"

Colin leaned in slightly, his tone soft but firm. "Honey, I think you've had enough for now."

"You're such a party pooper," Julie muttered, rolling her eyes dramatically as she staggered toward the deck stairs. Her tone, petulant and sharp, made her sound more like a sulky teenager than Colin's wife. "The fireworks haven't even started yet. Still, plenty of time to have fun."

"Sorry about that. She lost a patient a few days ago and has been hitting the bottle pretty hard," Colin said, running his hands through his thick head of hair, avoiding Olive's eyes.

"No worries, it is a party after all. And, between you and me, my father was an alcoholic. I've seen far worse drunks in my life." She wasn't sure why she revealed such an intimate secret, but Colin seemed relieved at her openness. "So, is your wife a doctor as well?"

"No. Nurse. But she takes it hard when she loses someone on her watch."

Just then, Terrance tumbled down the stairs, nearly crashing into Colin. Richie hurried over, pulled him to his feet, and pressed a bottle of water into his hand. The rest of the neighbors laughed it off as Terrance jumped up and joined in the laughter.

But the moment didn't pass so easily for Olive. It clung to her, heavy and uneasy. In the distance, the lake stretched out, vast and ominous, its surface barely discernible in the dimming twilight. As Olive's sights wandered to the shoreline, a sudden, inexplicable chill coursed through her, like a warning carried on the evening breeze. It felt as though the night had been teetering on the edge of something darker. She had thought to herself that she should head down to check on the kids, who, by that point, were all down by the dock.

CHAPTER 12

TUESDAY 6 P.M.
JUNE 27, 2023

"Welcome to A Peace of Serenity Al-Anon Family Group. This is a beginner's meeting, which means it is run a little differently than our regular meetings. Everyone is encouraged to share their story. This is a reminder that anonymity is the foundation of our tradition. However, it cannot be used as a legal basis to shield past or present criminal behavior. It is wise to remember that Al-Anon meetings are not above the law. We hope that you will find in this fellowship the peace and friendship we have been privileged to enjoy."

Olive casts a sidelong glance at Colin. She couldn't quite grasp why he had asked her to accompany him to this meeting. Yet she saw it as an opportunity to get closer to him.

Now in a small room within a church, she finds herself surrounded by mainly middle-aged, world-weary-looking people, alongside a few seasoned leaders seated at the front table. The primary guide stands in the center. With his white hair cascading back into a neat ponytail, it complements the rugged charm of his Harley Davidson leather vest, projecting the air of an effortless leader. Olive peers at the principles of Al-Anon hanging behind him, which she quickly skims. Her eyes freeze on the last one: *service to others.*

Was Colin bringing me here as his service to others step?

"For the newcomers, my name is Dodge," declares the man with the Harley Davidson persona. "I know some of you may be offended by that. I'm more of a Ford guy myself."

Olive can't help but release a soft chuckle. She has a soft spot for Ford. Her father had worked the assembly line until their Wixom branch was shut down and everyone was laid off. Her father used to come home smelling of diesel oil and nickel. For the life of her, she couldn't figure out why he couldn't hold down a real job after her mother passed, especially considering they lived in the motor city, the auto capital of the world. He would blame Olive for the inconvenience of her school schedule or looking after her, when, mostly, she was the one who looked after him. As an adult, she realized it was his alcohol consumption. When she was a child, she viewed him as the center of her world. The higher voice. Despite his consistent wrongdoings, she had believed he could do no wrong and that she was to blame for his failures.

Dodge continues, "Though we're not a religious organization, we are a spiritual one."

Olive inhales deeply, her breath faltering as if she can't draw enough air, like she is suffocating. The thought of Terrance momentarily haunts her. Was this how he had felt in his final few days or even moments? Was this why he sought clarity and consolation in hypnosis? It's curious how far we go to unearth buried memories from the past.

"Tonight, I would like to open a discussion about change. The principles you'll learn here can help you deal with changes as they come in life, sometimes major changes. Some of you may have lost a loved one or even your own identity. You all may not be able to change circumstances, but you can change your attitude about the situation. Accept the things you cannot change. But you do not have to accept unacceptable behavior. You have the right to make decisions that are in your best interest, to set boundaries, and to decide to no longer participate in the insanity of others. Have any of you found the courage to make such decisions? To change your distorted thinking?"

Colin and Olive exchange glances once more. Colin is fiddling with his wedding ring, which is now back on his finger. Olive scans the room, where she catches sight of two youthful women clad in nurse's uniforms, tucked away in a corner, murmuring. A flicker of concern crosses her mind. Have they recognized her? Would her presence here somehow get back to Richie?

Beside Colin, a woman who had been insistently tapping her feet together ceases the motion and raises her hand. She tells the group about how her teenage daughter had drunk herself into her third alcohol poisoning and now in her second stint at rehab. The women in the corner stop whispering and share how their mother had gone missing after they told her she could no longer live with them if she kept drinking. Olive can smell Colin's deodorant seeping through his collared shirt. She can tell he wants to share, but is nervous. Something is eating at him.

"I'll go," he manages to mutter. "I feel like I want to be courageous, at least for my daughter's sake. She's six-years-old. But sometimes I don't know if I'm the hero or the villain. Sometimes this particular person makes me feel like I'm the bad guy. But what if their actions are unforgivable? Is it courageous to let it go and forgive or to stand firm in your beliefs?" His eyes are directed at Dodge, seeking guidance.

"I'd say it takes courage to do both. Interestingly enough, villains and heroes actually have the same backstory: pain. They chose differently how to respond to it." Dodge looks down at his watch and continues. "But it all starts with forgiving. That's next week's topic: forgiveness. Don't you worry, son." He pauses, then states, "We have time for one more group share before we wrap up tonight's meeting. Would you care to share Miz—?" Dodge points to Olive. She feels all eyes on her. Her face flushes. She wasn't planning on sharing anything tonight, only getting Colin to divulge and shine some light on what Hannah had witnessed.

"Olive. I'm Olive."

The group responds in unison, "Hi, Olive."

"I'm … I'm not sure how to do this."

"Do what? Be vulnerable? Because vulnerability is more intriguing than perfection, ma'am," Dodge affirms. Olive closes her eyes. She visualizes herself as a girl of about fourteen with a French braid. It was a Sunday night. She remembered thinking then that it was an odd time for her father not to be home. It was also the night she realized her father *could* do wrong, that he had a problem.

"I guess you could say I lacked courage. It was a Sunday in

January. I cooked dinner for myself and made a plate for my dad, but he wasn't home. I was getting worried because the snow started to fall heavily. It was almost nine at night when I heard screaming next door. I grabbed my coat and ran outside. It was my dad in our neighbor's driveway. He was pounding on their garage door to get it to open. He thought it was our house and couldn't figure out why the garage wouldn't open. I walked over and pulled him into our house. He was screaming at me, demanding why I hadn't left my pink bike out front, so he would know which house was ours. He reeked of rubbing alcohol. I got him in the house and saw the neighbors peering out their window. I had never driven a car before, but I quickly figured it out that night. I managed to pull his car into our driveway before the neighbors could call the cops."

Colin stares at her with his intense blue eyes. They feel piercing.

"And how is your relationship with your father now?" Dodge questions.

"It's nonexistent … he's … he's passed." She pauses. "This is probably an overshare, but it happened the night I found out I was pregnant with my son. Again, it was January, with lots of snow. As I was walking back to my apartment at medical school, an officer called to tell me they found my father frozen to death near Commerce Lake. I knew right away that the lake was kitty-corner to his favorite party store. He must have gotten lost walking to it. My only thought was that at least he didn't drive this time. No one else got hurt."

A hush envelops the room, tangible and dense. Olive, who had never before voiced the events of those nights, now finds herself submerged in a profound silence.

"Alright, that's a lot to unpack. You're in the right place; thank you for sharing. Let's close this meeting until next week when we discuss forgiveness."

Colin still appears to be wrestling with the concept of courage, and it's evident all over his balmy face. He stares into the distance as they settle at a picnic table outside Darby's ice cream parlor. The church parking lot had quickly emptied, prompting Olive to suggest a detour before heading home.

The sun has just set, casting a soft glow over their ice cream, before Colin finally lets out a smile.

"So, what did you think?" he asks in a hopeful tone. He wipes his nose with his shirt sleeve.

"It was something," she replies with a saddened look.

"It's not your fault, you know," Colin interjects, his shoulder brushing hers a little as he leans forward for a napkin.

"It is my fault," Olive automatically replies, even though she's unsure what Colin is referring to. Deep down, though, she knew—the blame had always found its way back to her.

"With your dad, you should have felt safe as a kid, and you should feel safe now as an adult. Do you feel safe, Olive?" Colin's inspection was steady. His freckles adorned his sun-kissed cheeks, matching the hue of his hair. "You've created this false narrative, thinking you're responsible for all of it. But you're not, you know that, right?"

Olive senses an ulterior angle to his probing, yet she deflects with a query of her own. She mustn't let the surge of genuine emotions cloud her real intentions for accompanying her neighbor to this place—intentions that, she admits to herself, are not without their own hidden agenda that requires Colin to let down his guard. Hannah's warning about Colin still looms in the air, along with the allegation that he had some altercation with her husband on more than one occasion.

"Why haven't you tried your Vernors float?" she probes, taking a spoonful from Colin's dish. Instantly, she regrets it, feeling a tinge of adolescence, as if she were on a date. But this is not a date; it is a quest for information.

"It's decent. How's yours?" Colin questions, mimicking her actions by scooping up some of her freshly churned strawberry ice cream. His eyes light up. "That's amazing. Why did you tell me to get the Vernors pop float?"

Olive tilts her head back and snickers, something she also

hadn't done since her late teens. "Because you said you never tried one. That's weird." She stares down at the ginger ale bubbling over the cold vanilla ice cream.

Colin smirks. "Ah, I see. So, you wanted to relieve me of my Vernors float virginity. Right at your husband's family-owned ice cream parlor." He points over at the large Darby's sign.

"They don't own it anymore. Richie helped his mother sell it the second his father passed. I thought it would have been fun to keep it in the family, but Richie wanted nothing of the sort. He hated this place."

Taking a bite of the float, Colin nods. "You know, I used to bartend in college, and I've never heard of Vernors and vanilla ice cream paired."

The two go silent for a moment, and Olive decides to broach the topic that's weighing down the air between them. "What's the deal between you and Richie?"

Colin rolls his eyes and takes another bite of his float. "Did you tell him that you were joining me at the meeting tonight?" he asks, as though her response to his question will influence what he might reveal next.

"No. Richie doesn't believe in this kind of stuff," she replies.

"Getting ice cream with a neighbor or attending an Al-Anon meeting?" he jests.

"Probably both, to be honest. But he has a lot going on right now; he probably won't even notice I'm gone."

"We all have a lot going on. Do you want a partner who's only good to you when they have nothing else on their plate?" Colin responds defensively. She looks down in return, though Olive feels he's almost talking about Julie at this point.

"Did you decide what you're going to do when she returns home?" Olive questions, taking another bite of Colin's float. She had been unusually hungry all day, possibly another side effect surfacing from loosening the reins on her daily pill regimen.

He playfully hits her spoon away with his. "Julie? I'm processing it. Having her and Lucy both gone this summer has made me go a little nutty. Have you ever learned something so horrible about someone you love that it shatters the way you see them?"

Olive returns Colin's intense stare, observing his face as it suddenly contorts, as though he's seen a ghost. She has always perceived him as the laid-back professor type, with no worries in the world. However, despite being neighbors for years, she now realizes she knows very little about him. While she initially believed he was a professor at Oakland University, she had heard rumors that he was let go, so she didn't want to pry. Plus, her memory is shit now, so who knows how accurate that knowledge even is. But as she sits next to her neighbor, observing him play with his wedding band, a surprising affinity for Colin tugs at Olive's consciousness. Was it the common ground they shared in their struggles with alcoholic loved ones, an involuntary bond in a club neither had wished to join? Or was it his unexpected raw display of vulnerability, a rare glimpse of sensitivity she had never observed in a man?

She finally shakes her head no to his question before he continues. "Something terrible that you forgave a long time ago, only to discover something even worse?"

At this point, Olive doesn't know what he wants her to say or where he is going with this. It's like he wants her to remember something. "What are you talking about? How bad are we talking?" Olive finally asks.

Colin pushes his float away, as if to say he's sick to his stomach. What had Julie done? Before she works up the nerve to probe further, Colin's phone rings.

Though he stood a few feet away during the call, Olive observed his shifting body language—from tense to ease, then back to stressed. After hanging up, he returns to the table. "Sorry about that; she's only allowed one call a day at the rehab center. She said she's really been working on herself and that I should continue to do the same." Colin falls silent for a moment. "I'm sorry that was rude. I don't mean to make this about me. Tell me about you. How's the canvas going? I wanted to tell you the other day that I thought your painting was brilliant. The one of our willow tree."

Olive smiles and feels herself blushing. "Thanks. I used to sell them back in the day."

"Why did you stop?"

She takes another bite of the now-melted strawberry puddled cream, pondering the question. "I don't know. Richie wanted me to stay home with the kids. Kate's diagnosis meant she needed extra care. I started to paint as an outlet. Then I stopped. I needed to focus on Landon after …"

Colin clears his throat. A couple walks by them, whispering to each other while looking at the two. The need to get back home to Richie overwhelms her, whether he is there waiting for her or not. The two make their way back to Colin's Volvo, a car she thought was rather fitting—reliable and predictable, with a touch of class but no ostentation.

"Can you turn the air on?" Olive requests, a wave of warmth fueling her. She has trouble catching her breath, and her limbs feel prickly. Another day of skipping her afternoon medications. Yet, despite the physical discomfort, a faint sense of clarity bubbles just beneath her consciousness. He quickly flips the switch on, allowing the A/C to relieve her. The sun has officially set, but it is hotter than usual for a Midwest evening. Sweat clings to her back, and tiny perspiration beads glisten in the dim light on Colin's nose. He starts to put his seatbelt on when Olive finally musters up the courage to ask Colin another question she hopes he doesn't dodge.

"I have to ask. What do you remember about that night? The Fourth of July party at my house."

A car passes them, slowing down for a moment, then continues on its way. Colin opens his mouth, then pauses. He appears uncomfortable.

"We should head back." He quickly puts his hand on the gear shift.

"Colin." Olive places her hand on his arm.

"I'm not ready to talk about that night, I'm sorry."

"That's not fair. To drag me to a meeting so you feel comfortable, force me to talk about my childhood, and you sit there, sharing little half-truths. I don't know if you're the hero or the villain either." Her response comes swiftly, edged with defiance.

Colin flinches almost imperceptibly. His jaw tightens, and his hands clench the steering wheel before he slowly releases his grip. He doesn't look at her. Instead, he lowers his head, letting his gaze fall to the dash—retreating from her stare, as if bracing for something he can't put into words.

"You want to know why I'm here? I'm here because my wife is an alcoholic and had an affair. It's stupid and ridiculous and now I'm getting help because of the mess she created. She gets home from rehab in less than a week, and I have to decide if I forgive her or not. That's the truth. When I looked at you from my deck, I saw myself—two people mourning." Colin lets out a loud exhale. Another car whizzes by. Olive remains silent; she won't get any further information out of Colin tonight, but there's more he isn't sharing. A heavier secret. She needs Colin to trust her.

"I'm sorry. Let's talk more at the next meeting," he responds, still appearing a little on edge.

Olive feels a shudder of apprehension at the thought of enduring another meeting. Nonetheless, she commits internally, willing herself to navigate the discomfort to get to the bottom of her skepticism orbiting around Colin. It's been seven years. It's time to know the truth.

CHAPTER 13
RICHIE

TUESDAY 6 P.M.
JUNE 27, 2023

Dean had sent me a follow-up email, suggesting that *The New England Journal of Medicine* might want a non-work-related reference for a quote along with my interview. I drum my knuckles lightly against my mahogany desk as the sun gradually dips into dusk. Countless individuals cross my mind: neighbors, church members, my wife, although she has been somewhat erratic since Terrance's funeral, probably out on one of her lengthy walks at the moment. I can tell Olive hasn't been taking her medication this week, and honestly, it worries me—not for her, but for me. The last thing I need is for her to cause a scene. This moment is about *me*, after all. When Olive's off her meds, her judgment goes straight out the window. It didn't used to be like this. Back in the day, she was sharp. That's partially why I got her pregnant. Fun fact: children often inherit their intelligence from their mothers. I wanted my children to be bright, and Olive checked that box.

Now, I hope she's not out there doing something ridiculous. The kind of thing that could tarnish my reputation, or worse, the reputation of my family. People in this community hold me in high esteem, as they should. I've earned it. But appearances are everything, and it only takes one slip-up from Olive to undermine the respect I've built.

That said, there is one person's approval I'd care to have—my son. A kind word from him? That would be nice for my interview.

Landon and I have a complicated relationship. I can't pinpoint exactly where the disconnect began, but I would have to attribute it to that night largely. The way he looked at me when I couldn't save his sister is etched in my memory. Before that moment, I had thought of us as thick as thieves, as close as a father and son could be. However, I've come to realize that much of parenting is influenced by our own inner child; our personal goals, expectations, and dreams often overshadow the child in front of us.

I set my ego aside and dial him.

"Yeah, Dad, what's up?" he responds, as though I'm calling to offer him an extension on his car warranty, not like I'm the one covering his apartment and private college tuition.

"Hey, buddy. I was calling to catch up with you, check in after Terrance's funeral. Hannah looked really upset," I mention, my voice trailing off.

"Yeah, her dad passed away," he responds curtly. He's always brief with me, unlike with his mother.

"Right, challenging times. Anyway, could you do me a favor and provide a quote about your old man for a medical journal interview I have coming up?" I enquire, a hint of hope in my voice.

"Listen, Dad, I'm swamped with school and my summer job right now …"

"You got a job. Good for you. Where are you working?" I ask, mentally replaying my words to ensure they didn't sound condescending. In the background, I can hear a male voice calling my son's name.

"I've got to run. It's been a hectic day. Let's talk more about it when I come home for Mom's birthday," he replies, unaware that the magazine probably needs a quote before then. He hangs up. I find it rather irritating that he'll come home for his mother's birthday, but not mine, which was last month.

I sit there for a moment in silence, fixating on the picture on my desk of Kate and me. She had a way of making me feel truly special. Children have a knack for reflecting your emotions. It's why little kids throw tantrums; they feel powerless. Did I inadvertently convey to Landon that I was too preoccupied for him? And is he now doing the same? My intentions were never to neglect him, but intentions don't always align with how things are perceived.

CHAPTER 14

WEDNESDAY 11 A.M.
JUNE 28, 2023

Olive made the conscious decision not to take her second dose of a.m. pills, to give herself another day closer to freedom, closer to feeling a new emotion. Though, as a result, she found herself intently fixated on a piece of granite within the confines of the local kitchen design shop while Richie conversed in a firm tone with the shop attendant. He had insisted on an overhaul of their kitchen in the wake of upgrading their primary bathroom. However, Olive perceived it more as a diversion, a tactic to occupy his mind, steering it clear of the thoughts of Terrance, his work, or even his impending significant interview, which she had come to learn about.

And while Olive believed their kitchen was perfectly fine as is, she recognized that when Richie set his mind to something, persuasion wasn't an option. He mentioned a few neighbors who had recently revamped their kitchens, explaining that theirs needed to be the most impressive in the neighborhood to preserve its value.

Olive attributed much of Richie's behavior to his upbringing as an only child of sorts—accustomed to having his desires met and a stickler for order. And while Olive was an only child on paper, she seldom felt like one, having shared her early childhood home in Indiana with her cousins when her mom was still alive.

Despite his pampered aura, Richie Wentworth wasn't welcomed into this world as an only child. His older brother, Wells, was already the star of the family, naturally outshining him with an effortless blend of good looks, keen intellect, and a commanding athletic prowess—traits that, in their father's eyes, undoubtedly cast a long shadow over Richie. Their father never shied away from calling out Richie's perceived inadequacies against Wells' superiorities. But Wells, despite basking in their father's adulation, never lorded his favored status over Richie. Instead, he would often jest at their father's expense in a brotherly effort to buoy Richie's spirits, an act that Richie, in his heart, cherished. Wells was less a brother and more a surrogate father to him, a fact he once vulnerably shared with Olive so long ago. Yet, silently, Richie struggled with an inner conviction he also shared: his father was right. Wells was, and always would be, the better of the two Wentworth brothers, the son who shone more brightly.

And so, when, on a bitter winter morning, fifteen-year-old Wells plummeted through the ice at their cottage on Lake Superior, Richie's world disintegrated—forty-eight excruciating hours passed before the local search and rescue team recovered Wells' lifeless body. The tragedy permanently altered Mr. Wentworth Sr. for the worse. While Richie tried to cast light into the darkened shadows of their relationship, the chasm between father and son only deepened, filled with an intensified anger that often took the form of venomous words aimed at Richie: it should have been him beneath the ice, not Wells. Conversely, Richie's mother pivoted her entire emotional world around him, showering him with an almost suffocating affection and indulgence.

Yet, beneath the surface charm and easy smile, Richie harbored a tireless hunger to carve out his own worth. A full scholarship to the University of Michigan was his golden ticket, where his path serendipitously crossed with Olive one fall afternoon during a med school chemistry class. Olive was there as a first-year student, still getting her footing. Richie wasn't even enrolled in the class; he'd just stopped by to collect a letter of recommendation from the professor for his residency applications. But that brief encounter shifted everything. Their eyes met across the cluttered lab table, and something clicked. They found common ground, not just in their shared pursuit of medicine, but also in mutual grief—the losses of pivotal family members. Her mother and his brother. In this shared ache, they also discovered their respective fathers shared a particular unfortunate disposition, and they bonded over stories of angry patriarchal assholes. Men haunted by their own anger. It was the kind of pain that didn't need much explaining.

"This one has a more pronounced grain," Richie says, his fingers gently brushing the grey tones on the white quartz. "Do you like it?" His focus is intently locked onto the slab, a concentration that Olive keenly recognizes.

Observing the expansive sheet of material, Olive's mind is still in a whirlwind of thoughts since speaking with Hannah and Colin, making the task of selecting a mere surface detail feel inconsequential. She'd rather be anywhere else at this moment, yet she wants to be present with her husband, to demonstrate that she cares.

She looks to her right and notices a sparkling grey granite. *That one is much more my style and pleasing to the eye.* But Olive understood that when it came to Richie, compromise wasn't often attainable. It always felt like a no-win situation. And if she lost him, she would be nothing. She would *only* be the woman whose daughter drowned on Duck Lake. She knew he clearly liked the white marble, so she nodded apathetically.

"Yes, I like that one," she affirmed, her expression still blank. "It'll coordinate nicely with the bathrooms." Richie signals an associate across the store with a whistle, pointing towards the chosen marble slab. He turns to Olive and notices her distant demeanor.

"What's wrong?" he asks.

"Nothing, I just don't feel well today."

A tinge of annoyance creeps into his expression. "We've been over this. There is nothing physically or medically wrong with you. Just keep taking your prescriptions, and whatever you're feeling will subside." He pauses to see if she is receiving the information in the way one of his patients would.

Even though Olive hears the conviction in her husband's voice, she knows something is amiss, something beyond the reach of medication. Women are intuitive like that, and her own intuition can't be suppressed any longer. The ringing in her ears, the migraines, the numbness in her arms and legs, the sleepless nights. Those pills are not the answer anymore. She's aware Richie liked to fix things instead of listening. But how could her oncologist husband fail to see that she'd been deteriorating internally for years now?

Richie snaps his fingers in front of her. "Hello? Are you hearing me? It's a mental issue, all in your head. Take your medications; I've noticed you haven't been, and that makes me worried. You can't just skip doses. There will be severe side effects."

She nods as the sales associate approaches them. Richie gives him the specs and hands over his black Mastercard for the deposit. He then steps aside to take a call from the hospital. Olive suddenly feels like a burden. All day, her husband had to deal with sick people; it isn't exactly convenient to come home to it, too.

She stares off at the hardware options, a variety of knobs and handles in gold and bronze finishes. She catches a woman who looks familiar staring at her, but Olive can't quite place her.

"Olive Wentworth?" the woman says with a squeal. She approaches Olive and quickly grabs her for a sorority-type hug—waist out, bent knees, one hand. "It's Audrey, Audrey Assyrian!" she exclaims. Olive studies her appearance: a platinum blond bob, brown eyes, a bronze tan, and a J. Crew button-up dress. This was the mother of Landon's best friend growing up. They lived down the cul-de-sac in their neighborhood before moving to a newer lake community years ago. The two boys would run through the sprinklers in the summer and sled down the big hill in the winter. She has a younger daughter now, too, Olive believed, born post-Kate.

"It's been years! My God, you haven't aged at all. You bitch," Audrey jokes with a laugh. It was true, Olive did not look forty-two. She'd been blessed with her beautiful mother's genes and the gift of isolating herself from the sun and people. The only line that could be found on her was the small scar placed perfectly on her right cheekbone.

"And what about me? Not a day over thirty, right?" She winks at Olive, who agrees with a shy nod. Clearly, Audrey knew she looked good. "Joe has me doing all this alternative type therapy, you know, cold plunges and red-light therapy in the morning."

Olive highly suspected that some Botox was also involved somewhere in this regimen.

"I love this dress, so Martha's Vineyard!" Audrey reaches out, touching the soft sundress. Olive bites her tongue, trying not to appear awkward and say it was only $19 from TJ Maxx. She instead stares down at it, smoothing out a crease.

"Thanks. How have you been? How are the kids?" Olive attempts to navigate through the familiar rhythm of what a conversation between friends might sound like, keeping the questions flowing. She had discovered that people often enjoyed being the subject of discussion. Especially since Kate's funeral, understanding who genuinely stood by her side had become vividly clear. After the loss, many seemed to drift away, the shared pain perhaps too heavy a burden to bear in friendship. Audrey, while occasionally checking in, had maintained a calculated distance afterwards, especially visible during school events involving the boys. Eventually, when geography drew the boys to different middle school zones, their interactions withered away.

She had been at that fateful Fourth of July party. Audrey and her family had made an early exit after Audrey's unceremonious vomiting into Olive's plant bed. She had told everyone it was food poisoning, yet Olive quietly speculated she had been overserved. It was around the same time that Olive's own recollections of the night became hazy, blurred at the edges of her own imbibing.

"We are all so, so good. Ava is starting first grade… I know, terrifying. And little Joey, or JJ as he likes to be called now, was offered a full ride to Ohio State on a lacrosse scholarship." She smiles, waiting for Olive to update her as well.

"That's awesome," Olive exclaims.

"Yes … how is Landon? Once the boys all started driving, I swear I never see them anymore. Only the back of their heads as I yelled for them to 'watch out for deer, now.'"

Olive lets out a genuine laugh. "Watch out for deer" had become their shared quip, born from a comical irony when a woman had warned them in a children's museum parking lot about the presence of the animals on the road, only for them to almost collide with a deer on their way out. In Michigan, such incidents were as common as an insect striking a vehicle on the freeway. It had then turned into their customary farewell after leaving playdates, a lighthearted, humorous warning.

Audrey was like that, humorous, vivacious, candid, and saturated with a biting sarcasm that provided a counterbalance to Olive's quietude.

Her husband, Joe, often found himself playing the role of the moderator, trying to temper her lively antics with his inherent seriousness gently. Owning a chain of Coney Islands celebrated for serving the best Greek cuisine across the state, he was somewhat reserved, maybe even slightly aloof, in Olive's eyes. But then, there was a charming paradox in their differences that made the adage ring true: opposites do, indeed, attract.

"Landon is great, he got early admission at CCS and is doing a summer internship there before he officially starts in the fall." She pauses, making sure Richie is still out of earshot before continuing. "He's actually working on mechanical arms for amputees."

Audrey looks down at her phone and back up at Olive. "He always had such a giving heart. We all thought he would be a doctor. I remember when you and I did that field trip at the nature center and Landon was trying to save that little toad he found on our hike. The other toads were trying to eat the poor guy. Meanwhile, my kid was trying to stomp on all of them."

Olive gets a flash of a memory and laughs. "That's right! Joey always wore those huge green rainboots, stomping around everywhere."

Audrey rolls her eyes. "Those damn green boots were going to be the death of me; he wore them for a year straight. Maybe that's why we had to switch schools; the private one didn't want us anymore." The two sit there in a moment of silence, reminiscing about their younger mothering years.

"Audrey?" Richie's voice cuts through the conversation as he approaches the two women, his knack for remembering faces and names on full display. With a grin, he adds, "Shloonak?"—a familiar Chaldean greeting meaning 'how have you been?' Olive recognizes it immediately. Audrey is Chaldean, and her husband, Big Joe, is of Greek and Armenian descent—a mix that reflected Michigan's status as home to the second-largest Middle Eastern population in the country.

"Richie! Tova … good, good," Audrey replies warmly, her excitement evident. "Joe was just telling me about the huge feature piece they did on you in the *Detroit Free Press*!" Her eyes widen with admiration, her respect for Richie radiating in her expression.

"Yes, just covering the Gods of cancer, if you will. Not sure how I made the cut." Richie laughs along with Audrey.

"*The New England Journal of Medicine* is covering him next," Olive adds.

Audrey nods in awe, then turns to Olive. "Listen, Olive, why don't you meet Laura and me at the farmers' market tomorrow? You remember Laura, the twins' mom? She headed St. Thomas's Sunday School, or CCD, when the boys were little."

Olive looks over at Richie, who is now back on his phone. She can't think of a reason to say no. "Sure, I love the farmers' market. I haven't been in ages." Olive used to sell fresh bouquets and vegetables from her garden at the local Thursday summer farmer's market. It wasn't like they needed the money, but it was something for her to do. That and the paintings she would sell at the local Bees Knees art festival. This was all before Kate's passing, of course. After that, she spent her time sleeping the day away in her lake house, biting her nails to the stub, waiting for Landon to come home from school.

But now he had moved on. And as much as she yearned to shield him, she knew keeping him confined with her would be greater peril than letting him live his own life.

"Great, it's a date then. We'll see you tomorrow at ten0. Watch out for deer, now." Audrey winks, then grabs her small sample of granite board, tucks it in her hobo-style satchel, and walks out. Richie is still looking down intently at his phone.

"Is there a problem?" Olive asks, trying to peer over at his phone. He quickly tucks it away and wraps his arm around her small waist.

"Just figuring out my first interview for the journal. They're trying to move it up sooner, possibly to later this afternoon."

Olive hesitates, considering how to delicately introduce the next subject. Richie already appears a little on edge with this big interview approaching. "I was saying farewell to Hannah the other evening, and she mentioned something about witnessing a confrontation between you and Colin, our neighbor, around Christmas. Does that ring any bells for you?"

"Nothing for you to worry about, my love. Just a little dispute over property lines. Now, I need to take this call to confirm the new interview time."

Then why do I feel worried?

CHAPTER 15
RICHIE

WEDNESDAY 4 P.M.
JUNE 28, 2023

The interview's well underway by the time I ease back into my leather chair, eyes drifting toward the awards lining the bay view window. I can't help but reflect on how odd the young journalist's questions have been so far. His voice is driving me insane—it's way too nasally. You know that old saying, "he had a face for radio?" Well, this guy has a voice for silent film. To top it off, he barely sounds older than his mid-twenties, if that. Back in medical school, I learned that the frontal lobes don't fully mature until around age twenty-six, which means one can't truly grasp significant decisions until then, or conduct a proper interview, for that matter. Had I agreed to the Zoom call, I'd have a clearer sense of his age; however, my laptop camera had been acting up, so we settled on a phone call. Also, his name has slipped my mind and usually I'm good with people's names.

"Would your pursuit for this cure border on obsession?" he asks.

"Obsessed, no. I'd describe myself as focused. Determined. It could have saved people I cared about, so it became a top priority. A way to prevent such a tragedy from recurring."

"By people, you mean your daughter, Katherine?" he asks impassively. I confirm, but it's not just her. It could have saved my brother, Wells, too. He carried the gene. Technically, he didn't succumb to it, but he would have eventually. Only my parents and I knew of his condition. He was my hero and my father's golden child.

They say parents fight with the child they're most like. If that's the case, I must have been a spitting image of my father. Not the looks, of course. I was a carbon copy of my mother, receiving her amazing, thick hair and brooding eyes. I got away with a lot based on my eyes. But looks can only get you so far. I always felt you don't just inherit your mother's beautiful eyes and your father's jet-black hair. You get physical traits, but also the iniquities of your parents—a tendency to be bent or twisted in certain ways. It was in the air I breathed, the words I heard, the arguments I saw, the brother I once had. What I wish I had known then was that your parents determine your history, but your choices determine your future. No matter where you come from, your decisions are more powerful than statistics. You can have a "bad seed" of a father and still choose not to repeat history, to do what is right.

"Apologies, just reviewing my notes here. It does seem like you were laser-focused on this. Your medical school dissertation even centered around discovering this specific cure." I now really regret not opting for the Zoom interview so I could read this guy's expression.

"Impressive. You really know all the little facts and details, Mr.—"

"Conch, Maxwell Conch. The devil's in the details."

"Shall I call you Lucifer then?" I jest, half-serious. He releases a long sigh, as if I'm boring him. I need to refocus. It's been hard after burying a good friend, especially with my wife's erratic behavior. She's been out of the house more than ever, which is unlike her. I figured Terrance's death might dredge up old emotions about Kate, but I still can't wrap my head around why she can't just move on from death the way I have. The way Landon has. I mean, as *Star Wars* so eloquently stated, "There is no death, there is the Force." Death isn't an end—it's just a transition.

Ironically, Mr. Conch opened the interview by asking about my favorite movie. I told him all the *Star Wars* films, which didn't seem to win me any points. Landon and I used to watch them together, back when things were easier, before the blame settled in his eyes. Before he started resenting me for not saving his sister. Or at least, that's what I tell myself.

"We pose this next question to all oncologists. What's your take on the causes of cancer?"

"Well, there are both environmental factors, diet, and genetics, of course."

"Yes, I'm aware."

I ignore his jab and strive to stay on track. "One of the first things I learned in medical school at the University of Michigan was that our nervous systems start to form as early as three weeks in the womb. This highly sensitive system is designed to check for safety and detect cancer cells. We take in our mother's nervous system and continue to be impacted by our family environment during our formative years. If, for instance, our mother was emotionally unstable and did not receive adequate support and love, we may develop a 'short fuse' too. Therefore, it is evident that our emotional reactions as well as genetic conditions as adults are not necessarily our own doing." At least that's what I tell myself.

"The classic nature versus nurture debate. I'm intrigued," he responds. I draw a relieved breath.

"Let's schedule a second interview for …" He makes a swishing sound, as if slotting me into his bustling summer schedule. My eyes fall on the clock. Somehow, an hour has flown by. "How about the day before the Fourth of July, Monday the third?"

"Perfect," I reply. I'll remember because it's my wife's birthday.

CHAPTER 16

WEDNESDAY 4 P.M.
JUNE 28, 2023

Olive disregards her husband's expert advice, now leaving her p.m. tacklebox of meds full. She has a burst of energy after an afternoon cup of coffee and decides to tackle the backyard and revamp her vegetable garden until her husband's interview is over. She can hear Richie speaking sternly on the phone in his study as she peers out at the peaceful expanse of the lake. The once-manicured garden is now overrun with stubborn weeds encroaching along the human-made shoreline. The garden holds a significance that pulls at Olive's heart. She'd been wanting to tidy it up for many summers, but it reminded her too much of when the kids were little.

Amidst the encroaching weeds, a few resilient strawberries and flowers have managed to thrive. She recognizes the parallel between their tenacity and the lingering grip of grief. Just like a weed, grief could be temporarily subdued, but unless the root were addressed, it would resurface with a vengeance. Today, Olive resolves to at least confront the unruly garden, which would somewhat mitigate her pain.

As she climbs around the deck, pushing through the foliage, her eyes catch a groove in the wood where the first step meets the patio. It marks the spot where Terrance had face-planted down the stairs, his beer shattering against the stained lumber. Usually fine with four beers, that particular night he'd mixed them with the oxycodone he'd taken for his knee surgery. Richie had sent him with a bottle of water to sit by the lake, but Olive's memory of what happened after was a haze. Now, the morning sun illuminates the scars of that night, etched into the deck.

Lulu quacks from the water. Olive knows it most likely isn't the original Lulu, considering ducks only live about ten years, but the idea of it being *her* is all she needs. She's back—this time with two smaller brown ducks. Olive takes off her gardening gloves and slowly walks down to the shoreline, following the ducklings.

"It's been ages since I've seen them here!" Mrs. Schmidt screams from her yard. She approaches the shore as the ducks enter at the beginning of her property. She, too, is out gardening and is wearing a glittered visor and a large lavender Mumu dress.

"I know, they're beautiful." Olive smiles.

"I wouldn't go that far. They usually shit all over the dock." Mrs. Schmidt isn't one to censor herself. "Since Harold moved out, I've started noticing the few useful things he actually did around here—like cleaning this damn mess. Now it's my glamorous new chore." She strides toward the ducks, gesturing at them crowding her shoreline.

Harold Schmidt was always a quiet, mellow-mannered guy. He was a retired park ranger and had mentioned to Olive once that the lack of ducks could be due to the recent uptick in pollution on the lake from the wakeboarder boats, which were also slowly eroding and ruining the shorelines and lake bottom. Every summer, he'd canvassed the neighborhood, clipboard in hand, gathering signatures to impose a ban, yet he never garnered enough support. Once retired, Terrance assumed the mantle of neighborhood association president and took particular care to thwart Mr. Schmidt's persistent attempts to outlaw his cherished boat. He made it a point to caution the neighbors to keep their pens at bay whenever Mr. Schmidt and the clipboard made their rounds. But Mr. Schmidt seemed like a decent man. Olive couldn't imagine what he'd done to be kicked out of his house. Despite her love for discussing other people, Mrs. Schmidt didn't share her own personal issues.

"So how are you holding up, hun? I still cannot believe Terrance is gone. I saw him *that* morning; I wish I could've done something to save him."

Olive absorbs the detail, a flicker of interest sparking behind her eyes. Without fully realizing it, she crosses the property line into the Schmidts' yard, drawn in by something unspoken. Her eyes meet the woman standing there, broad-shouldered and solid.

"You saw Terrance that morning?"

"Well, yes. I told the police officer he was pounding on my door the morning before he passed. They didn't give a flying rat's ass about that. They say he was intoxicated and fell into the lake. End of story."

Olive thinks back to that morning. "How early in the morning was this?"

Mrs. Schmidt peels off her gardening gloves and settles into her lawn chair. "Just about dawn; I reckon it was around six. His surprise was quite evident when I opened the door. I thought maybe he was returning the crockpot he borrowed for Memorial Day, then I noticed my car had a flat tire in the driveway. I thought he might be offering a helping hand. Would you believe six nails in one tire? Certainly seems deliberate. And not your everyday I-696 construction mishap nails, mind you."

Olive releases a breath and forces a smile, trying to steer old Mrs. Schmidt back on track. "So, you saw Terrance at your door . . ."

"Yes, he gave me this hollow-eyed look, then staggered back down the steps and continued on his way, saying nothing. Rather odd, but I suppose substances can distort one's senses, the poor soul."

Olive contemplates the possibility of Terrance knocking on her door that same morning—that unexpected knock at such an early hour.

"Oh dear, I promised Hannah I would haul the trash bins out before she left." Mrs. Schmidt glances at her watch and then up the imposing hill. It's Wednesday, just trash day. No recycle.

"No worries, I can do it."

"Are you sure? I don't want to make it a bother. But I suppose if it doesn't get taken out, we'll have some raccoons scavenging the neighborhood. And I do need to head to Kohl's shortly; gotta use up my Kohl's cash before it expires tomorrow."

"Not a problem at all. Hannah gave me a key to the house for showings."

Mrs. Schmidt exhales, her body sinking heavily into the lawn chair. The thought of hiking back up the hill and over to Terrance's may have put her into cardiac arrest.

Right as Olive turns to walk up the steep incline, she hears Mrs. Schmidt mumbling to herself in a hushed tone, "Two deaths at this lake, what in the world?"

It triggers her to remember that small mention from Mrs. Schmidt at the funeral. "Sheri, what was it you were saying the other day? Something about how I had known about Kate being gone before the drowning happened? Before anyone found her."

Mrs. Schmidt tilts her head as if concentrating hard, her glitter visor reflecting onto the lake. "You should speak to Jimmy, my nephew. He was one of the EMTs who took care of you that night. You were saying a lot of crazy things to him. Then again, if I were half in the bag and found my daughter dead at my own party, I probably would be too." Again, no filter for Mrs. Schmidt. Never delicate, just straight to the point. "He now works at the Rite Aid off Grand River as a pharmacist's assistant. I think the EMT gig was too much for his sensitive heart to handle. Tell him Auntie Sheri sent you. He's good people."

Good people was a phrase Olive hadn't heard since she was a kid. A Midwest phrase, mainly because Midwesterners were known for being genuine and good people. And Michigan was full of small towns with good people. But what Olive was starting to come to terms with was that not *all* people in her small community were good people. They were people with secrets. And in small towns, there are no secrets that stay buried.

Nurturing her thirst with a glass of ice-cold water, Olive commences her journey down the street towards Terrance's home beneath the suburban sun. With the garbage collection not until the later hours on Fridays, she has ample time. Her path intersects with Colin, and they exchange a smile and a wave.

He seems to be surprisingly visible this summer. Olive hadn't seen him out this frequently before, but it had also been quite a while since her last leisurely late-day stroll. Back when she did walk this late in the day, neighborly interactions typically consisted of a customary Michigan wave, then continuing without delay. During the peak of the pandemic, if anyone did halt her, it was to direct questions towards Richie's medical expertise: vaccine readiness, booster safety. Not a soul sought to enquire about her own well-being. Likewise, no one had shown interest in Terrance's circumstances until they dredged his body from the neighborhood's collective waters. And now Olive was at his home.

Extracting the key from her leggings' pocket, she unlocks the side garage door, immediately being assaulted by a pungent, nauseating odor. The stench is so potent that her eyes involuntarily tear up. Tracing the source, she cautiously approaches the trash, nudging the lid open with trepidation. An unbagged, decomposing rotisserie chicken and an open container of Brussel sprouts greet her. It strikes her as an odd selection for what turned out to be a final meal, although Terrance couldn't have known that. With one hand clamped over her nose and mouth, she maneuvers the hefty trash can with the other, wheeling it to the curb. Gazing at her hands in disgust, she steps back into the garage, searching for the recycling bin. It would be easier to just leave it out until Friday, she thinks—easier than coming back here for a second time. The thought of Terrance never setting foot in this house again twists her stomach into knots. She scans the dim garage, her eyes flicking over the shadows and clutter, but the bin is nowhere to be found.

Acting on an unplanned impulse, she ascends the steps and opens the door that leads into the house, crossing the threshold into her deceased neighbor's dwelling. Maybe the recycle bin had been thrown into the mud room.

The interior is somewhat unkempt, although not as disorderly as she might have expected from a bachelor's residence. A junk drawer protrudes in the kitchen, flanked by a modest pile of dirty dishes. This is her first glimpse into Terrance's home.

Richie, on the other hand, had frequented the space on numerous occasions, engaging in poker nights and football viewings.

There's no recycling bin in sight, yet she continues further into the home, curious about Terrance's final hours. A floorboard creaks under her foot as she moves past the dining room, which contains an elegant baby grand piano. She pauses, allowing her fingers to dance across the keys in a fleeting moment. While it has been years since she's played, memories of teaching her children, especially Kate's enthusiastic embrace of the instrument, surface in her mind. Richie had relegated their own piano to the darkened confines of the basement, concealed under a white linen blanket. A single comment he made after the drowning still pierces her like a sharply thrust dagger.

"Why did you teach our daughter to play the piano rather than swim?" he had questioned her one evening, staring out at the darkened lake.

Perhaps he had a point, but at the time, exposing her to a public pool amidst cancer treatments had seemed a formidable proposition. As for the lake, that wasn't much better. Kate could never focus long enough to learn. She was more interested in the ducks and frogs than listening to instructions, often pretending she was a lily pad herself, drifting through the reeds in her own little world. But playing the piano had been their shared activity, an intimate union in the comfort of their home, fingers coaxing melodies like "Chopsticks," or Kate's favorite, "Down by the Bay." A twinge of guilt accompanies the memory, that jab feeling deserved. Safeguarding Kate had been her primary responsibility as a mother.

She removes her hand from the black-and-white keys and approaches the corner of the room to find Terrance's den ahead. It's exactly as she thought it would be, a room that embodied his pride and accomplishments. Trophies, plaques, and framed jerseys adorn the walls and a small picture of Hannah rests on his mahogany desk. He was a proud man, and this den displays it. There are bills scattered across the desk and an open moving box in the corner of the room, as if someone started packing, then stopped. It has to be Hannah's as it contains many of her childhood items.

She leans over the desk to get a closer look at the box, and her eyes fall upon a familiar name: Landon, written in a child's scrawl on a sealed, wrinkled envelope. She's both intrigued and puzzled.

Olive hears a car pull up and peers out the front window. It's Terrance's aunt. *Shit. Why am I trying to play Nancy Drew?* She quickly grabs the envelope, tucking it into her fanny pack, and runs to the garage. To her surprise, she immediately spots the green recycle bin full of empty, expensive liquor and wine bottles. It had been tucked behind Terrance's leased Lamborghini. She only knew it was leased because Richie gave him a hard time about it when he was over at their home this past spring for a U of M March Madness game. She grabs the bin and quickly walks out to the driveway as the elder aunt approaches her.

"Who the hell are you?" the woman says while pointing at Olive.

"Hi, you're Terrance's aunt? I'm Olive. I met you at the funeral. I live across the street, and Hannah asked me to take the trash out and check on the house until the realtor comes by." She reaches her hand out to shake the woman's hand, the other gripping the recycle bin.

"Aunt Pearl," she replies, emphasizing the "au" in the word, instead of how Michiganders pronounce it, like "ant." She must not be from around here.

The woman stares her up and down, then leans in for the shake. "Forgive me, my manners have been all over the place lately. I didn't realize how many neighbors Hannah had helping out with the home. This has really shaken up our family. Hannah asked if I could start boxing up some of Terrance's personal items before they show the house. My poor sister couldn't handle the deed."

"Yes, of course," Olive says, nodding. There is an odd silence as the two grieving women stand there, the afternoon sun starting to peer out onto them from behind heavy clouds.

"Well, I'll just take this to the curb and be on my way. Let me know if you need any help," Olive says.

The elder woman nods back and heads towards the garage.

Olive exhales and walks the long stretch to the end of the driveway so she can drop the heavy bin down next to the trash can. As the bin hits the cement, she hears a rattling noise. Something has fallen out. It appears to be a pill bottle. She reaches down and picks it up. There's one lone pill inside it, and half the label is missing—the name of the prescription and patient peeled off. But one thing hits her immediately—the patient's date of birth: 7.3.1982.

Her birthdate.

She knew she didn't share a birthdate with Terrance. He was a Christmas baby and years older than her. She looks at the bottom of the bottle, which reads Rite Aid. It looks like she'll be seeing Mrs. Schmidt's nephew sooner rather than later.

The moment she walks into her home, Olive finds herself back in Landon's silent bedroom. Clutching the envelope, aged and inscribed with "Landon" in the uneven script of a crayon, she hesitates, contemplating calling him before opening it. Resolute, she finally splits the seal with a swift, deliberate motion. Her eyes land at the bottom of the letter first, simply signed "your summer best friend, Hannah," the writing's imperfections hinting at a rushed farewell:

Dear Landon,

I've been thinking about you a lot. I know we'll see Kate again. I'm sorry I have to leave so quickly. I'll miss our adventures by the lake and all the fun we had together this summer.

I want you to know that I don't want to leave, but my dad said it's for my safety. He said sometimes accidents happen and sometimes good people do bad things. I don't really understand what he means, but I trust him.

I can't wait for the day we can play again. I hope it's soon, or maybe you can come visit me in Florida. I made a drawing on the back of us by the lake, so you won't forget me. You'll always be my summer best friend.

– Your Summer Best Friend, Hannah
PS Your mom knows. Please talk to her.
PSS Remember to give Lulu a hug goodbye from me.

After absorbing it all, Olive deciphers that this note marked Hannah's final goodbye to Landon. He did wonder why she left so abruptly that fateful summer.

What did she know? The room begins to spin around her.

CHAPTER 17

THURSDAY 10 A.M.
JUNE 29, 2023

Olive had always cherished her visits to the local farmers' market. It used to be an opportunity for her to catch up on the latest happenings, sample new fruits and vegetables, and show her support for the close-knit community of the small lakeside town. This particular Thursday feels like a trip down memory lane, and with good company. Meeting up with Audrey and Laura seemed like a pleasant diversion from the labyrinth of unanswered questions that had been entwining her thoughts. She had texted Landon to confirm he would be home this weekend for the lake's fireworks. She received a single thumbs-up emoji in return. Perhaps he could shed some light on Hannah's artifact of a letter; it was, after all, meant for him. Meanwhile, her lead on Jimmy would also have to wait—she had learned after calling the pharmacy that he wouldn't be back from vacation until tomorrow.

As Olive strolls through the market, the scent of baked goods and fresh herbs fills the air. As she admires a basket of vibrant raspberries, she hears a familiar voice calling her name.

"Olive! I haven't seen you in years!" a voice calls out, high with surprise. Olive turns to find her old friend Laura, flanked by Audrey and a tall, scholarly-looking woman she doesn't recognize. The three of them look so natural together, and Olive can't blame them for filling the space she left behind.

Laura pulls Olive into a tight hug, holding on a beat too long. When she pulls back, her eyes are glassy, and her smile trembles at the corners—as if seeing Olive has shaken something loose she didn't expect.

Olive takes in her old friend's new appearance, amazed at how much she has changed: a breast enhancement job, bangs, and a few extra pounds in all the right places. All the ups and downs and add-ons of being a middle-aged woman.

The third unknown woman stays put, observing Olive.

"Hi, I'm Olive." Olive extends her hand out.

"Oops, forgot my manners, I'm sorry, this is Shay Everly. Actually, Dr. Everly," Audrey interjects.

Shay reaches for Olive's hand firmly. "It's a pleasure, Olive. I've heard great things about you," she says with a raspy voice. Olive winces at the statement. She already knows what she's heard about her.

Amidst the bustling market crowd, the four women find themselves standing awkwardly as people pass around them like fish swimming upstream.

"Ladies! Come try my special jam!" Mrs. Schmidt's hoarse voice catches the women by surprise, prompting them to move away from the center of the market. She holds out her jam on a tasting spoon she pulled from a jar, reading *Sheri's Special Jelly.*

"I'm staying away from sugars right now," Laura replies.

Audrey pulls out a wad of twenties and hands one over to Mrs. Schmidt. "I'll take two, Sheri. My daughter loves your special jam."

Mrs. Schmidt smiles proudly. "Have you seen Jimmy yet?" Mrs. Schmidt asks Olive.

"It's on my to-do list," she replies, fully cognizant that Jimmy's upcoming shift back to work is scheduled for tomorrow morning.

"Here, on the house for the doctor's wife." Mrs. Schmidt hands her a small jar of tangerine jam.

Olive notices Shay's unwavering eyes upon her.

"Why don't we head over to the picnic tables?" Audrey suggests. Seated around the tables, the women catch up over homemade lemonade. Olive discovers that Shay and Audrey's daughters are good friends and that she, too, went to U of M for medical school. The conversation shifts to school safety concerns.

"We're thinking about moving our daughters to a private school for the rest of their higher education. You can't be too careful these days with all the shootings. The thought of losing a child—" Audrey stops herself.

Laura and Shay turn their attention to Olive, whose face turns crimson. "Oh gosh, I'm sorry, Olive. I didn't mean to bring anything up like that."

Olive reassures them with a strained smile that it's okay. Audrey swiftly changes the subject, briefly discussing JJ moving out, earning a subtle eye roll from Laura.

After about forty-five minutes of chitchat, Olive glances at her watch. Reconnecting with her old friends has been nice, reminding her of the value of human connection. However, her social energy has reached its limit for the day.

She begins to feel dizzy, and her legs tingle. She notices a high-pitched noise, but knows only she can hear it, like a dog whistle. She's a slave to the stimuli; every sight and sound is like nails on a chalkboard, while Laura's monologue about their new cottage in Muskegon continued, along with the subtle jab about its quaintness compared to Audrey's cottage in Glen Arbor.

"Are you okay?" Shay whispers. *Leave it to the doctor to ask.* Olive struggles to respond. She feels almost intoxicated, barely able to string a sentence together. Is this withdrawal or something else? It is also day two of her period; her symptoms always heightened at this time of the month. Her stomach tightens, twisting into a tense knot.

"Yes, just feeling a bit tired. I get these weird dizzy spells sometimes."

Shay offers her a serene smile, exuding a soothing presence. Since taking a seat, she's been relatively quiet, but there is authenticity and candor in her eyes that put Olive at ease. Perhaps it's the color of Shay's deep brown irises that are like Landon's.

"You know," Shay says softly, her voice steady, "our brains operate on two fuels: fear and love. But never at the same time. You can't heal while you're stuck in fear."

"Olive, Shay's a psychiatrist," Audrey chimes in, her tone light but with an undercurrent of meaning. "Maybe she could offer some insight. Not that you need help, of course! You know what I mean …" The stumble in Audrey's words hints at the possibility that this reunion was more of an intervention than a simple get-together.

"Here. Call me anytime." Shay pushes her thick business card across the picnic table. Olive stares down at it. Shay Everly, Psychiatrist. Below that, in smaller letters, reads "Specializing in grief counseling."

There it is. Her heart beats faster. She quickly picks up the card and tosses it into her fanny pack. The women bid their farewells, Olive promising not to be a stranger.

"By the way, Olive, I'm still running the CCD group at St. Thomas. I see Richie most Sundays, but never you," Laura states, judgment noticeable in her tone. Audrey stands next to her, nodding in agreement.

Laura had long been a pillar of faith, always at the helm of the Confraternity of Christian Doctrine and deeply involved in the education department at St. Thomas. She was equally gifted in conversation, able to weave words that could captivate your attention completely. However, her penchant for sharing one's confidences with the next listener was a less celebrated trait.

"I would never want you to think we ditched you. Richie just told us you needed some space," Laura adds, her words now carrying a hint of concern.

"Yes, I need to make more of an effort to get back there," Olive responds, clutching her small bag of fruit tightly as her body sways a little.

"Yes, well. As they say, wives must honor their husbands. You should join him at the next service," Laura suggests with a smile.

Olive nods, realizing it is officially time to depart.

CHAPTER 18

THURSDAY 6 P.M.
JUNE 28, 2023

After an afternoon nap, Olive is ensconced once more in the confines of the local Al-Anon meeting room. She sits next to Colin, who smells of freshly cut grass and mint. *He must have mowed his lawn today*, she thinks, inhaling his scent. The atmosphere is uncharacteristically stuffy, hinting at an air conditioning malfunction. Overhead, the harsh glow of fluorescent lights intermittently glistens, momentarily distracting Olive. Colin's voice, imbued with a hint of concern in a hushed tone, interrupts her overstimulation. "Everything okay?"

She responds with a nod, her legs wound tightly beneath her, an embodiment of her restless anxiety. This evening is reserved for unraveling the deeper content of Colin's connection not just to Richie, but also his evident discomfort surrounding the Fourth of July party so many years ago.

At the front of the room, Dodge takes his position. "My friends, today's discussion centers around forgiveness and self-care. Some of you have some big things to forgive. And trust is a problem we all walk in here with. All the lies, the betrayals, the secrets … my God, the secrets." Dodge takes a step back to inhale lukewarm air. She has to give it to him. He does have an incredible speaking voice. It is as powerful as Morgan Freeman's. But the concept of forgiveness seemed better left unaddressed, festering within her. She had already forgiven her father for being a drunk years ago. He did the best he could with what little he had.

She struggled to extend the same grace to herself. How could she forgive her own actions —the unwatchful mother who got recklessly drunk, the wife who disrupted her husband's career? Kate's drowning derailed Richie's research, resulting in another seven years of research, as she had found out at his recent award ceremony. She knew her daughter's condition was unique, as were candidates willing to try experimental testing.

Richie was a good man with the misfortune of losing a child, which had hardened him and made him distant. However, lately, since Terrance's passing, he had almost seemed more aloof. Then again, losing a friend can do that. And here Olive sat, not on any of her meds, out at nighttime with another man—quite the opposite of what Richie expected of her. The doctor's good wife. But she couldn't worry about that now; she needed to focus on *why* she was here.

"Does anyone want to share something they have forgiven and moved on from?" Dodge asks, then adds, "Remember, the loneliness that comes from speaking your truth is way more peaceful than the companionship that comes from living a lie."

Colin looks over at Olive and smiles, but she can tell it's forced.

"Well, I for one feel like my relationship has been co-dependent," Colin starts, glancing over at her briefly before continuing. "How do I start fresh to forgive someone? Don't you have to be in a safe place to do that? Otherwise, how can you possibly be vulnerable with them again?" Colin probes. A few others nod in agreement.

"It starts with stepping back from putting the person with the problem before your own needs," Dodge replies. Olive takes in Colin's intense expression. She then thinks of Julie's purple mouth the night of the party and feels for him. He's fully engaged, absorbing the words as if they were tailored for him. She muses that perhaps his focus on his wife's recovery and the heartache of her betrayal had left him little room for his own growth. After all, you can't grow your own garden if you don't water it.

Dodge continues, "If you can't draw a line in the sand and set boundaries, it is guaranteed to make you sick. To quote someone I can't remember, your body keeps the score—and it's crazy how intertwined our bodies and minds truly are."

A heavyset woman raises her hand, and Dodge points at her. "But what if the person needs help? What if they're gonna kill themselves if they keep using? We're just supposed to ignore them and focus on ourselves?" Her face is a mix of confusion and utter despair.

"Listen, it's you or them. You forgive and move on. Sometimes you have to let someone sink if they refuse to swim. They have to decide to change; you can't do that for them. The fastest way to dysregulate your nervous system is to have empathy for others without boundaries for yourself," Dodge says, his wisdom reverberating in the air. He settles back into his seat and pulls a rag from his weathered jeans to wipe the sweat from his forehead. Olive reflects on his bold statement. She always wondered if there was anything more she could have done for her father. Then again, she could also hear her dad whispering in her ear how these people seeking help at an Al-Anon meeting were not built Ford tough. But *these people* who surround her in this overheated room weren't looking for advice. They were looking for empathy.

As individuals recounted tales of restless nights, dwindling funds, and deteriorating health, Olive saw the echo of herself in their narratives. The weariness she'd attributed to underlying health issues or shifting medications was now tinged with new understanding. Since recently liberating herself from all of those dependencies cold turkey, memories were reemerging like pieces of a puzzle she'd lost long ago. Was her body trying to reassemble a long-buried truth? Something she had failed to acknowledge or had intentionally suppressed?

As the sharing continued, one voice resonated more profoundly and burlier than the rest, pulling Olive out of her introspection. It was unmistakably Big Joe, Audrey's husband. He was hidden in the back of the room, wedged in between two older gentlemen.

"So you're permitting us to wipe our hands clean? Just walk away from the person. Doesn't that make us just as bad?" he asks, his voice sharp, almost cracking, like he's barely keeping something down. His foot taps, restless, and his eyes won't stay still.

"Sometimes people vilify others to alleviate their own guilt," Dodge responds nonchalantly. Joe stares back with his poker face, clearly not happy with the answer. His mirrored sunglasses and disheveled appearance simulate his inner turmoil. He doesn't seem to notice Olive. *Who was he here for?* Olive wondered. Audrey liked to have a good time, no doubt about that, but she didn't appear to have a problem.

"Listen, whatever this person is going through, it's not about you. It's about them trying to escape their own pain," Dodge adds. "When someone is in active addiction, what they're really experiencing is active grief, using the addiction to mask that pain. It could be something from their past."

A quiet settles over the room as people begin to stand and make their way out.

"Hey folks, before everyone heads out, this is a reminder that we will not have a meeting next week due to the holiday. Also, Ms. Rita has an announcement," Dodge says. Sweat is now seeping from his neck onto his shirt, the room now a temperature adjacent to that of the sun.

An older woman with an overbearing amount of makeup on stands up. "Hello, everyone. I'm Rita Harris." She smiles wide, revealing lipstick on her teeth. "I just wanted to remind those who have RSVP'd and invite all of you newcomers to our Up North July retreat. This is not affiliated with Al-Anon, but it's a retreat designed to help you heal and work on yourself. A healing, wellness retreat, if you will."

Colin reaches out and takes a pamphlet from her.

"Now the only cost to you is lodging at the cabins in Traverse City. Our generous donors have covered everything. We would love to have you all join and heal as a community. The retreat starts July second and will end on the fourth."

Once in the confines of his car, Colin and Olive stare at the pamphlet. Its cover is adorned with imagery of a campfire, canoes, and someone receiving a massage.

"You're not seriously contemplating going to this thing?"

Olive says, keeping her tone calm and assertive. "It seems weird. You'd be out there in the middle of nowhere, surrounded by a group of damaged people dealing with some depressing stuff."

"We're all carrying our wounds, Olive. Maybe you should chat with your husband about damaged people," he responds.

Olive crosses her arms. "What's that supposed to mean? What is your issue with Richie? And what happened between the two of you the night of the Fourth of July party? Or even Christmas break, for that matter?" As she awaits his reply, her eyes wander, taking in the strength and definition of Colin's chest beneath his snug white jersey shirt. With her medications in the rearview, her long-dormant desires have returned, yearning for connection. She had tried to rekindle this with Richie just the night before, but he had been unresponsive and preoccupied.

"You need to take that up with him. I'm not going to get involved in a marriage. I've already had that happen to me."

"Well, you kind of already have. You've been dragging me here and ..."

Before Olive can finish her probing, Colin's ringtone cuts through the air. She can tell by the way his body tenses up when he looks at his phone that it must be Julie. He lowers the volume, shielding her from Julie's side of the conversation.

Colin's voice is strained, but it's the expression on his face that says everything—tight-lipped, shoulders hunched, eyes fixed somewhere far beyond the windshield. Whatever this call is, it's unraveling fast. Olive shifts in her seat, the silence pressing in on her, thick and awkward. She doesn't belong here. Not in this conversation. Not in this space. Her fingers fidget at her side until she catches movement out the window. Big Joe is sauntering toward his truck, his back turned. She seizes the moment. The car door groans as she pushes it open.

"Joe! Joe, wait up," she calls, her voice rising just enough to carry, a flicker of relief blooming as she steps out into the open air.

He turns around, still wearing the cop-like sunglasses, and his mouth quivers a bit. "Olive. I knew I would run into someone going to the local meeting."

A hesitant hug ensues between them.

"This is a tad awkward. I won't lie," Joe continues, his hand clutching his car keys so tight she can see the veins in his hand bulging.

"I'm not here to judge you, Joe. I'm here for similar reasons. You know what they say: when the house is on fire, we don't tell people to watch their tone as they yell for help. Everyone reacts to crises differently." She tries to sound empathetic.

Joe manages a strained smile. "Listen, no parent wants to believe there is something terribly wrong with their child. But there's a difference between believing it and knowing it. I can't just sit around in denial like Audrey."

His weary expression evokes sympathy from Olive. Whatever is troubling him has been a heavy burden to bear. She wonders why Audrey didn't seem to be going through the same distress. "Is it with JJ? What happened?"

Before he can respond, a sudden slam of Colin's car door, accompanied by curses, stalls the conversation. Joe seizes the opportunity to edge toward his vehicle, waving goodbye.

"I'm off to Meijer's," he says, now entering his truck.

Olive's eyes follow Joe as he peels out, leaving her to ponder what has become of young Joey — JJ, as Audrey now refers to him. She then reenters Colin's car.

"This is why we have to choose ourselves," Colin says, as if she had walked in mid-monologue. "Maybe we're not the broken ones, we're just done shrinking to keep the peace." He exhales. "I can't be here when she gets out of rehab. I'm going to the retreat. This time, I choose me."

Colin picks the pamphlet back up, hands trembling in the aftermath of the phone call.

Olive reaches over and places her hand on his. "It's going to be okay. What happened with Julie?"

Colin removes his hand from underneath hers and runs it through his hair.

"She's unsure about moving back in once she leaves her facility, and mentioned staying with her parents for a while. Then she told me there's something else she needs to discuss in person. Like, there might be something even worse than what I've already uncovered. I … I have to get home." Colin suddenly pushes against Olive, his cheek grazing hers as he secures her tightly in her seat and accelerates.

"I can buckle myself," Olive responds, noticing Colin taking deep breaths, his focus laser-sharp on the road.

"I don't understand her, Olive. The most isolating feeling is waiting for someone to love you the way you hope," Colin says with frustration, navigating the dark roads erratically.

They both say nothing for the rest of the drive. As they round the bend into the neighborhood, Olive glimpses something small in the road. "Colin, slow down."

His jaw is clenched tight, a muscle twitching near his temple. Hands gripping the wheel like it's the only thing anchoring him, he doesn't ease off the accelerator. His eyes stay fixed, rigid and unblinking, as if he's daring the road to challenge him.

She speaks louder. "Colin, I see something. Please." A sickening thud follows as the car makes contact with the small object. Every inch of Olive feels the impact.

A mixture of fear and frustration mars Colin's face as he quickly brings the car to a halt and exits. Olive follows, her eyes moving between the ground and Colin. She bends down, her heart sinking at the sight of a wounded duck. For a split second, she thinks it may have been Lulu's look-alike, but this one has more hints of hazel in its feathers, with a burnt toast color on its tail feathers. No orange bill and no dark mark on its wing. Anger brews in her chest as she watches Colin inspect the damage to the car, refusing to meet Olive's eyes.

"Colin, do you realize you nearly took a life?" Her voice shakes, but she fights to keep it steady. She reminds herself; she has a full year of medical school under her belt. She'd studied trauma response, suturing, and anatomy. But all of that vanished the moment Richie insisted she leave school, insisted she stay home once she got pregnant with Landon. And now, faced with this grisly scene—the blood, the stillness—panic claws its way up her throat. Whatever training she once had feels distant, drowned out by the rush of adrenaline and the raw fear pounding in her chest.

Colin's eyes remain on his car's front grille, and his silence speaks volumes. Her attention returns to the duck, its condition worsening as blood starts to pool under its stomach. Olive's voice quivers when she says, "We have to do something."

Colin stands there, hesitant. Olive reaches for her phone, fingers hastily typing as she shoots off a text to the only person she knows can help them the quickest. Time is of the essence.

"What are you doing?" he asks, his tone high-pitched.

Colin peels off his shirt and gently presses it over the duck's wound, careful but firm, applying pressure as blood seeps through the fabric. A pair of headlights slices through the dark, casting long beams across the road as a car approaches.

Colin's head snaps up. "Olive, get out of the road."

Ignoring his words, Olive raises her hand, signaling the vehicle to stop. The car door opens, and Richie steps out of his Porsche SUV with an air of authority. He glares at Colin's shirtless figure, then over at the injured duck.

"What the hell is going on?!" he demands.

"Richie, please. It's suffering. Please help it."

Richie's stern expression softens as he lifts Colin's bloodied white shirt to inspect the duck's wounds. The duck lies motionless, its pain unmistakable. Richie's tone remains clinical, "Its breathing is shallow, injuries severe. Even if we rushed it to the vet, survival chances would be minimal." He stands up and looks around.

"What should we do?" Olive asks, tears filling her eyes.

"We have to make a difficult decision. But it's the right one." He retrieves a heavy rock from the roadside and walks back to the duck, lifting it over his head.

"Wait!" Colin exclaims.

Olive exhales, hoping Colin can salvage the mess he created in the first place. "I have a handgun in my trunk, wouldn't that be more … humane?"

Richie looks him dead in the eyes. "More humane? The humane thing would have been not hitting it in the first place, Colin." Taking a heavy measured breath, he raises the large rock again and brings it down with swift and definitive force, striking the duck and ending its life instantly.

For Olive, the world seems to dissolve from underneath her.

The rest of the night seems like an obscure painting to Olive. Something she couldn't figure out or definitively decide on. The two men seemed to share an unspoken agreement on their actions, a shared belief that it was the right thing to do. Her heart feels heavy. The sight of the little duck has stirred something within, a trauma echoing in her. Colin's intense rage was driving through the neighborhood, his readiness to employ a firearm. And it was either heroic or unusual that her husband was able to make such a quick, hard decision to end something's life.

Regardless of the interpretation, Richie held nothing back when they returned home. His reproach was fiery, a storm unleashed upon her. She was sure the sight of finding her, his homebody wife, with a shirtless Colin, a man he seemed to have some vendetta against, brought a fire to Richie's soul.

"I don't want you around that guy. I forbid it!" Richie screams while pacing back and forth in the kitchen. Blood spatter is noticeably visible on the hem of his khaki pants. "Do you understand me? He has a temper. I've seen it firsthand."

Olive sits there on the couch like a child being scolded. "What happened between you two? Obviously, something," Olive replies in a low tone, her lips quivering.

"The guy is psycho. End of story. And why are you questioning me when you were the one who was out with him? What were you doing together?" Richie continues firing questions and rules at her rather than giving her any real answers. Outwardly, she makes herself appear stoic, weathering the storm. When he's finished, she apologizes and retreats down to the dock.

A desperate need for a calming relief pulses through her as she sifts through an old fishing box, her trembling hand pulling out a joint. She recalled having stumbled upon Landon and his friends smoking by the dock last summer, fishing being their cover. She hadn't found anything particularly wrong with them smoking weed, but she'd assumed the role of a responsible parent. She confiscated and hid it, wondering if it would be healthier than taking a pill. And now, freshly out of Valium, she desperately needed something to calm her nerves.

Sitting at the brink of the wood pier, Olive dangles her feet, letting her toes flirt with the cool lake surface. She gazes at her reflection shimmering on the water, studying the version of herself she's still learning to accept. A woman grappling with a husband who seems to be hiding something and a neighbor who has just taken a living creature's life.

She lights the joint hastily, just as she once had in college, the act of inhaling causing her to cough violently. Glancing over her shoulder, she looks at her own house and Colin's adjacent to it, both structures swallowed by darkness.

Drawing another drag, a cacophony of coughs escaping afterward, Olive inadvertently knocks the small tackle box over. Lures and hooks come tumbling out, along with a worn-out-looking business card. *Shay Everly, Psychiatrist.*

CHAPTER 19

FRIDAY 3 A.M.
JUNE 30, 2023

Olive awoke at her customary time of 3:03, the memory of the familiar reels still vivid, the scent and sensations lingering. The aroma of fresh strawberries, the sizzle of sparklers, and the sound of red wine being uncorked fill her mind. Then swiftly and vividly, it ends with screams and sirens.

She paces the house softly, wearing her plushest slippers. The dream that had abruptly woken her started almost the same as before: the one where she felt her daughter's gentle hands against her cheeks, urging her to stay awake. However, this time, her daughter conveyed fear. Olive whispered back to her, "Think of something that makes you feel happy, like watermelon seeds, smores, Lulu …" Her daughter's response was tender, "And you, Mommy. You always make me feel safe." Olive's fingers brushed against her daughter's little dimple. It had become a ritual, a way to comfort Kate during the nerve-racking experiences of medical procedures, examinations, and blood tests.

Olive can't shake the feeling that, as of late, her daughter is trying to tell her something. "Kate, what do you want me to know?" Olive whispers as she sits in the dimness of her family room, engulfed by feelings of shame and confusion. For a moment, she half expects the old family photo to crash to the floor again, just as it had before. But nothing moves. Deep down, she knows it's not the room that's haunted. It's her own mind trying to speak.

Melancholy was a word she once heard and decided it perfectly described how she felt. *Gloomiest of spirits wrapped up in sorrowful thoughts*. She swears she can faintly hear the piano playing in the basement. The gentle patter of raindrops against the window eases her a little. An early morning storm has arrived. She had always loved watching the disturbances form in the clouds as a kid.

It is almost six when Olive realizes she needs to start the coffee. Richie's departure is imminent. A sudden two-day medical conference at the Cleveland Clinic demands his attention. Fortunately, he will be spending the night. Olive can't manage any more unpredictable mood swings from men right now.

Around 6:30 a.m., Richie descends, looking sharp in his navy suit, tie, Gucci shoes, and matching belt. The scent of strong cologne wafts from him as he clutches a small rollaway bag.

"Good morning, my love," he greets her warmly, planting a kiss on her unkept hair. His demeanor has shifted drastically from the night before as he pours a cup of coffee into a to-go mug. Checking his Rolex, he remarks, "I'm off. Wish me luck. I should be back by tomorrow evening." He exits the room but then returns. "Oh, I know you're swamped, but if you could find the time to pick up my dry cleaning, I'd appreciate it." Olive notes the sarcasm in his tone.

"Good luck, drive safe," she manages to mutter.

"Listen, you just have to trust me about that guy." He nods his head towards Colin's house, his eyes wide. He's treating her like an object, one he wants to keep to himself.

"I apologize for yelling yesterday. Gotta run." With his briefcase and coffee in hand, he leaves before she can engage.

The second the door closes behind him, Olive retrieves her purse. From it, she produces two identical business cards for Dr. Everly, one considerably more worn than the other. The presence of Shay's card among their fishing gear nags at her. Her penetrating gaze at the farmers' market seemed to carry a secret empathy and knowledge, as if she saw through Olive's façade of composure. Despite the early morning hour, Olive punches in the number. Shay's excited tone of voice on the other end is unexpected.

"I actually had a cancellation. Could you make it at noon?"

Olive hesitates for a moment, but this is a task that can't be delayed. "Yes, that would work."

Shay takes a long pause. "I'm so glad you reached out. Looking forward to seeing you this afternoon."

Olive ends the call and steps onto the deck, her eyes fixated on the lake. She'll have just enough time to pay a visit to Jimmy before meeting Dr. Everly. She takes in a big gulp of pure Michigan air. The sounds of water sports and children's laughter fill the neighborhood, marking the early beginning of the Fourth of July week. Waves brush against the dock, gently rocking their boat. Warm, humid breezes carry the fragrance of water and blooming hydrangeas. Her attention shifts slowly to Colin's house, still cloaked in darkness. Weeds and foliage encircled his porch, reminiscent of a snake coiling around its prey.

Stepping into the neighborhood Rite Aid, Olive's heart pounds slightly as she prepares to meet Mrs. Schmidt's nephew. As she makes her way through the store, it appears nearly deserted. She heads towards the back, where an older man wearing a pharmacist's jacket greets her.

"Hi, are you Jimmy?" she asks politely.

"No. I'm Boris," he responds, pointing to the name "Boris" on his jacket. "Jimmy is out back. It's his lunch break. Look for a blue Bronco if you don't see him eating on the curb."

Olive thanks Boris and starts to make her way to the side exit when she notices Laura pass by, walking down the medicine aisle. A few short weeks ago, she would have avoided the run-in, content with being invisible and unnoticed. But things were different now. Perhaps it was serendipity that led her to spot Laura—but Olive didn't believe in coincidences. She recalled how Laura rolled her eyes quite a bit at the farmers' market whenever Audrey spoke about JJ. Now, after hearing what Big Joe had to say, Olive had an inkling as to why.

"Laura, hey! My allergies are terrible right now, too," Olive says, attempting to lighten the mood. "I think it's all the ragweed."

Laura places a box of Zyrtec back on the shelf and smiles. "Funny seeing you twice in a week," she remarks, picking up the generic version. "This pharmacy is almost out of everything. Should've gone to Meijer."

Olive seizes the opportunity to engage. "Speaking of Meijer, I bumped into Joe around there yesterday." It wasn't a lie; she just didn't specify the details. "He seemed a little stressed … about Joey, er, JJ. Do you know anything about that?" The image of Big Joe's disheveled face now seizes Olive's mind momentarily.

Laura looks around, as if hesitant to say what her bright red lips were about to expose.

"I really shouldn't say anything. You know how it is—loose lips sink ships."

Olive nods, waiting for her to continue because she knows Laura can't help herself.

"But between you and me, JJ isn't going to Ohio State like Audrey's been telling everyone. He did get a scholarship, but they revoked it due to his latest arrest."

"Latest?"

"Well, yes. He's had several. They've been very hush-hush about it. Aggravated assault twice—somehow, they got him out of those, maybe community service or something. But this last one was a doozy. DUI." She pauses for effect and leans in closer. "And it gets worse. He tried to fight the arresting officer with his lacrosse stick. I don't know if you're well-versed in the law, but that's assault on an officer and resisting arrest." Laura often brought up legal terms since her husband is an attorney.

"And don't get me wrong, I love them. Love the family. These are just facts. JJ has always had a bad temper that has just escalated throughout the years. I suppose being cooped up during the pandemic didn't help him much. You remember how aggressively he used to play with our boys? Landon was my best CCD student, while I wanted to kick JJ out on several occasions." Laura rolls her eyes once more.

She wasn't wrong. Joey was a rough child. She and Audrey used to joke that Landon was the brains and Joey was the brute. She chalked it up to some children playing rougher than others.

As Olive continued to listen to Laura divulge more, her empathy for Audrey and Joe grew, combined with a queasy feeling in her stomach. It puzzled her, this façade of tranquility Audrey managed to maintain on both occasions of their meeting, belying the tumult that evidently lay beneath.

"That must be super hard on Audrey and Joe," she finally responds.

"Audrey doesn't really acknowledge it, to be honest. She lives in her own world when it comes to JJ and focuses a lot on Ava. Last I heard, JJ was just sentenced to juvie by a judge earlier this week." Her eyes widen as she looks around once more.

"Well, I'll be praying for them," Olive offered, hoping it would suffice with Laura.

"That's all we can do, hon. And you know what they say, we have to deal with the plank in our own eye before judging the specks in others."

Olive nods, unaware of what Laura is referring to.

With farewells exchanged, Olive goes outside to the back of the pharmacy and finds a man near a blue Bronco. He appears much younger than she envisioned as he takes a bite of his sandwich while perched on the curb beside a large dumpster.

"Jimmy? I'm Olive, your Aunt Sheri sent me," Olive says, approaching the young man with shaggy hair.

"Heyyy, it's Olive, don't cha know?" Jimmy stands up, wiping his hands off on his slacks. She notices his thick Yooper accent right away, similar to her grandmother's with its distinct mix of Minnesotan and Manitoban pronunciations. Olive could almost predict that if she asked where he was from, he'd use his hand as a map—Michigan being a mitten—and he'd point to the upper part. But she wasn't there for small talk.

"My Aunt Sheri said yous been lookin' for me. Sorry, I was out earlier this week."

Olive nods. "Mind if I join you?"

Jimmy pulls up a heavy box for her to sit on as he perches back on the curb. "You can put your bag down if you like? What's goin' on? I heard about your neighbor. Looks like they made the official ruling of an accidental overdose. Still, though, odd how he ended up in the lake."

Olive hesitates at the announcement. "Yes, it is. His death has stirred up some stuff for me. And, I'm a little embarrassed to admit this … I've been searching for closure about …"

"That night. My goodness gracious, I will never forget that night," Jimmy says, interrupting her. "The looks on all yous guys' faces were like you'd seen a ghost. And that little red-headed girl." Jimmy puts his face in his palms, shaking his head.

"Kate. Her name was Kate. Do you remember anything about that night? It's all quite frankly a blur to me, and your aunt mentioned I was talking about—"

"Yes, everyone thought you were either drunk out of your mind or in shock." Jimmy sets down his Faygo and takes out a cigarette and lights it. "Suppose I should ask if you mind?" She shakes her head no, as if she can say anything after it's already lit. "I know what yous thinking. A guy like me shouldn't be smoking, working in health and all. But the truth is I need somethin' to take the edge off." Before Olive can interject, he continues. "And I also know what else yous thinking. Why do I work here now after I had the EMT gig?" Olive looks down at her watch as Jimmy takes a drag. "The truth of the matter was, after that night at your house, I was done. That job was pretty fucked up most nights, but I made a difference. That night … I couldn't do much. But want to know what might be more messed up? I work here now pushing all these pharmaceuticals on people who either don't need them or really do need them but their insurance don't cover half their shit. Over medicating and under healing, doncha know."

With a sense of urgency and limited time before her appointment with Dr. Everly, Olive presses harder. "Listen, Jimmy, you seem like a smart guy. A guy with a good memory. Do you remember anything I might have said when you took me from my house to the hospital? If you recall, I took a little stumble down my hill and my glass cup somehow wound up in my cheek." She is downplaying her accident; it had been a spectacular tumble.

Jimmy snorts. "That's what I was getting to. Everyone thought you were drunk, but I knew the truth. That's why I issued a blood test on you."

"You knew what?"

"That you were drugged. I've seen it before: women who think they were drugged at a nightclub or bar and their friend calls an ambulance. You had that same vibe. And I was right. Your blood tested positive for GHB. It was a small amount, but enough. You also had some alcohol in your system, and the mix of the two explains the memory loss. I personally called your home a few days later account of you being my aunt's neighbor and all."

Olive stares at him, trying to process this revelation.

"I mean, everyone was a fucking mess that night though—the big linebacker dude had cuts on his neck, the pretty boy hotshot had a black eye, that one lady …"

Olive puts up her hand for Jimmy to stop talking. "I'm sorry, I was drugged? And you told someone in my home?"

"Well, yeah, of course. I thought you knew this. It was an older woman who answered the phone; she said she was a family member. Figured it was your mom. She said you were resting, and she would pass along the info and gave me an email to send the results to from the hospital.

Olive stares at the sky blankly. An older woman answered her home phone. Then it hit her like a ton of bricks. "Trudy."

Jimmy chuckles. "She sounded like a real Trudy, ya know?"

Olive's blood begins to simmer. "Aren't you supposed to have my HIPAA consent or something before sharing my medical info?"

A thick gulp rises in his throat. "Aw geez, I don't want any trouble, alright? I just thought someone in your family oughta know, that's all. Didn't mean nothin' by it." Jimmy starts backing away. "I should get back in there. Real glad you're doin' okay, though. They sewed ya up pretty good at the hospital, too."

He gestures towards her cheek, then drops his cigarette on the pavement, putting it out with his shoe. Olive sits there for a moment, taking in this new information. Looking at her watch, she sees that she still has time to pay Trudy a quick visit before her next appointment.

CHAPTER 20

FRIDAY 12 P.M.
JUNE 30, 2023

Trudy Wentworth had been in an assisted living home for years. Not because she needed assistance, but because she enjoyed the lifestyle. The liberation from culinary duties, the weekly pampering sessions for her hair and nails—a luxury she didn't have to step outdoors for—the track outside for leisurely walks and exchanges with her fellow seniors. She relished her role as the embodiment of "Michigan nice," dishing out compliments upon her fellow residents before sneaking in a touch of subtle gossip or a well-placed dig. The upscale living arrangement was made possible by Richie's financial support, a fact that went without a thank you from Trudy.

Approaching the building, Olive is welcomed by an exquisitely manicured garden boasting vibrant flowers and lush greenery. The driveway leads her to a grand entrance, featuring double doors crafted from rich mahogany that are courteously opened for her by a staff member. Stepping inside, Olive finds herself in a spacious lobby, tastefully adorned with elegant furnishings. The receptionists, unfailingly affable, address her as "Mrs. Wentworth," likely because Trudy occupies the most expensive unit in the facility. Olive is aware that Trudy's penchant for complaining likely makes her a challenge for the besieged staff.

With a wave and a sign-in, Olive proceeds. Inside the elevator, classical melodies create a soothing ambiance for others, though all Olive hears is a ticking bomb.

She knocks on Trudy's door, which holds a festive Fourth of July wreath. Trudy quickly answers, wearing a sweater and pearls, her nails freshly done. "Olive, to what do I owe this surprise?

And is my handsome son with you?"

Brushing past Trudy, Olive enters the private and spacious room, choosing a vintage leather chair beside the front window.

"We need to talk. Please have a seat." Olive gestures to the couch opposite her, but Trudy's expression sours when she realizes neither Richie nor Landon is in tow; just her daughter-in-law. Olive has often sensed that Trudy views her as a vessel to produce her grandkids and nothing more. Despite Olive's hopes for a deeper connection, given her own absence of a mother, that aspiration had never come to fruition.

"Did you happen to bring those mints I like from the CVS pharmacy?" Trudy inquires, her frown lingering.

"No, I'm here to discuss something important." Olive straightens her posture, anchoring herself.

"Oh dear, is it Richie? Landon? Is everything okay?"

"Yes, they're both fine. It's about *that* night. I recently stumbled upon some new information."

Trudy sighs and rolls her eyes.

Olive recounts her conversation with Jimmy and the positive GHB test. Across from her, Trudy shifts in her seat, tapping a fingernail against her mug of tea. Her eyes flick to the muted television in the corner, where *Days of Our Lives* plays with exaggerated gestures and dramatic glances, then back to Olive with a tight-lipped smile. "GHB is the date rape drug," Olive says. "It's used to incapacitate someone's memory or induce unconsciousness when mixed with alcohol." Trudy leans in, not with concern, but as if she's waiting for the headline—the part worth sharing over coffee.

"Now, why would someone target you at a neighborhood gathering? It's not like you were at the club." Trudy mimics a fist pump, as if insinuating that such incidents were more acceptable in club settings. The comment ignites fury within Olive, especially given Trudy's implication that date rape might be justifiable under certain circumstances.

"Listen, I don't have all the details. This is what I've been told, and apparently, you were told too." Olive pauses, hoping for the proverbial lightbulb moment to illuminate Trudy's memory.

With her impeccably permed hair unmoving, she shakes her head in denial instead. "I have no idea what you're talking about. And to be honest, Olive, I'm a bit concerned about your mental state. Richie mentioned you've been neglecting your medications. Your behavior tends to veer towards paranoia, and quite frankly, delusion, when you skip doses." She takes a small sip of tea before delivering her final blow. "And should I mention the rumor that you've been going on dates with another man?"

"Excuse me?" Olive senses her temper flaring, a simmering fury rising from within. She recognizes Trudy's tactics—those subtle deflections meant to sidetrack the conversation. Something shifts within her, subtle but undeniable, an emotion she's been yearning for: anger.

"Oh yes, don't assume I'm oblivious to the scene you made at Darby's. Cynthia informed me that she saw you sharing ice cream with a younger man, and the two of you seemed rather close. My son is a saint; he treats you like royalty." She scans Olive head to toe, as if silently asserting her own status as Queen Mother.

"I was out with a neighbor friend. It's nothing like that." Olive checks herself, steering back to the main issue. "The EMT told me he spoke to you on the phone, Trudy. He informed you about the drugging and confirmed the email address on file to send over the findings. Wouldn't that be something worth mentioning to Richie or me?"

Trudy throws her hands up. "Listen, dear. That was a long time ago. You weren't thinking straight. Losing Kate, with her being so close by, is understandable. Believe me, I would know; I've lost a child too. In a perfect world, children would always be safe. But this world is broken. That's why we chose not to tell you. It had nothing to do with Kate. We just… needed to move forward."

"We?"

"Yes, Richie and me. I told him later on about the results, and he figured it was a prank. Perhaps a mischievous neighborhood kid, or heaven forbid, someone with ulterior motives. We … we didn't want to distress you any further during that difficult time."

Olive stands up, her hands fisted, anger boiling over. "Fuck you, Trudy. You both knew I was drugged, then led me to believe I got too drunk, blacked out, and couldn't watch after my own child? What kind of twisted rationale is that?"

Trudy stands up, her lips trembling. Instead of speaking, she gives Olive a knowing look. It was the same look she'd given all those years ago, when Olive first announced she was pregnant—"fallen pregnant," Trudy had put it, as though it were something careless, like tripping over a crack in the sidewalk or catching a seasonal cold. That summer, just before Olive's second year of medical school, Richie had proposed. He was deep into his residency, and the gesture came with urgency: marriage, a baby, a home. It was dressed up as love but carried the heavy weight of haste. Med school could wait. Or, in Olive's case, disappear entirely.

And Trudy did object, openly and sharply. She warned Olive that if she chose to keep the baby and marry her son, she wouldn't just be gaining a partner—she'd be inheriting Richie's grief, too. His brother's death had carved something empty in him, and Trudy made it clear: that kind of shadow doesn't just vanish. It lingers. It spreads. And eventually, it would darken and shade Olive's life as well.

Back then, Olive couldn't quite grasp the depth of Trudy's words. She believed loving Richie would be enough … enough to fill the gaps, to heal what came before. What she didn't understand was that when you marry someone, it's more than just a commitment to their present self. It's an intricate dance with their history, their concealed truths, and the emotional ghosts they carry. And the weight of it all can ultimately be crushing. She couldn't mend Richie's thought processes or redeem him through kindness and compassion, just as she couldn't with her own father, and no more than she could rescue her own daughter.

Once in the sanctuary of her car, Olive repeatedly dials Richie, but each call goes unanswered. Finally, she tosses the phone back in her purse in frustration. A tumult of emotions churns inside her—anger, bewilderment, a profound sense of betrayal—yet amidst this storm, a weight seems to dissolve from her chest. She steadies her breathing and contemplates, recognizing with cold clarity that she hadn't been responsible for her own inebriation that night. Someone had drugged her and manipulated her reality. And all this time, Richie has held this truth. Olive is haunted by the question: what other truths is he concealing from her?

A sharp buzzing abruptly rouses her; her phone is buried within her purse alongside the disconcerting identical business cards from Dr. Everly. "Hello?"

"Yes, Olive? It's Shay … I mean, Dr. Everly. Is everything alright? You were scheduled to be here over thirty minutes ago."

Shit. The rush of new intel had rendered her oblivious to her appointment.

"I'm so sorry. Something came up. I should have called. I can still make it?"

"I have my next client coming here shortly and then I need to prep for a retreat in Traverse City. Could we reschedule you for later next week?"

The word "retreat" sparks her curiosity. How many retreats could the small town of Traverse City accommodate this weekend? No coincidences, she reminds herself.

"Is Rita Harris the host of that retreat by chance?" Olive asks.

"Why, yes. Yes, she is." Doctor Everly sounds surprised.

"Maybe I'll see you there. I've been invited."

"Well, that would be great. Let me know." And with that, Dr. Everly hangs up. The retreat now holds a tantalizing allure. Not only would Dr. Everly be there, but Olive now understands the sentiment Colin had expressed: the desire to escape his current reality. And as Dodge said, how long can one stay bound by fear, uncertainty, and sadness before seeking change? After all, fear doesn't stop death. It only stops living. A change of scenery would be nice right about now. The perfect place for healing and respite. She would no longer be complacent.

She turns on the radio and spaces out, driving home, but having no real memory of the drive.

CHAPTER 21

MONDAY 8 P.M.
JULY 4, 2016

THEN

Olive slid the glass door shut behind her and stepped into the kitchen. The blast of air conditioning hit her like a fresh smack in the face, raising goosebumps on her arms. She flicked on the overhead light, only to jump back with a small gasp when two figures emerged from the shadows.

"Hey, stranger," Audrey said, already uncorking a bottle of red wine. "Just looking for more drinks."

Big Joe stood beside her, peering through the window toward the lake, where the kids were still down by the dock, their laughter echoing faintly through the night air.

"Lord, you scared me, Audrey," Olive exhaled, pressing a hand to her chest. "Even more than having to talk to Dean, Richie's new board president at the hospital. He just left."

The screen door snapped open again with a loud rattle as a neighbor across the lake launched a few small fireworks. Bursts of color briefly lit up the sky, and the children's excited cheers drifted up from the shoreline.

Julie stumbled in through the doorway, looking flushed and even drunker than before. "My girls! Are we popping bottles in here?"

Right on cue, Audrey smiled and gave the wine bottle a celebratory pop. "Why actually, yes. I was going to make a sangria for the birthday girl."

"Delicious!" Julie squealed, her voice bubbling with delight. She turned to Olive and added brightly, "Happy birthday!"

Olive gave a small smile and said, "Thank you. It was yesterday, actually."

Audrey chimed in, undeterred, "Yes, but we can still celebrate you today!"

Big Joe, less than amused, muttered something under his breath and headed toward the porch. A few lightning bugs blinked lazily around him as he opened the screen door and disappeared into the humid dusk.

"Shoot, where's your brandy?" Audrey asked, glancing around the kitchen.

A row of mismatched mugs lined a narrow pine shelf above the sink, and a bowl of fresh strawberries sat on the island, picked that morning from the garden. The scent of lake air still lingered faintly through the open window screens, mixing with the floral sweetness of Audrey's perfume and the earthy bite of red wine.

"Richie keeps the good stuff in the basement bar. Help yourself," Olive answered absently, turning toward the junk drawer. She rummaged past half-spent birthday candles, rubber bands, and dried-out glue sticks—searching for sparklers but feeling Julie's gaze prickling against her like a sunburn.

"So, I heard you're a Spartan?" Julie asked, casually leaning against the kitchen island. Her tall frame and long strawberry-blonde hair gave her the air of someone used to commanding attention. Her tone, though pleasant, had an edge … something performative curling beneath it. "Michigan State for undergrad, right?" Without waiting for Audrey, Julie grabbed the bottle of Malbec, poured a generous splash into a cup, and took a casual sip.

Olive didn't look up. She grabbed a dusty box of sparklers and shut the drawer. "That's right. Go Green."

"Go White," Julie replied with a knowing smirk, sipping her wine as if it were a secret. Her lips turned the same shade as the Malbec—dark, bruised. Then, without hesitation, she tilted her glass and poured half the contents down her throat in one gulp, her neck arched like a snake unhinging its jaw for prey. "I'm not even a big wine drinker," she said, licking a droplet from the corner of her mouth. "But I might be now." She lifted the bottle, squinting at the label. "1989. Same year I was born. Great year."

The basement door creaked open. Richie emerged with flushed cheeks and fireworks energy, calling down to Audrey about the brandy. His shirt was wrinkled, and his flip-flops slapped against the floor like punctuation marks. "What are you ladies up to in here?" he asked brightly.

"Just getting to know your beautiful wife a little better," Julie purred, glancing at Olive over her rimmed glass.

Colin entered then, brushing past a departing neighbor. He looked tired, like the life had been wrung from him. His eyes sought Julie, then landed on Olive before darting back. "There you are," he muttered. "Uh, where's the restroom?"

Olive and Richie pointed in unison. "By the office."

Colin reached out to guide Julie, but she batted him away with a roll of her eyes. "Let's just go home," he said under his breath.

"Don't be silly, it's no big deal to use our restroom," Richie chimed in, too casually.

"Found the brandy!" Audrey shouted, bursting up from the basement, hair wild, cheeks glowing. She held the bottle high like a trophy. "Okay, everyone, let's have a toast!"

"Great idea, Audrey," Richie added, already pulling glasses from the cabinet.

Colin stepped in, eyeing the ingredients with a smirk. "Careful with that," he said, nodding toward the brandy. "If you want a real sangria, it's got to be balanced. I used to bartend in college—give it here."

Audrey handed over the bottle, amused, as Colin expertly poured a generous, but measured amount into the wine and fruit mixture. Audrey resumed stirring, the chunks of citrus and berries swirling like confetti in a carnival glass bowl.

Five glasses. Five pours.

"To friends and neighbors," Julie said, raising her glass, her smile dazzling in the kitchen's candlelight.

The clinks rang out. Glass met glass. Colin, still stiff, shoved his hands into his pockets. "I'm not much of a wine drinker," he muttered.

"You want a beer instead?" Richie offered, pointing toward the fridge.

"Just drink the damn sangria," Julie cut in, pouring herself another round with theatrical flair.

Olive took a sip. Rich, fruity, and tart—too bold for her liking. Her mouth stained instantly. She let out a half-laugh, dabbing at her lips with a cocktail napkin, but something was off. Her limbs felt too heavy for just one sip. Her eyes lingered on Julie, whose tongue now curled against her wine-stained teeth, eyes glinting beneath the dim kitchen lights.

Just then, Big Joe came in through the back door, looking a little winded. Richie handed him a drink without bothering to ask what he wanted. Out in the yard, Trudy's voice rose above the murmur of conversation, loudly complaining about the mosquitoes to Mrs. Schmidt.

"Anyone seen Terrance?" Big Joe asked, glancing around. "The Slip 'N Slide came loose. Someone's gonna break a leg out there in the dark."

"Good thing Laura's husband isn't here," Audrey quipped from the pantry, referencing the neighborhood lawyer infamous for his litigious streak.

Julie laughed a beat too late, her smile wobbly with uncertainty. Olive doubted she even got the joke. She took another sip of her birthday cocktail, feeling Colin's unnervingly blue eyes fixed on her. When she glanced back at Julie, she caught her smirking behind her wine glass, her tongue sliding along the inside of her purple-painted mouth. *PAM,* Olive thought. That name suited her much better.

Olive looked away, her pulse tapping a nervous beat. Maybe it was the wine. Perhaps it was nothing. Or maybe, she thought as she wiped her palms on her jean shorts, the kitchen had just gotten a little too warm.

"We need more," Audrey said, popping open another bottle of wine.

Olive shook her head and reached for the Malbec instead. She preferred its warmth to the tart bite of sangria. One glass of that had been more than enough.

Outside, another firework cracked, followed by a wave of cheers from the kids.

Over the noise, one voice rang out louder than the rest:

"Ready or not, here I come!"

CHAPTER 22

FRIDAY 4 P.M.
JUNE 30, 2023

As Olive steers homeward, she calls Landon to confirm his arrival later that evening, and his familiar voice casts a serene spell over her. Their brief exchange lingers in her thoughts, a soothing balm, as she glides into the garage's shelter. Just as the door closes behind her, the first whispers of the evening tempest murmur across the lake's surface.

The sky is dark, and the wind has picked up. Lightning crackles in the distance as the first drops of rain fall on the calm surface of Duck Lake. Standing in her kitchen, still holding her purse, she watches the gentle storm begin to intensify. She slides open the glass door leading to the deck, grabbing the towels before the wind can carry them away. The breeze carries the scent of burning sparklers and the faint crackle of poppers.

Her thoughts retrace once more to that fateful morning. Olive and Kate had planted red and white hibiscus along the water's edge after a brief nap in the hammock. The image of Colin and Julie on their deck, Colin visibly distressed, lingers. It was the first whole summer the couple had spent in their lakeside home since moving from the west side of the state. At the time, Olive had kept her distance, viewing them as carefree newlyweds—childless, untethered, and worlds apart from the rhythm of her own life. Now, getting to know Colin, she felt bad for not being warmer and more welcoming. Still, she remained plagued by nagging questions about him, particularly the drastic change in his persona that she had glimpsed the evening prior, the night of the duck's demise.

Apart from Colin and Julie, she'd shared a close rapport with all her neighbors and trusted them implicitly. The perplexing question remained, however. Among these familiar faces, she struggled to identify anyone who might have orchestrated such a sinister prank involving GHB or anything darker.

Terrance's effusive drunkenness was a fixture at the gathering, his jubilant spirit a well-known aspect of most neighborhood events. Richie and Colin had apparently locked horns about something later in the evening, per Hannah. Olive briefly recalled rushing inside to grab a drink and more sparklers for the kids. Julie then entered, looking for the bathroom. They exchanged pleasantries, bonding over their shared undergraduate Alma Mater, Michigan State. Julie's lipstick was long gone, replaced by a deep maroon stain from the wine she kept topping off. Richie, Colin, Audrey, and Big Joe filtered in and out of the kitchen, a blur of laughter, sangria, and raised glasses.

Now, thinking back, that small exchange with Julie stood out as one of the last fully coherent conversations Olive could remember from the night. That, and saying a hasty goodbye to Audrey's family—just before Audrey doubled over in the rose bushes, vomiting violently.

Who would have guessed that a party that started with laughter would end in bloodcurdling screams?

Olive's attention snaps to the sudden clatter of their boat slamming against the dock bumpers, the Malibu Wakesetter tugging free from its lift. The once-calm water has turned turbulent, waves pounding the shoreline and tossing the boat with growing aggression. The lift, long overdue for repairs, groans under the strain—its faulty grip on the stern giving way each time the lake grows restless.

Should she head out there to throw an extra line on the boat? She hesitates. Maybe she should call Richie again. By now, he must have been warned by his mother about what she uncovered.

She glances at her phone, realizing how unusually quiet it has been. Richie always made an effort to check in during work conferences when he was away, so the lack of returned calls and texts speaks volumes.

The thunder roars again, and lightning brilliantly lights up the sky, casting an eerie glow over the lake. A figure in a green raincoat runs towards her dock as little ducks take shelter under the large willow tree. Quickly throwing on her own coat, she heads down to the dock to find Colin attempting to tie up the boat properly.

"What are you doing?" Olive yells through the loud wind.

"What does it look like?" Colin asks, annoyed. She can see that he is struggling to get the back fender placed perfectly to cushion the boat against the dock. The bow is now coming loose as the waves hit harder with each wind gust. Colin jumps into action, tying the dock line from the cleat. He ensures that there is enough slack to account for the rising water level.

Olive is impressed, especially since he's only a jet ski owner. They stand in the rain, staring off as birds fly frantically and fish jump high out of the water. "Care for fishing?" Colin asks with a smirk.

"I'm thinking a hot coffee instead." The rain has managed to get inside Olive's jacket and Hunter boots. Despite the ferocity of the storm, there is something exhilarating about being out on the water during such a natural display of power. The rain is cold and stinging on her skin, but there's a feeling of being alive, of being part of something much greater than herself. She looks down at her neglected garden and senses something new stirring within her. Maybe, just maybe, everything flourishes after a little rain.

Colin gestures for her to follow him. "Come on, let's get you something warm." He leads her into his home. She goes willingly, preferring the uncertainty of Colin's company in his house to the oppressive quietness waiting for her. The anger towards her husband's silence sits at the surface of her mood, fueling her steps into Colin's kitchen.

She'd never been inside Colin's house and, for some reason, expected it to be more modern—dark wood with black accents. But it's charming and done in hues of greys and creams. He hands her a towel as she takes off her wet jacket and boots. He starts to hum as he brews the coffee. As she waits, Olive walks around, taking in pictures of Lucy everywhere on the walls and a stack of unopened mail sprawled across the kitchen counter.

"Here you go." Colin hands over the comforting warmth of the cup and guides her toward his screened-in porch. As they cross the threshold, an undeniable tension hangs in the air, one that can't be attributed solely to the crackling static of the storm.

"You know," Olive begins, her voice carrying a hint of defiance, "I don't need saving. I could have handled the boat."

Colin turns to her; his eyes filled with puppy-like earnestness. "That's perfectly fine. I won't be doing any more saving. But can I at least sit with you? Watch this toad-strangler of a tempest together," he replies, his tone soft. The two sit and watch the storm attempt to shake the boat loose once more. This time it stays put. Olive glances at Colin, catching the wheels turning in his mind as he absentmindedly runs a hand through his hair. She wishes, for a moment, that she could dive into his thoughts and see what lingers there.

"Well, thanks. For the coffee, and I guess for the boat help." She smiles and takes a sip, noting her mug reads 'World's Best Euchre Partner.' She also notices Colin isn't drinking anything—his hands are empty.

"No problem. And I'm sorry for the mess. I wasn't really expecting a visitor. Lucy gets back from camp soon. I really need to pick up. It looks like such a bachelor pad." He runs his tan hands through his beautiful, thick head of hair once more. "I want to apologize about the other night. I feel horrible. I let my emotions get the best of me. I'm just feeling nervous about Julie coming home … I don't know if she's really changed. Do you ever feel like you're just waiting for the other shoe to drop? Questioning how long this good moment will truly last? It's like living in a constant state of fear," he admits, pushing aside a patio pillow that separates them.

Olive shrugs her shoulders and inches closer. She can see his chest rising in sharp breaths through his wet shirt. His scent has somehow grown familiar and comforting to her, along with his vulnerability. A huge lightning bolt startles them both, and they laugh it off together. Colin puts his hands on her shoulders and squeezes them tightly. "Are you warming up? Do you want a blanket? Is everything okay? Am I asking too many questions?"

Olive laughs. "Yes. I mean, yes, I'm warming up. No, not everything is okay."

Colin puts his face in his palms. "Are you still mad about the duck? I'm so sorry. I didn't mean to hit it. If I could go back in time, I would. Please don't hate me." He clasps his hands together, pleading with her.

She pushes his hands away and forces another smile. "No. It's not about the duck. I … I found out Richie kept something important from me about the night Kate drowned."

Colin shoots up from his seat and digs his hands into his pockets. "What was it? Do you want to talk about it?" He sounds genuinely concerned.

"No. Not really." Olive responds tersely, her thoughts still shrouded in uncertainty over who might have tainted her drink.

Colin exhales loudly and sits back down, this time his knees touching hers. "Olive, you can stay here if you don't feel safe."

Olive stares into his deep blue eyes. "Funny, Richie told me you weren't safe and to stay away from you." He doesn't respond. Another boom shakes the house, lighting up the sky. Olive breaks the silence by taking another sip of her coffee.

"Listen, I do have ulterior motives for inviting you over. And I know you have a lot going on, trying to piece together stuff. But I need a favor."

Olive inches closer to him. "What?" she whispers.

"I need you to come with me to pick Julie up tomorrow. She's super happy you have been on this journey with me, with our meetings, and she has decided to come back home. I just … I can't do it alone. I haven't seen her in sixty days, I … " He begins to shake.

Olive pushes his knee with hers, feeling like a kid again. "Yes. I'll go with you."

Colin smiles and exhales. Olive isn't sure if she is the dumbest neighbor alive or a really good person for saying yes. She no longer knows her own motives with Colin. All her questions just led to more questions when it came to *him*.

"Thank you so much; you don't know how much this means to me. Do you want some more coffee?" He points down to her empty cup.

"No. I'm good. I won't be able to sleep tonight. I probably should head home." She stands up and places the empty mug down, thinking of all the cleaning she too needs to do before Landon is home.

They walk back inside. "Are you sure you don't want to stay for dinner? I could order some deep-dish pizza, extra ranch," Colin offers, raising an eyebrow to sweeten the suggestion.

Olive rolls her eyes with a playful grin.

"I know, too many questions," he adds quickly. "Okay, at least wait here one more minute. I want to grab you another line in case the boat comes loose again. I won't be around later tonight to help." He steps toward the garage.

Alone in the room, Olive stares at the photographs of Lucy and gets the uneasy feeling that the little girl is staring back at her. Amid the snapshots, one image captures her attention: Colin and Julie, wrapped in an embrace so intimate, it seemed to defy the world's troubles. It stirs an unexpected surge of jealousy within her.

The thought crosses her mind that Julie doesn't truly deserve Colin. Olive isn't opposed to second chances, but witnessing how Julie's past actions have profoundly affected Colin triggers a protective instinct within her. Leaning wearily against the cool surface of the kitchen island, a sudden wave of dizziness overtakes her, and the room sways a bit.

In the moment, Olive realizes with a twinge of regret that she should have probably tapered off her last long-standing prescription. It had been her constant companion for so long, and now, amid these emotions, it is starting to distort her perception and intensify her unease.

She looks down, taking in all the mail scattered before her, her vision still blurred a little, and notices a loose check. She pulls it closer, recognizing the name at the top, and her heart drops. The check is made out to Colin Baker, from Richard Wentworth, for $10,000. Dated last week. Was Richie paying Colin to stay away from her? Or was he paying Colin for something much worse? The two seemed to despise each other, so what kind of arrangement could there be between them?

She sifts through the mail further, hoping to find some other kind of clue. A manila envelope draws her in. She pulls the first page out to find a medical record and chart. It appears to be an oncology report, but for whom she is unsure.

She hears Colin walk in and shoves the papers away, acting like she's sorting them into neater piles.

He wears a big smile on his face, holding the boat rope. "Here you go."

She looks up at Colin and feels a sense of unease. There's obviously something he's keeping from her. She isn't dumb enough to confront him now. Not during a storm, in his house, with a rope in his hand and a gun in his car. She had watched way too many episodes of *Dateline* to make that mistake. She takes the dock line and forces a slight grin.

"Okay. I'll see you tomorrow then. Bright and early," Colin says and escorts her out.

As soon as her boots hit the grass, she feels the urge to run, but doesn't. The storm has passed, and the sun has begun to peek through the clouds. The air smells fresh and clean. The world seems renewed on the outside. But inside Olive, a different storm begins to stir, heavy and unresolved.

CHAPTER 23

FRIDAY 6 P.M.
JUNE 30, 2023

The sun has now disappeared, obscured by the lingering storm clouds that persist above. Olive is in her husband's sanctum, his sacred office. She's rifling through his belongings, searching for any insight behind the check and oncology report discovered at Colin's house. She still hasn't heard from him, only confirming what Trudy had said—Richie was aware of her being drugged.

The desk stands locked, resisting her, and the search for the elusive key becomes a grueling quest. Eventually, her persistence bears fruit: a key taped beneath a frame holding a picture of Kate and him. She turns the key, and the desk surrenders its secrets. Before her, she finds Richie's medical script pad. The last entry's outline was faint, but the date stood clear: June 11. The patient's name, however, remains a scribbled enigma, too hard to make out. She sifts through a stack of mundane papers—bank statements, investments, and a key fob to Richie's work office—nothing out of the ordinary.

When she reaches the last locked drawer, she finds Kate's file, front and center, and dust-ridden. Taking a sip from a nearby water bottle, she pulls it out and opens it to the first page of Kate's medical chart. It is painful to revisit the file, to confront the initial diagnosis. Richie had been unwavering in his determination to find a cure, and Olive sensed his guilt over being the gene carrier. No one blamed him. The genes we end up with are, after all, a random act of God or a capricious twist of fate. They had prepared themselves for the worst and cherished every moment with Kate. Then their miracle had come with Richie's medical help, and she had improved, only to be snatched away forever. It was an emotional rollercoaster, and Olive felt like she was strapped back onto a janky Cedar Point ride.

As she tucks the file back in the cabinet, her eyes land on another behind it labeled "Baker." A quiet tension creeps up her spine. Richie had never before mentioned seeing Colin as a patient. Carefully, she pulls the file free, her fingers trembling slightly as she lowers herself to the floor. Page after page of clinical notes unfold in her lap. Lab results, treatment plans, oncology consults. Her breath catches. This wasn't Colin's file. It's a child's. Olive blinks hard, her throat tightening as the name finally clicks into place. Lucy Baker.

She then recalls Colin's emotional turmoil during meetings, his subtle outreach. She had attributed it all to Julie's addiction, but now she knows the extent of what he has been grappling with. Richie had always kept his patients' information confidential, but why hadn't Colin at least told her about his daughter's condition? Lucy, it appeared, had been cured, thanks to Richie's medical prowess. As Olive reaches the last page of the report, she can't help but feel a wave of pride that Richie is indeed a miracle doctor and able to save little Lucy. Yet the tension between Colin and Richie remains unresolved. Did something go awry between them during Lucy's treatment? And what about the mysterious check written to Colin?

Olive's leg grows numb from her awkward posture as she stares at the files. She looks over at the small closet in the room. She had nearly forgotten to check Richie's safe. It was mostly for shotguns and rifles, which he used for hunting in November.

After opening the closet, she tries the garage code, Richie's birthdate. It yields. Inside, she finds guns, passports, and Rolex watches. But the sight of the guns gives her pause. A flash of memory surfaces: her father, his idea of bonding wrapped in camouflage and gunpowder. She remembers being twelve, sitting silently beside him in the freezing woods, watching him sip from a silver flask and whisper about the fawn just beyond the tree line. He never told stories, only pointed at prey. She shakes the image loose and looks back at the safe. Beneath the usual contents lies a larger envelope marked "Hernandez." Why would he need to keep this locked in the safe, rather than with the other files?

A hazy fragment from the award ceremony at the Townsend flickers back. The two women whispering about Lisa Hernandez over the hum of a bathroom hand dryer. She pours the contents out, revealing candid photos of a brunette, labeled Doctor Lisa Hernandez, and her husband, along with financial records. Altogether, they appear to be the work of a private investigator.

What were Richie's ties with this family? Olive realizes she's stirring a hornet's nest, and there's no turning back at this point. She'll have to face the consequences, however devastating. Years of detachment have fallen away. She's acutely aware of her surroundings now and is determined not to retreat into the darkness, or her crutch, the pills, especially not after learning what Jimmy revealed.

She googles the name *Lisa Hernandez,* and up pops her profile as part of the oncology board and research team at Henry Ford Hospital, where Richie works. But who was Lisa Hernandez *to* Richie exactly?

Trudy begins calling insistently around 8 p.m., but Olive rejects them all, embodying a newfound sense of control. She emails Rita to secure her spot at the wellness retreat this coming weekend. If Richie can run and hide, so can she. Still no word from him. She calculates how many hours it's been, possibly the longest she's gone without speaking to him in years.

As she contemplates texting Colin, her thumb hovering over his contact, a sudden vision floods her thoughts: the sight of Julie staring at her and Colin in the dim sterility of the rehab center. Julie, still shouldering the weight of not only addiction and marital vows, but also the profound agony of a child who just went through cancer's ruthless onslaught. With Olive's contemplations swirling, the shrill ring of her phone cuts through, banishing the mental image as swiftly as sunlight dispels darkness. An unfamiliar number glimmers on the display, yet she resolves to take the call.

"Hi, is this Mrs. Wentworth? This is Dr. Ashbury from ProMedica Toledo Hospital. Your husband was in an accident."

A tidal wave of panic crashes over Olive as the doctor informs her that Richie's car was heading northbound earlier this evening near Toledo, when he was deliberately run off the road by an unknown driver, resulting in Richie hitting a median at high speed. He had suffered a broken foot and a dislocated shoulder and was to stay overnight for observation per concussion protocol. Now she understood why she hadn't heard from him for at least the latter part of the day. And for the barrage of calls from Trudy. Olive quickly throws some items into her purse and grabs her keys.

CHAPTER 24

SATURDAY 9 P.M.
JUNE 30 2023

An hour later, Olive steps through the entrance of Toledo Hospital, where she is quickly guided to Richie's room. She's immediately struck by the antiseptic aroma that pervades the air, the intermittent beeps of machines, and the hushed exchanges between doctors and nurses. It all creates a disorienting symphony around her. Her heart quickens its pace, a maelstrom of emotions swirling within. She's unsure what to expect. Images of his Porsche SUV, crumpled on the northbound lanes of 696 with airbags deployed and her husband incapacitated, flash before her. Despite knowing the rough extent of his injuries, she remains oblivious to his current state of mind, his consciousness.

When she finally enters his room, she finds him propped up on pillows, his leg encased in a cast, and a sling supporting his shoulder. Lines of pain and weariness etch his features. Upon spotting her, he turns his head, his eyes feeble as a faint smile tugs at his lips. "Hey," his voice emerges in a soft whisper.

Olive approaches his bedside, her emotions conflicted, carrying a mix of indignation and a somber weight at his disconcerting condition. "Hey," she echoes, placing her purse beside a beeping apparatus and resting her hand atop his.

"How are you holding up?" she asks, her tone tender.

He shrugs, a veneer of nonchalance masking his evident discomfort. "Could be better. The painkillers do their part, but this foot of mine is putting up a hell of a fight."

Observing his foot, ensnared in a bulky cast, she says, "I'm sorry."

A grimace of pain twists Richie's features as he manages to

edge closer to her, his left hand seeking hers. "Don't apologize. I'm the one who should be sorry. I should have shared those blood results with you. My mom withheld them from me, too, initially. Then I stumbled upon the hospital report in my spam email box later on. By that point, I was more concerned about sparing you worry than anything else. You weren't in a good place then, Olive. I left the conference early to talk to you in person. Then I was run off the road by some lunatic."

Richie's eyes fill with tears. His hand is cold and clammy, and Olive can feel his pulse racing beneath her fingertips. She shakes her head. She wants to ream him out. She wants to express the unfairness of withholding such vital information that has haunted her. But an aching sympathy emerges for the figure before her.

On some level, she understood his decision. Unearthing the identity of her assailant wouldn't bring back Kate. She reasoned further that learning such information so soon after the drowning might have tipped her over the edge. He had sought to protect her, even if it meant withholding the truth from her. Yet she still wished he had told her once the initial pain had subsided.

"It wasn't my fault. I needed to know that, Richie," she asserts.

"It was never your fault," he counters earnestly. "I was just angry and took it out on you. I'm sorry—no more secrets. You just being here means everything to me. We will get through this together, just like we always have."

Olive maintains her silence, wrestling with the sea of questions swirling about in her mind.

"And Terrance?" she enquires, prompting a look of confusion from Richie. "Was that him? At our house early in the morning, before he …"

Richie's nod is immediate. "I caught him attempting to steal some of your medications one afternoon when he was over at the house during March Madness. I then prescribed a few drugs to wean him off the painkillers, but he kept taking more. So, I cut him off. I told him that very morning—no more. I couldn't jeopardize my medical license. And then, well, he was gone." A heavy sigh accompanies Richie's words, followed by a wince of pain. The empty bottle of her medication in Terrance's recycling bin now makes sense.

"And why are you keeping tabs on this Lisa Hernandez?" Olive blurts out.

Richie's response materializes as a blend of surprise and a quick flicker of his chapped lips. "A colleague of mine. The board suspected her of sharing confidential research with external investors without proper clearance. I felt compelled to investigate personally. You know me, I like to be thorough. Vigilance is key," he states matter-of-factly.

Olive studies his face, searching for substance—regret, guilt, anything. But his expression is unreadable, as if carved from stone. Not a twitch, not a blink. A fortress behind his eyes. Her anger softens, dissolving under the weight of familiarity. He isn't just hiding, he's protecting. It's written not in words but in the stillness of his stance, the way he holds himself like a shield. Richie has always tried to guard what he loves, even when it meant bearing the blame alone. It's what made him a good doctor. This compulsion to fix, to carry burdens that don't belong solely to him. However, in doing so, he has always walked a tightrope between protecting and deceiving, between healing and harm.

Now, the doctor is the patient, sitting there injured and vulnerable. She knows firsthand the toll exacted by the medical profession, both physically and mentally. The relentless hours, the unforgiving pressure, the constant demand for perfection; it was a heavy burden. But being wedded to it was equally weighty.

"And Colin Baker? Tell me *everything*," she requests firmly.

Richie inhales. "Julie approached me when Lucy was diagnosed with cancer early last year. She didn't want anyone to know, but she believed I could assist, given my personal experience in pediatrics. I promised her I would do everything I could to save Lucy …"

"I know. And you did. But what about the check? To Colin. And your feud?"

A sigh escapes his lips. "Listen, Colin and I don't see eye

to eye on much, except when it comes to Lucy. The treatment expenses were high and took a financial toll on them. Then, recently, Julie decided to enter rehab, following my advice. She mentioned it was costly; insurance didn't cover it, just like many of Lucy's treatments. And Colin has been unemployed since Christmas when he lost his teaching position."

Understanding dawned on Olive. The frequent sightings of Colin were now explained. It was during Christmas break that Hannah had recounted witnessing a confrontation between Colin and Richie as well.

"So, what? You were lending them a helping hand? I thought you despised Colin," Olive asks, now removing her hand from his, sweat accumulating.

"I don't hate the guy. He harbors resentment towards me. He seems possessive. He didn't like the idea of Lucy and Julie spending time with me at the hospital. Julie and I have a work history from Beaumont; he hated our proximity and collaboration. He never trusted Julie, you know, she can be a bit of a flirt, and she's indicated in the past that their marriage hasn't been the best. When she turned to me regarding Lucy's diagnosis, I had to persuade Colin to allow me to treat her. After all that, when Julie called me one day from rehab, I wrote the check and placed it in their mailbox. A loan, a gesture of goodwill. I don't even know if they cashed it. He has a thing against me." Richie throws his hands up. "I thought after saving his daughter, he would finally cut me a break. I think he's just a jealous, controlling guy, to be frank. I heard he lost his job after he went ballistic on Julie in front of his students. They gave him mandatory leave and I questioned him about it during Christmas break, which he also did not like. I also question his intentions with you."

Olive hesitates, absorbing the avalanche of new disclosures. The additional detail of Julie's work association with Richie is a bit of a surprise. Though she knew Julie was a nurse, the dots had never fully connected.

A buzzing noise diverts their attention—a text from Landon inquiring about Olive's whereabouts. "Shoot. I told Landon to come home this evening. We probably just missed each other. I left in such a rush ..."

Richie raises his good hand, interrupting her thought. "Don't worry, I'll get them to release me here shortly. Tell Landon we'll bring him home some late-night Joe's Coney dogs."

A smile breaks across Olive's face. Joe's chili dogs were Landon's favorite when he was little. Maybe Richie did care more than he let on.

"Hell, tomorrow's July. Let's celebrate for once. Why don't we invite some people over tomorrow for boating and do a big bonfire?" Richie suggests.

"Slow down there, I think the pain meds are affecting your judgment. You were just in an accident. Maybe we should take it easy. I also have to pack tomorrow. I'm headed to a retreat with my Al-Anon group on Sunday."

"That's ridiculous," Richie retorts, shaking his head sternly. "Let's discuss the retreat tomorrow. We are definitely going to have a party. Tell Landon to invite some of his buddies over, like old times."

The look on Richie's face is one of decisiveness. He's decided on this party, so there will be a party. She shrugs. "Are you sure? I mean, I guess it could be fun."

Richie smiles at her, his eyes softening. "I'm sure," he whispers, leaning in to kiss her gently. "We need to celebrate life."

Olive takes in his suggestion. He is right. She's spent enough time in the past seven years grieving. Grief is cruel. And sneaky. And life must go on, despite it. There is a delicate balance between the two. It's time to celebrate.

CHAPTER 25

SATURDAY 11 A.M.
JULY 1, 2023

Olive had dedicated the previous night to tending to Richie and reaching out to some folks for their impromptu July party the following evening. Despite its last-minute nature, she was pleasantly surprised by the number of affirmative responses she'd received by this morning —largely due to the town's firework show being held on July first at their very lake. She had also informed Colin late last night about Richie's accident and her inability to join him in picking up Julie. Nevertheless, she had invited them both to the party if they were up for it.

Now that the morning had arrived, anxiety about the plans she had orchestrated crept in. A party. A retreat. She didn't recognize herself anymore, but that must mean she was on the right path. She'd slept until 6—no dreams. Her own transformation is becoming increasingly evident. Her racing heart slows as she lays her eyes on the enormous willow tree she can see from her spot on the deck.

Her attention shifts to Colin and Lucy near the tree, practicing soccer and laughing. It seems everyone in the Baker household is home. The jarring sound of her sliding glass door makes her jump as Landon strolls out with two cups of coffee. Strangely, he somehow appears taller than the previous night when he was indulging in chili dogs.

"Good morning," he says, handing over a cup.

"Thank you, my love. What a beautiful morning for boating. Did you invite some friends over? The twins … Laura's boys? I can't ever remember their names. Or maybe a girl …" She grins, taking a satisfying gulp of the brew.

Landon laughs. "Ethan and Aaron are their names, Mom. And no, no girls. The twins are also having a party tonight, so they'll stay for a few, then bounce." Now it made sense why Laura had said no to her party; she seemed to be having one of her own. After a brief pause, Olive's thoughts shift to JJ. She ponders whether he truly was sent away or if he could possibly show up this evening, accompanied by Audrey and Joe, both of whom confirmed their attendance. She hadn't laid eyes on little Joey since he was a child.

"By the way, have you been in touch with Joey at all? I know he switched schools in middle school, but you two were inseparable. What's he been up to?"

Landon's expression contorts in a manner she has never witnessed before. He deliberates for a moment before taking a sip of his coffee.

"Joey's been off my radar since ninth grade. Last time I saw him was the homecoming game when our schools played each other. I messaged him for a pre-game meetup in the parking lot beforehand. Total disaster." He takes another swig of his coffee, which seems to age him beyond his eighteen years prematurely. "He was ready to brawl with some kid from my school, convinced the guy was hitting on his girlfriend. Aaron and Ethan intervened just before the police arrived. There was this intensity in Joey's eyes; I'd never seen him like that, Mom. But I heard he's had several brushes with the law since then. Last I checked, he's completely off the grid now—no social media at all. I heard he was being sent away to some special youth center. Even lost his lacrosse scholarship."

"I see. That's unfortunate," Olive responds, her mind pulsing. Perhaps Audrey's distancing wasn't solely because of Kate. Maybe it had all been due to her preoccupying problems with Joey.

"That was a nice dinner last night. Can never go wrong with Joe's Coney dogs," Landon comments, breaking her thoughts.

"Yes. You and Dad seemed to be good."

"Yeah, I guess. Felt like old times a bit."

Olive smiles, reaching down into her bathrobe that held the

note from Hannah. She slides it across the glass patio table towards him. "Speaking of old times."

Landon looks down at it with a puzzled expression and begins reading. He stands up quickly and leans against the railing of the warm deck. "So, did Hannah give this to you?" he asks, sounding a bit distant.

"No, I found it while I was at Terrance's house picking up a little for the realtor," she answers, bending the truth slightly. "I thought you should have it after all these years. I mean, it *was* addressed to you."

Landon looks at her with angst, briefly scans it, then rips the letter in half. "This is just a reminder of the worst day of my life, Mom." He sits back down beside her, taking a huge gulp of his coffee.

"Hey. I didn't mean for this to stir up bad memories, but to be honest, I'm finally starting to heal after thinking about that night over and over again the past few weeks … I need to know what this means." She gestures to the note's closing line: "PS your mom knows, please talk to her."

"We were kids. I have no idea what she was talking about. That was, like, a traumatic time."

Olive's eyes begin to fill with tears.

Landon inches closer to her. "Mom, it was not your fault. You have to know that." And she did, now.

"Then whose fault was it?" she asks, staring into her tall, handsome son's eyes.

"Hello!" Both Olive and Landon turn to find Pam—or rather Julie—standing beside the deck, on the easement. Landon immediately stands up and hurries inside.

"Good morning," Olive replies, placing her hand up to block the mid-morning sun.

"Colin said you guys are having a little get-together later. Count us in!"

Olive extends a thumbs-up. She'd extended the invite, but now she's not so sure. After everything she's learned, however, it might be the closure they all need. Julie's unruly blond hair dances wildly in the wind. She appears older than Olive remembers, but she also hasn't had a face-to-face talk with Julie in years.

"Is there anything I can bring over? A casserole, perhaps?"

"Just yourselves!" Olive replies. Julie flashes a grin and strolls back towards her home. She seemed pleasant enough. As is the weather report for the day.

In the back of her mind, however, Olive hoped that this event wouldn't conclude in the same manner as their previous Fourth of July party.

CHAPTER 26

SATURDAY 6 P.M.
JULY 1, 2023

The party exploded into a raucous affair before the Wentworths could blink. Traditionally, in a Midwestern neighborhood, when someone hosts a neighborhood gathering, it is understood that anyone from the area is welcome to drop in, and the turnout is typically tremendous. Year after year, the neighborhood's youth surged, while Olive's social skills had withered like forgotten petals. Still, she puts on her best efforts at the ritualistic small talk. The new post-pandemic faces, blissfully ignorant of the haunting history from seven years prior, revel in her and Richie's lavish half-acre lakeside haven. They have one of the best lots in the neighborhood, with the perfect vantage point for the impending fireworks show once the sun surrenders to the horizon. With less than a day's notice, Richie had worked a little magic, securing a last-minute food truck for BBQ sandwiches parked out front, while a mammoth-sized volleyball net took residence in the back. The wide grin on his face is evidence that he has reclaimed his element.

Olive wrestles with a bag of ice, dumping its contents into a cooler stocked with drinks down by the beach. Her eyes turn towards Richie, who stands up the long hill by the deck, engrossed in conversation with Audrey and her burly husband, Big Joe. Yet, Olive can't ignore the peculiar unease emanating from Joe's refusal to meet her eyes when they arrived. Discomfort clung to him like a second skin, almost as if he had been forced into the event against his will. There is no sight of JJ, and little Ava is said to be left at home with a babysitter.

Richie is spinning tales of his horrific accident to Audrey's delight. His raven-colored hair is slicked back and his linen shirt clings to his fit frame, a perfect blend of casual and crisp.

He leans heavily on one crutch as Mrs. Schmidt abruptly intrudes, elbowing her way past Audrey to deliver her prized cherry pie directly to Richie's hands, her voluminous dress clinging to her in the July humidity. He gracefully thanks her, while Audrey indulges in her third White Claw, her transformation into a party persona palpable. Audrey only had two modes: prim and proper or full-on Jersey Shore. Tonight, proper was left behind.

"So, where's the booze?" asks Colin, digging through the cooler beside her. He looks very dapper tonight. His Vineyard Vines polo and boating shoes add sophistication to his appearance: freshly trimmed hair and a blond, five o'clock shadow of stubble frame his face. Olive can't help but smirk at his query.

"Didn't your wife just get out of rehab?" she playfully returns.

"That's precisely why I'm asking."

They both force a smile, a familiar camaraderie in their awkward stance on the sand, the distant echoes of their children's laughter on the boat serving as a beautiful backdrop. The water before them seems almost stagnant, symbolic of the feeling that Olive had often sensed in her own life, until now.

"I saw you on the email chain for the retreat tomorrow. We should carpool?" he suggests.

"Yeah, that could work. I have to confirm everything with Richie," she replies, wondering how he would feel about her alone in a car with Colin for the more than three-hour trek up north. Or maybe he wouldn't care. Since their heart-to-heart in the hospital, they'd shifted onto peaceful terrain. Yet, something still tugged, a nagging intuition gnawing at Olive's core, an ache traversing her disposition that seemed to spread throughout her body. Something she couldn't unearth. Something off that she couldn't quite place.

"So, how's the doc feeling?" Colin gestures uphill, where Richie animatedly recounts his road-rage escapade to a new and engrossed crowd. Most of the attendees seem to be clustered around the deck, drawn by the allure of alcohol, or beneath it, where the walkout basement offers tables for enjoying the BBQ.

"He'll survive," Olive chimes, donning a smile with stitches of restraint.

Colin traces her figure with his eyes. She decided to wear her hair naturally curly tonight and put on a little makeup for once. She's donning a white linen dress with red-and-blue flip-flops.

"He told me …" she says, hesitantly. "He told me everything about Lucy."

Colin's confusion splinters into surprise. "He told you. About Lucy?"

Olive nods. "Yes, why didn't you tell me about the cancer?" Her small hand rests briefly on his shoulder before trailing down his arm. "He told me about your job, about Julie—"

Olive feels a sudden hand on her back, which startles her. She turns to find Julie in a vibrant yellow sundress; her hair elegantly gathered in a high ponytail. The dress is notably short, prompting Olive to glance at her own longer one that concealed her insecurities.

"Did someone say my name? My ears are ringing," Julie chimes in with a smile. Olive's ears seem to buzz as well, and her face is aflame. She prays it hasn't turned beet red.

"I must say, Olive, thank you. Thank you for being there for Colin while I was away." Julie enthusiastically clutches Olive's hand. Olive surveys Julie's freshly manicured nails and her princess-cut wedding ring. In chunky Tori Burch sandals, Julie stands at least 5'9. Olive, barely 5'2, tilts her head up to address her.

"Of course. Turned out to be mutually beneficial. I had my own childhood demons thanks to dear old Dad," Olive responds.

"We all have our skeletons," Julie immediately replies, squeezing her hand. *Is this excessive friendliness or is there a hidden agenda beneath her warmth?*

"Dad! Help!" Lucy's voice carries from the boat, drawing Colin's immediate attention. She's struggling with a wakeboard, dismissing the boys' aid. Aaron and Landon cling to the dock as Colin hurries to assist.

Julie seizes on Olive's momentary solitude, drawing her close. Her eyes scan the surroundings for anyone in earshot. "I overheard you telling Colin that Richie spilled everything?"

Olive nods, curiosity knitting her brows.

An exhale of relief escapes Julie's dewy lips. "Thank God. I've been dreading all of this. The real reason I asked Colin to bring you to my facility. It's part of my Twelve Step ordeal, seeking forgiveness and making amends. I've done that with Colin, but wanted the same with you." Julie sucks in more air, words tumbling out further. "You're only as sick as the secrets you keep. I couldn't keep that secret any longer, Olive. I don't know how much detail Richie divulged, but what happened between us was a drunken mistake on my part. Alcohol was my mask for suffering. I was never in love with Richie; it was purely physical. I love Colin. Don't misunderstand me, I love Richie for saving Lucy. Our fling ended long before I sought his aid for her. I just needed you to know that. And I'm sorry."

Olive feels the ground give way beneath her feet as the revelation hits her: an affair, a drunken blunder with her husband of seventeen years. Julie's grip tightens, searching Olive's eyes as though she were seeking to extract the amends from her soul.

A whirlwind of local fireworks explodes in the distance, stealing Olive's breath. The willow tree behind Julie seems to be entangling them both. Olive's eyes start to sting as she holds back tears.

"I had … I had no idea," she manages to stammer out.

Julie stares back, confusion evident on her face. "I think you knew, Olive. You saw us. You were drunk, but you saw us. That night … the night of everything, and you said nothing."

She shakes her head no. She can't speak. A lump begins to form in her throat. How could she be so oblivious? Julie stares at her with pity, obviously not knowing what else to say. What else can you say after such a confession?

"Hey, ladies!" Audrey's sudden interruption is a welcome lifeline, White Claw in each hand. She hands one to Olive, who shakes her head no. Audrey then repositions it in front of Julie.

"No thanks, I don't drink."

Audrey looks around, disappointed. "Wow, isn't this a lively bunch. Thought we were sparking up down here. Don't worry, I brought edibles." Audrey begins to rummage through her clutch.

Olive notices Julie fixated on her left hand. Most likely laughing at the overly large, three-carat cushion-cut ring. An upgrade from Richie on their tenth wedding anniversary. At the time, she truly loved the gesture. Now, it seems like a flashy joke. Right about now, she is fighting the urge to toss it into the dimness of the lake.

"I love this. I used to have one just like it." It wasn't the ring that caught her eye. Julie touches the bracelet on Olive's wrist—her birthday bracelet.

Olive's heart drops, sudden and jarring, like an elevator skipping floors and jerking to a halt somewhere it shouldn't.

"Sorry, guys, I can't find the edibles. My bad. It would've been a trip to cruise on the boat while high. I've done it before, it's wild." She finishes what's left of her current White Claw. "Anyway, I'd better skedaddle to Laura's party, she can be a real biatch about not being on time."

Olive quickly reaches out and grabs onto Audrey's arm. She needs to get away from Julie. "I'll walk you out," she offers. Both women climb the hefty hill of soft grass, leaving Julie to contemplate her amends by the water's edge.

As the night drapes its cloak over the waning party, Olive finds herself seated alone beneath the walkout deck's shelter. A few stragglers remain, not yet lured by Laura's competing soirée. The fireworks had fallen victim to the erratic weather forecast, postponing them by an hour. Mrs. Schmidt chats animatedly by the fire pit with Landon, while Lucy, with a marshmallow on a skewer, dances along with the flames. Nearby, Colin and Mrs. Schmidt's reclaimed husband, Harold, plunges into a dialogue about the reformation of the Detroit Red Wings.

A chill hangs in the air from the dropping temperature, and Olive's hands quiver. Her eyes fall to the bracelet, a silent witness in all of it. She watches as Richie limps towards Julie, who emerges from her garage with sparkling water. Their embrace is soft, words hushed. Colin's posture shifts, a swell of pride inflating his chest as he observes Richie conversing with his wife.

The jigsaw pieces, so long a jumbled mess, align like stars in a cosmic tableau. The visible tension that had long simmered between Colin and Richie, so thick it seemed she could cut it with a blade, now has a proper narrative. The architects of this maze of betrayal and pain were none other than Richie and Julie. Young Hannah must have witnessed Colin's assault on Richie seven years prior, during that fateful Fourth of July gathering. That must have been the moment Colin discovered the clandestine affair. And, supposedly, Olive saw it with her own eyes, too, according to Julie.

Had the embers of that old relationship reignited when Julie turned to Richie for medical advice, sparking Colin's explosive rage last Christmas? Or had Julie been genuine in seeking out Richie's specialized skills for Lucy's treatment, despite an abundance of qualified oncologists in both Michigan and nearby Ohio? Regardless of the actual circumstances, it was not her own doing; she was simply an innocent insect, a casualty ensnared in a web spun by others.

"Mom? You okay?" Landon's voice trembles as he joins her, offering a s'more on a navy plate. She remains wordless, a captive audience to the drama unfolding before her. Richie and Julie are still talking intimately. Landon watches too, equally stunned.

"You *know*. About Dad and Julie, don't you?" he asks, his voice cracking a little with the burden of his question.

She stares at her grown son. "Yes," she affirms. His gulp is audible. If her body could still produce tears, this might be the moment when they'd flow. Yet, it's been quite some time since her body has permitted such an emotional release. She once came across a quote that struck a chord: "Cursed are those who feel oceans but can only express a drop."

"I'm sorry, Mom. I wanted to tell you, but I didn't want you to feel any more hurt. Hannah and I saw them together; that's what she referred to in the note. At first, I didn't know what they were doing. I was young … but then it became clear. We were playing hide and seek. Dad didn't know we were there, on the side of the house. I left when I saw them, but Hannah stayed." Landon pauses to take a bite of his s'more before continuing. "Hannah said that you saw them. That you knew, but you didn't confront them. You just walked away, like you had an understanding."

Olive sits frozen, shock gripping her. She truly had no recollection of any of this.

"And there's something else from that night. We never discuss it. You told me Kate was gone before anyone found her. Your words were quiet, almost incoherent, but Grandma Trudy and I heard you, maybe Mrs. Schmidt too. You said Kate was dead."

How did I know she was dead? Was it a mother's intuition, or something I'd done? Olive stares down at her charred s'more as the possible implications weigh on her. The question also remains, whether relevant or not, who had drugged her that night. She reasoned the internal memory loss had to be an effect of her spiked drink. Or could it be something her mind just didn't want her to remember? And what brought Kate down to the dock in the first place? She would never have wandered down alone in the dark.

"We don't have to talk about it, Mom. My therapist back then told me not to push things for people who aren't ready. You just seemed out of it after that. I didn't want to bring it up, and Dad, well, I always thought he was a bad guy after what I witnessed. But Dr. Everly said time would heal it all." He takes another bite, causing an audible crunch of graham crackers.

She knew Dr. Everly looked familiar. But in her brain fog of a mess, she didn't even remember who her son was seeking grief therapy from at the time. She remembered waiting for him in the car. The thought of walking into the office made her physically sick. Most of the time, she would even have Trudy take him.

Olive watches as Colin, now broken free from his hockey talk, engages Richie on the driveway. A flash of discomfort crosses Richie's face as he meets Olive's glare. *Recognition.* He recognizes that her knowledge and awareness now exceed what he'd disclosed in that confessional hospital room. The truth he shared was actually a cocktail of half-truths, bound by one monumental lie.

"Anyway, I should go clean up the boat. The guys left a bunch of food in there." Landon stands up, his eyes meeting Harold Schmidt's. "Mom, what is Mr. Schmidt doing here? Aren't they, like, separated? I saw him the other evening too …" He trails off as he turns to her. "Hey, what would you like to do for your birthday? It's right around the corner, and all I want is to see you happy."

Olive snaps out of her self-inflicted turmoil, assuming her role as mother. She wraps her arms around her almost adult son, who will forever be her child.

"I am happy," she fibs, trying to reassure him. "Sometimes life throws us challenges we can't explain—bad things happen, and we never truly know why. And that's okay," she adds softly, whispering the words into his ear with a calm she doesn't quite feel.

Landon's phone buzzes several times in quick succession, rattling against the fold-out table. Without looking, he flips it over.

"Who's that?" Olive asks, gently brushing a stray lock of his dark hair aside.

"Hannah. She might come back one more time before summer ends. I told her I'd pick her up from the airport and help her pack up what's left of her dad's stuff." He forces a smile, but Olive can see the concern for her lingering in his eyes.

"You're a good person, Landon. She's lucky to have you as a friend right now. I'm proud of you." She snags a small chunk of chocolate from the remnants of the s'more on his plate.

Just then, the night erupts into life as fireworks explode over the lake. The sky bursts into brilliant hues, a kaleidoscope of colors and shimmering light reflecting off the water's surface. The booms and crackles echo across the dark expanse, but Olive's thoughts drift elsewhere.

She stares out at the lake, the dazzling light shows unable to distract her from a singular thought: how deep it goes, and what other secrets might be hidden far below its surface.

PART TWO

CHAPTER 27

SUNDAY 9 A.M.
JULY 2, 2023

As the final car pulled away and silence settled over the house, Olive lingered near the bedroom doorway. The air still carried a trace of perfume and cologne from the evening's crowd, but the warmth of company had long vanished. She turned to gather her things for bed, ready to collapse—until Richie walked in behind her, posture tense, hands in his pockets.

"I need to tell you something," he said.

She turned, startled by the weight in his voice.

"It was just sex," he blurted out. "It didn't mean anything. I should've told you."

For a moment, Olive just stared at him. The words floated in the air, as if they belonged to someone else's story. Her mouth opened, then closed. It wasn't the shock of the betrayal, but the offhand way he said it. Like he was commenting on the weather.

"You and I weren't even having sex," he added, almost defensively. "I mean … I'm a guy, Olive. I'm not making excuses, but it wasn't emotional. We were friends who had a few drinks after work, and … it just happened. I kind of thought you just turned a blind eye to it all."

She took a step back, hand finding the edge of the dresser for balance.

"You thought I turned a blind eye?" she asked, her voice cracking. "You thought because I was grieving, I wouldn't care that my husband was sleeping with someone else?"

"I didn't think you'd notice anything," he said flatly. "You were in your own world. After Kate … you stopped seeing me. I needed someone to talk to. You shut me out."

"Of course I shut you out!" Olive snapped, tears stinging the corners of her eyes. "My daughter died—our daughter. And I'm sorry I wasn't in the mood to be touched, to perform, to pretend like everything was normal. But that doesn't permit you to go looking for comfort in someone else's bed."

Richie sighed, like this was a conversation he'd hoped would go differently. "Look, I'm just being honest. It's been over. It meant nothing, and it will never happen again. And now, we're in a better place, right? Our marriage is fine."

Olive shook her head, her lips tight, trying to block out the weight of his words. How could she trust this promise? She wasn't sure of anything anymore. Turning away, she gripped a sweatshirt in her hands, folding it carefully, though her fingers trembled—more out of the need to do something, anything, than out of any real intention to tidy up.

"No," she said quietly. "You don't get to decide that everything is now fine." When she turned back to face him, her eyes had steadied. "I need space, Richie. I need time to think, without you in my ear, without the noise of this house."

He looked confused. "What are you saying?"

"I'm going to the retreat. This … this just made the decision clearer. I need to heal. Not just from this. From everything."

He nodded, but she could see he didn't truly get it. Not in the way she needed him to.

And deep down, she knew the truth: it wasn't just about Richie. It was about that night—**the Fourth of July.** The night Kate drowned. Every conversation, every clue lately had started circling back to that moment. Her mind couldn't stop pressing on it, like a bruise that hadn't healed right. Something was missing. Something more.

And now, away from Richie, away from the weight of his justifications and her guilt, maybe she'd finally be able to see it clearly.

Olive's phone interrupts her reverie in the passenger seat of Colin's getaway car. She's not quite sure what she's getting away from. Everything will still be there when she returns: Richie,

Julie, the lake … but maybe, just maybe, her doubts won't be.

She looks down to find a text from Richie: "I have a surprise for you when you return for your birthday. I love you." *It better be a different surprise than the bracelet*, she thinks to herself, prying her wedding ring off and securing it away in her purse. Ever since she learned about Julie, it had felt like the ring was scalding her finger, as if her own skin were rejecting the symbol of their marriage.

She promptly turns off her phone, feeling a sense of relief as they cross the threshold into the tranquil northern Michigan landscape. A sea of towering pine trees stretches for miles, a stark contrast to the southern Michigan scenery. She takes in the breathtaking view—the rows and rows of trees against the clear sky, the tantalizing hint of the blue water in the distance, as rich in hue as the Caribbean Sea.

She realizes that she's not just escaping her lake house, she's discarding the expectations and constraints that have defined her for so long. The road ahead is uncertain, but she likes that. The surge of newfound freedom courses through her spirit. It has been decades since she's ventured up north, and it feels like a chance to not only reclaim herself but recover the truth of the past. A truth she hopes Dr. Everly can help her uncover once and for all.

Olive rolls down the windows, inviting the warm summer breeze and the rejuvenating touch of the sun. The air brings the fresh scent of pine and wildflowers, filling the car with the essence of nature.

"I'm glad the weather forecast changed, looks like clear skies for the rest of the week," Olive states with a smile. It was a classic Midwest deflection to talk about the weather over feelings. Colin doesn't take the bait.

"So, I know you don't want to talk about it yet … but I heard you found out *everything* last night. I hope this doesn't make things weird. I didn't want to be the one to tell you about Richie and Julie. Now you can understand why I'm not a fan of the guy." Colin grips the steering wheel hard as he navigates through the winding roads that snake through the dense forest.

"You're right. I don't want to talk about it." She wants this trip to be about her for once, not her husband's poor decisions. She also doesn't hold any ill will towards Colin for not telling her. It wasn't his place. It was her husband's. She imagines that if the roles were reversed, it would be a hard spot to be put in.

"Alright, well, when you're ready, I'm here. They say being married to an addict is like death by a thousand cuts. So, I'm still struggling myself."

She supposed he had a point about the slow and painful nature of it. However, her husband had made the deliberate choice to betray her trust. At the same time, she assumed Julie's involvement seemed to be mainly fueled by alcohol—an addiction that, in her opinion, is one of the worst, given her father's history. Alcohol is socially acceptable and readily available almost everywhere, making it a challenge to confront. Imagine telling yourself that alcohol is the problem.

"I guess anyone can be addicted to anything, though," Colin muses. "Power, money, sex. Anything you put above your moral compass, or someone you love."

She nods in agreement, reaching for a box of Milk Duds. Colin hits the cruise control and casts a glance her way as she leans against the window. Journey's "Don't Stop Believin'" plays on the radio in the background. She can't help but chuckle at the lyric's humorous inaccuracy—every Michigander recognizes South Detroit would be Canada.

But she *would* take the midnight train going anywhere at this point in her life. She stares ahead blankly, her exact final destination up north still known only by Colin.

"Can I ask you one more question?" Colin asks in an edgy tone.

Olive rolls her eyes and nods.

"Why do you stay with him? Why are you choosing to stay with Richie? I know you'll go back to him."

Olive finds herself unexpectedly protective, not just of her husband, but also of the seventeen years they've shared, the life they built, their home, their children. "You don't know anything about Richie and me," she retorts defensively. "He's made mistakes. We all have. But he's a good person." Still, could a genuinely good person hurt someone they love in the way he did her?

"No, he's not. He's good to everyone besides you. You need to understand the difference. A wife becomes a reflection of how her husband treats her. Of her environment. How do you feel?"

"I'm sorry." Olive chokes back a laugh. "Is that a line from one of your self-help books? How did you feel when your wife was fooling around on you? And how do you know she hasn't done it with anyone else in one of her sloppy drunken stupors?" Olive regrets the last sentence the moment the words leave her lips, but she couldn't help herself. Colin looks over at her, his face flushed.

Before Colin can say anything, Olive continues, "Richie is my husband. He's a good doctor."

"He treats people like objects for his own amusement."

"He saves people's lives. Your daughter's included," Olive retorts.

"He's a pompous liar and a conniving cheat," Colin quickly responds.

"So's your wife."

Colin visibly deflates and he slaps his knee hard. "Touché." He unrolls the windows a tad, inhaling the fresh air.

"All I'm saying is I think you can do better. Richie keeps you small, so you don't outshine him. And maybe you're right about Julie, but she got help for her problems, and we're working on it."

Olive starts biting her nails vigorously, the taste of metal creeping into her mouth. "I … I don't know who I am without Richie. I know that sounds silly, but we've been together forever. We've been through the worst thing a couple can experience. We lost a child. I think we can get through infidelity." Olive feels her own words deep within her soul. Who was she, stripped of the layers she'd worn for so long? The question gnaws at her as she stares out of Colin's car window, silence filling the space between them. The concept of her own identity seems as elusive as smoke and mirrors. It all seems to be an illusion—the picture-perfect wife of a doctor—a lifelong people-pleaser shaped by the scars of growing up with an alcoholic parent. Lately, the medicated spouse, numbing her own scars from losing a child, is driving her into the contours of her home.

"Welp, good thing we're driving up here in the summer. Last time I came up north, it was mid-January. Cold as hail," Colin remarks, shifting to the weather-based deflection tactic.

"Don't you mean cold as hell?"

"No," Colin replies firmly. "It's cold as hail. Hail is a form of frozen precipitation, making it a natural and logical reference for describing extreme cold."

"Touché," Olive says, allowing Colin his biology professor win for the day.

During the prolonged quietness that follows, Olive flips through the radio stations, searching for a song to match her mood. She begins with a Motown hit before switching to a classic rock station, turning up the volume and nodding along to the rhythm. Colin glances at her, taken aback by her carefree demeanor and the irony of the song choice—Phil Collins' "In the Air Tonight." Olive sings along loudly. Colin eventually decides to join in for an air drum solo and they both laugh. Olive looks down to find goosebumps on her arms.

Colin lowers the volume and looks to her with an odd smile. "Do you know what this song is about?"

"I think it's about Phil Collins' divorce," she replies, now reaching for a bag of Chex Mix.

"No, it's about how he saw the guy who was having an affair with his wife drowning and didn't help him," Colin responds.

Olive laughs. "That's just an urban legend."

"No, even Eminem rapped about it in his song 'Stan.'" Olive smirks, reveling in the fact that Eminem was considered a God to most local men. Anyone who made it out of Michigan and became famous was someone you could reference for truth and admiration. The funny thing is, even when people made it out of the mitten, they always chose to return.

"But if you look at the stats, the chances of you getting pulled under while trying to save someone are way higher than actually managing to pull them out," Colin continues. "So, I understand why Phil wouldn't want to try to help someone he despises. You can't put your own life at risk." Colin's statement is grounded in cold statistics, far from the heroic ideals Olive wants to hear. They instantly transport her back to the night he struck the vulnerable little duck.

"I think there are many theories about what the song is about. I guess it will remain a mystery," she finalizes sternly.

Colin continues to contemplate her comment when Olive swiftly turns to him, her hand resting on his plugged-in phone.

"I have to ask … where did you go the other night? The night you helped me with the boat. And Richie ended up getting in his car accident."

Colin looks over at her, his blond hair reflecting hints of champagne. "To meet one of Lucy's other doctors. She had updated bloodwork and some new files. The insurance company was giving me a hard time about covering some stuff the doctor deemed medically necessary." He turns the side visor around to block the sun, keeping his vision on the road.

"Everything's alright though, with Lucy?" Olive asks, now concerned.

He smiles, nods, and turns the radio volume up.

Olive couldn't help but wonder who was that *other* doctor?

Olive's eyes flutter open after a thirty-minute catnap, a jarring noise from the car having woken her. Her last recollection is of Colin delving into one of his professor-like lectures, this time about halogenic toad venom, a topic apparently gaining buzz in the realms of psychedelics and modern medicine. The only tidbit she found interesting in his lecture, however, was that toads normally wouldn't stand a chance against the scorching Mexican desert heat, but these special ones defy the odds by spending ten months buried underground, emerging for just two months to eat and reproduce. Olive can't help but think that these toads, with their brief moments of life, shared a kinship with her. She also thinks of Landon, who used to love amphibians.

They pull onto a dirt pathway, the gravel spraying from behind. It appears to be a private road. She can see sprawling mansions on the lakefront. They turn once more into a gated compound that is nestled away and has several log cabins spread out on the site. Behind the cabins, she can see a glimpse of the shimmering blue of a lake.

Colin quickly parks the car and leaves to find Rita. Olive stays put, taking in the view of the cabins, which are labeled A-F in one section and G-K on the other side, reminiscent of her childhood summer camp experience. The one summer her mom worked overtime as a dental hygienist so that she could attend.

"Olive, come here, honey." Rita waves her down. Olive hesitantly leaves the sanctuary of the car. As she approaches, Rita's strong lavender perfume wafts towards her, a fragrance that brings Trudy to mind, making her skin crawl.

"So, there's been a slight issue, dear. I didn't realize we were at capacity when you emailed me. I just told Colin you guys are going to be bunking together. I hope that's okay. Unless you want to sleep in a sleeping bag on the floor in my room? I'm just so thrilled so many of our group wanted to participate in this."

Olive looks over at Colin, who appears slightly uncomfortable, judging by the way he's running his hands through his hair. "Oh, um, yeah, that's fine. We'll make it work," she responds.

Rita leads them to their quaint little cabin, furnished with child-sized wooden bunk beds and one large king-sized bed. Olive could work with this; it wasn't like they were sharing the same bed. "So, they typically use this cabin for families with kids. I apologize for the sleeping arrangement since this is an adult-only retreat this week."

"Rita, are you kidding me? This is fantastic. We are so thrilled to be here," Colin says as he smiles at the kind older woman.

"Alright, well, I'll let you guys get settled and then Dodge will want you all out by the water later. We're going to do a bonfire and introduce everyone to our team. You guys can just relax until then, and Olive, I know Dr. Everly has an appointment set up for you as well. I just want you both to find your inner peace and calm here." Rita clasps her hands together and offers a warm smile before departing.

"So, I can take the top bunk," Olive says somewhat awkwardly.

Colin casually tosses his duffel bag onto the king-sized bed and replies, "Suit yourself. You're welcome to take the big bed, too."

Olive contemplates it for a moment and then puts her bag down on the bottom bunk. Her attention drifts to Colin's large briefcase next to his suitcase as he pulls his sandals out. She can see that it's filled with a plethora of paperwork in two large folders.

"Are you planning on doing some work while you're here?" she probes.

"Something like that. I do have to fine-tune my resume for Wayne State, but those are mostly Lucy's medical records and bills, for the insurance issue I mentioned. I've been meaning to sift through all of them. Just haven't been in the right headspace."

Olive thinks of the mountain of medical bills piled up in his kitchen, as well as the check that her husband had so *generously* written them.

"I'm just happy Lucy will get to spend some one-on-one time with her mom. It's been a while since Julie has been truly present," Colin adds, his expression softening.

Olive returns the smile and glances down at her hands, now tanned and void of a wedding ring. No more regifted bracelets either. If Julie could find a path to redemption in sixty days away, Olive wondered just how much she could change in the span of forty-eight hours.

CHAPTER 28
RICHIE

SUNDAY 10 A.M.
JULY 2, 2023

I stare out at the vast lake, mulling over my life choices as I gear up for the next part of this phone interview. My wife, the woman I've known half my life, has taken off with a man I loathe after uncovering a brief affair I thought I could bury. If only she had stayed on her medications, stayed in her lane, like the ducklings trailing their mother down by the dock. They follow their leader, with no hesitation and no straying.

I glance toward the Bakers' house, half-wondering if Julie is there, staring back at me as I sip my morning coffee. My phone buzzes, pulling me from the thought—an unknown number. It might be *The New England Journal of Medicine* calling early, although a day ahead of schedule seems unlikely. "Hello?"

"Yes, is this Doctor Wentworth? It's Father Paul from St. Thomas. I was curious if you'd consider sponsoring our youth trip this fall?"

"Sure. Sign me up," I answer curtly. If throwing money at something makes me look good and maybe saves my soul, so be it.

"Great. I'll have Laura Lang reach out with more details." He coughs, hacking loudly. I wonder briefly if my time with Father Paul may be coming to an end in more ways than one. The thought lingers, turning my mind to fatherhood. What is a good father, anyway? A son's first hero. A daughter's first love. I suppose I was both, once. I'm not so sure anymore.

I hang up and turn around to find my son, my only living heir—Landon.

"Hey, Dad. There are some guys at the door. Said they're here to install the new countertops."

I notice he won't even look me in the eyes. *He knows* … or at least, I think he does.

"Alright, let them in. They better be done today; I've got my last big interview tomorrow …" I trail off, waiting for my son to look at me the way a son should, with admiration. But he doesn't.

"Cool. I gotta head back to school."

He turns to leave, but I gently grab his shoulder, deciding to bring up the only topic I know he cares about. "How's Mom? How did she seem when you spoke to her last night?"

This time, he stares back at me—really looks at me—our matching eyes meeting as a blue jay flits overhead and lands on the bird feeder. "She knows."

I hesitate, unsure what to say. I settle for the truth. "I know. Do you think she'll be okay?"

He nods, pressing his lips together as if deciding whether to say more. Before the silence becomes unbearable, I interject, grasping at a minor distraction.

"Alright, I digress. Twenty bucks if you can name that bird." I point to a new one that's joined the blue jay at the feeder.

Landon takes a moment to study it. "House sparrow."

"Correct!" I say, though I haven't a clue what kind of bird it is. I'm just relieved he went along with it. I pull out my wallet and hand him the money.

"Alright, see ya," he says, already turning to leave.

"Wait. Real quick—how's school? The internship?"

"It's good. Working with amputee patients, helping with 3D imaging. That sort of stuff. I really have to go. I'll call you."

I know he won't.

We hug, and he heads down the deck toward the driveway. I watch him go, replaying his words in my head. I didn't even know he was doing medical work. It's always the kid you clash with the most who ends up being the most like you.

CHAPTER 29

SUNDAY 3 P.M.
JULY 2, 2023

Shay Everly is two years younger than Olive, and both attended medical school at U of M around the same time. The two of them now sit together in a log cabin, face to face. Doctor. Everly is donning a professional demeanor with her thick black glasses and meticulously styled hair, worlds apart from the mom Olive had met at the farmer's market. Doctor Everly opens her notebook as Olive fidgets in her chair, wishing she had joined Colin for a canoe ride. She is new to this, and the prospect of opening up to a therapist leaves her uncertain.

"I'm so glad you agreed to be my first one-on-one session here. I know these circumstances are … unique," Dr. Everly says. Olive still struggles to recognize herself in this new professional guise. She clutches her hands tightly together.

"I've never done anything like this before. I'm not really sure how these things work."

"Talk to a doctor? Forgive me, but it says in the paperwork you sent over that you've been on …" Doctor Everly pauses and pushes her glasses down to the tip of her nose, scrutinizing the long list of medications Olive had been prescribed over the years. "Well, you've been on a lot of different medications."

Olive squints and nods, trying to make it seem normal. But it was far from normal for her husband to write half of her prescriptions, with the other half prescribed by his friend Dr. Eisenberg. Nor was it normal for Olive to be sitting across from the same woman her son had seen seven years prior. She's waiting for Dr. Everly to acknowledge the shared history.

"Right, I know. I've never really spoken about a lot of my

feelings," Olive admits. "That was just the norm growing up," she continues. "My dad used to say, 'We Greens are mean. Don't let them see any emotion.'" The mention of her maiden name brings back memories. She had been teased about it throughout her childhood. To be named Olive Green was an invitation for ridicule. The only time she enjoyed it was during her undergraduate time at Michigan State University, where the slogan was "Go Green." She had dreamt of the day when she'd get married and change her last name to match her husband's. No feminist principles or hyphenations for her. She willingly and happily became Olive Wentworth when the opportunity finally presented itself.

"When you're taught not to show emotion—even anger—you end up drowning in it. It seeps into your nervous system. Your body ultimately pays the price, carrying all that unresolved weight. Funny, isn't it? Anger is justified in men, but when women hold it in, it festers into chronic illness."

The doctor's words linger in Olive's mind. Maybe there's truth to it—after all, 80% of chronic autoimmune disorders affect women. She tugs at the sleeve of her sun shirt, trying to absorb it all, resisting the urge to stay at the surface. Instead, she knows she has to dig deeper, to uncover the root. "I guess I've never really talked about the death before," she admits quietly. "I've just kept it all inside."

"When you say you haven't spoken of the death … do you mean your daughter's?"

Olive contemplates the question. She hasn't truly gotten over or spoken about her own mother's death either. Or her father's, for that matter. Or even the possible death of her marriage.

"Olive, listen. This is only going to work if you feel safe with me. This is a safe place." The word *safe* makes Olive feel queasy. She hadn't felt truly *safe* in years. Not the kind of safe you feel in a gated community, but the safe where you can take a deep breath and know everything is okay in the world. The safe feeling a child gets when their mother holds them in their protective arms. And she remembered every day when she awoke at 3 a.m. that she'd failed to keep her daughter *safe*, even if it genuinely wasn't her fault.

"I'm going to be straightforward with you, Olive. You may or may not remember, but I treated Landon after Kate's death. I know this is a little unorthodox, but I'm familiar with the events leading up to that night. How familiar are you with that night? At what stage of grief do you believe you are at?"

Doctor. Everly hands a chart over to Olive that lists the different stages of grief. So many emotions listed on one single piece of paper. She had felt all of them at one time or another—anger, depression, guilt, shock. There were two listed she hadn't landed on yet—rage and acceptance.

One would think finding out your husband's mother didn't mention to you that you were drugged and not drunk the night your daughter drowned would cause rage. If that didn't do it, finding out your husband was having an affair with your neighbor that very same night might. Olive did feel a sense of anger, but more than anything, she just felt hollow. She may have been a sparkling, beautiful shell at one point, but now she was one of those dried-up ones with holes you find at the beach and toss aside.

She felt completely emptied of emotions to display. And *acceptance*. That would never happen. Most men seem to move on relatively easily. She recalled Richie telling her that she needed to get over Kate's death so they could all move on. It was easier for him. He had distractions. But if someone experiences enough grief and trauma, they cannot simply "get over it." Just like Richie wouldn't expect someone in a terrible car accident at the ER, their body mangled, to "get over it." It would be cruel to expect them to. *Why can we understand the physical damage that a traumatic accident can cause, but we struggle to understand the emotional repercussions?*

Doctor Everly begins tapping her pen that holds the initials SEE on it. It makes her wonder what Dr. Shay Everly's middle name is.

"So, I think it's fair to say you may still be in the shock phase?" the doctor asks gently. Then she adds, "Grief has a way of living in the body. It stays stored in waves. Give it permission to exist, and it can finally move through you."

"Shay—I mean Dr. Everly, I don't remember much of that evening. I recently found out I was drugged with GHB that night."

Doctor. Everly looks up, her brows lifting slightly and her lips parting just enough to betray a flicker of surprise. A beat passes before she straightens her posture, quickly smoothing the expression from her face, professionalism sliding back into place like a mask. "I see. You know, trauma can suppress episodic memory, especially in cases like yours. The sequence of events may fragment, even disappear. But there are ways to recover it. Even if you were drugged, your brain stayed alert. The body remembers everything. It holds what the mind can't."

Olive's ears perk up. "You're saying you can get the memory back of that night?"

Doctor Everly quickly shakes her head no and drops her monogrammed pen. "I can't get your memory back. *You* have to do that with our other licensed professional, who, to your luck, is here at this retreat. Her name is Goya. She specializes in EMDR memory recall work and craniosacral somatic therapy. I'll get you guys lined up for tomorrow, and then I'd like to see you after, if that works?"

Olive takes a moment to contemplate. The idea of delving into her subconscious memories is daunting, especially with the most agonizing memory she's ever experienced lurking within. But maybe that's exactly where the truth has been hiding all along—in the quiet corners of what she's avoided. Her thoughts drift back to what Julie said down by the beach: you're only as sick as the secrets you keep.

"Yes, that would be wonderful." Maybe there is hope—something she also hasn't felt in years.

"Our brains are capable of hiding things deep in there. But Olive, I still have to warn you. Even if you get pieces of that night back, it's still going to be subjective. Meaning you may remember things that are not quite accurate. I want you to know that. Our memory can have a way of tricking us sometimes to protect ourselves. It's nature for our body to do anything to protect itself. But there's hope. Secrets within us do have a way of resurfacing if you give them time. And if you feel something was off about that night, that's an intuitive feeling you need to listen to."

Olive nods and stands up. She hasn't done much talking, yet she already feels a sense of relief. There is still hope of finding out what had happened that night—who drugged her, and if she was somehow responsible for any of the events.

Kate would never have gone to the dock alone. They'd had repeated talks about water safety and she knew the rule: no lake without an adult or Landon by her side. And Kate, for all her adventurous spirit, had always been cautious when it came to the lake. She understood the dangers. She respected them. That's what made everything so impossible to make sense of. Something, or someone, had to have changed the plan.

Dodge inhales a lungful of thick smoke drifting off the firepit, then doubles over coughing, struggling to clear his throat as the burn clings to his chest. It is 8 p.m., and Olive yearns for the comfort of her twin-sized bunk bed, her body and soul already worn down by the day's trials. But once again, Colin has coaxed her out of her comfort zone. She had put on a forced smile and engaged in small talk during the earlier outdoor dinner.

Now, she finds herself encircled by both familiar faces from past meetings as well as new ones, a mix of men and women from diverse backgrounds. But that's the thing about addiction. It doesn't discriminate. It casts its wide net, ensnaring and uniting people with its devastating grip.

A faint hope lingers within her that Big Joe might make an appearance. After all, his and Audrey's cottage isn't too far from here, and Audrey had mentioned they might head up for the fourth.

Olive still carries a trace of guilt for not enquiring about JJ the previous night when Audrey had rescued her from Julie's unsettling confession. Yet, a newfound certainty begins to take hold. For once, she feels as though she is in the exact place she needs to be. To her left, Colin's face glimmers in the fire's dancing light, while on her right, Rita takes a seat.

Dodge says, "I hope your bellies are full. Thank you, Ms. Rita, for that wonderful, fresh fried fish. That was superb! I know we all have meetings lined up over the next few days with our counselors and a trip to the dunes, but I wanted to have one big group meeting tonight to talk about the two A's: Acceptance and Anger. We all need to accept the difference between the things that we can and cannot change in our current situation. We all know the verse, come on my people …"

Dodge puts his hand out, waiting for the group to take the reins. Rita and a few others begin to fill in the space. "God grant me the serenity to accept the things I cannot change, courage to change the things I can, and the wisdom to know the difference."

"Good! Now, we can't accept things until we deal with that other pesky A word: Anger. Now, I'm *not* tellin' you people that anger is bad. No, no, no. On the contrary. Anger is natural. Look at nature. Look around at these beautiful trees, beautiful lake, animals. Everything beautiful can get angry—even the weather. But as humans, we have the power to take responsibility for that emotion and choose to live a harmonious life. And what breaks our hearts can fix our vision."

Rita, now makeup and fragrance-free, stands up and begins distributing pieces of paper and pens to each person curled around the campfire. A quick gust of wind pushes the burning blaze close to Olive's skin. It is a slow burn, and the smell reminds her of fireworks. She closes her eyes briefly and reopens them to find a piece of paper in her lap. Colin must have sensed her discomfort, as he promptly drapes his hoodie over her shoulders.

"Now, on this piece of paper, I want you to write down something that angers you that you want to release. Until you choose to grieve and release anger, you will always feel guilty. You are not meant to carry that. You can release both with no fear, no judgment. Accept the anger, then let it out."

Olive sits there staring at the blank piece of paper. The fire crackles and sparks fly into the night sky, resembling fireflies in the darkness. Colin starts diligently writing down many things, while Rita sits down next to her and pens the word "grief." She then looks up and makes direct eye contact with Olive, her pupils appearing grey. "It gets into your body. Grief. It gets buried deep. It's not good to hang on to. It will make you sick," she says, throwing the piece of paper into the fiery inferno.

One by one, members of the group begin discarding their notes into the roaring flames. Olive suddenly feels exposed, vulnerable to her innermost feelings. But this is what she came here for, she reminds herself. Catharsis. Release. Truth. She takes a deep inhale and tries to allow herself to *feel*, finally. Slowly but inevitably, anger begins to rise—anger at the sheer unfairness of life. How, in one moment, everything could be perfect—a loving husband, two healthy kids—and in the next, it could all be torn away.

She feels like she is drowning, not in water, but in an oppressive, suffocating void. She finally scrawls a word on her paper and lets it drift into the consuming flames, releasing.

As the night progresses, the group continues to share their stories. Olive mostly listens, her sense of calm gradually deepening. She supposes Dodge was right when he told them that shared struggles released oxytocin in the brain. Allowing someone to sit and struggle with you has the power to bond souls, especially when it comes to grief. She knows that everyone experiences it differently, but one thing is sure: grief cannot lie buried. It demands to be seen and heard. It requires a witness. And they are all witnesses for one another.

It is nearly eleven when most of the group wanders off to their cabins. Olive spots Colin still engaged in a conversation with Dodge, and waits for him to finish so they can turn in together. She hadn't noticed that Dr. Everly had been present at the bonfire, in her street clothes, discreetly positioned behind a large water cooler. She approaches Olive with a smile on her face and the scent of cannabis clinging to her body, appearing to have something important to convey. But she remains silent. Olive questions the doctor's use of cannabis in a work environment. They stand there for a few more moments until Olive decides to break the silence.

"So, what's your affiliation with this group? You know an addict?" Olive asks, hoping Dr. Everly caught the sarcasm in her tone. The doctor laughs, understanding the jest. "No. I know a good person." She points over at Rita, who is tidying up the leftover food and packing it into a cooler. "She's my aunt, almost like a mother to me. She's been through hell and back, lost a child, my cousin, to a drunk driver when we were younger. She's the director at the church where you have your meetings. But she strongly believes in the cause, helping others overcome tragedies, and so do I," she explains.

"I'm sorry to hear that," Olive replies, absorbing the revelation about Rita's shared experience of losing a child.

"Listen, human connection is the one thing that can hurt us as well as heal us and pull us out of an isolation pit of self-defeatism," Dr. Everly replies, retrieving a vape pen from her hoodie. "Sorry if that was a little intense. Sometimes it's hard to take off the doctor hat. Or so I've been told by Laura." Both women snicker.

"That's okay. Apparently, I'm not honoring my husband enough, according to Laura, too."

Doctor. Everly takes a puff from the vaporizer, filling the air with a skunky grape musk. Olive raises an eyebrow, her curiosity still piqued by the doctor's choice of relaxation methods in a church retreat setting.

"Yeah, what she failed to mention was the other half of that verse. It drives me crazy when people focus too much on the rules and legalities of religion rather than their personal journey with God. It should be grace over guilt." She hands her pen over to Olive, who shakes her head no.

"Funny. I wouldn't have taken you as a religious person. Being in the medical profession and all the scientific … ness … is that a word?" Olive laughs awkwardly.

Doctor Everly chuckles, her laughter mingling with the dissipating vapor. "I believe the medical profession and spirituality are very closely intertwined. We either are playing God or work alongside Him, and it's our choice. Just as we choose between doing good or bad."

The hair rises on the back of Olive's neck. The doctor's words feel eerily similar to the sentiments in Hannah's letter. *Sometimes, good people do bad things.* Olive hesitates before finally voicing her thoughts with a tinge of uncertainty. "Can I ask you a question, Shay, uh, Dr. Everly?"

Doctor Everly places her warm hands on Olive's shoulders, exuding a comforting presence. "Ask me anything," she responds, as if daring Olive to ask the doctor what she *really* knew.

"Do you think good people can do bad things? What if …" Olive feels the doctor's hands squeeze her shoulders, then release.

Then Dr. Everly says, "No. I mean … sometimes. But for the most part, people do things because they want to. If someone chooses to do something bad, well, that's not for me to judge. But Olive, you're good. Don't ever question that. From what I've seen, you're a true empath. You take on everyone else's emotions, and that can be exhausting. Just because you feel someone else's pain doesn't mean it's your responsibility to fix it." Doctor Everly places her hands in her hoodie pockets, shivering for a moment before continuing. "You need to give yourself some grace. It seems to me like you give it to everyone else except yourself."

Maybe she is right. Or maybe Olive was a good person who had done a bad thing once. Maybe this was all karma. *If only I could remember.* Olive knows she isn't a terrible person, but years of hearing one narrative about herself have left her grappling with not only her identity but the truth.

Doctor Everly takes one more draw of her pen, inhaling for what seems like an eternity. "You know, bad things happen to good people. Just look at my aunt," she says, her voice steady but knowing. "It's how you rise from it that defines you. There's a saying I like—if you fall into a ditch, don't start decorating it." Olive looks toward the trees outside, their branches swaying wildly in the gusty wind. The words settle in, heavy but true. "And you, my friend, have been living in this pit of isolation for far too long," Dr. Everly continues, her hands gently resting on Olive's narrow shoulders. There's warmth in her touch, but also finality. Olive feels the weight of the moment shift, sensing that her conversation with the doctor might have reached its conclusion for the night.

Rita approaches them, appearing a little annoyed. "Alright, dears, it's quite late. Why don't we all get tucked in now for the night? We have the dunes in the morning." She grips the back of Dr. Everly's hoodie, a silent signal not to blur the lines between business and pleasure.

Colin, sensing the cue, approaches and places a reassuring hand on Olive's back.

Walking together along the dimly lit dirt pathway, a spark of hope flares anew within Olive. She and Colin turn the corner, approaching their cabin. Tomorrow's prospect of reclaiming her lost memories with Goya fills her with anticipation and a little bit of fear of what she may uncover.

CHAPTER 30

MONDAY 3 A.M.
JULY 3, 2023

Somehow, even after releasing her anger to the bonfire, Olive finds herself awake at the usual time—3:03 a.m. She's officially forty-two years old. No one here knows, and she likes it that way. She's always hated her birthday; it was the day her mom was diagnosed with ALS.

Peeking through the blinds, she observes a landscape shrouded in the morning fog. She reaches for her phone and powers it on. Multiple texts from Richie flood through:

-I miss you.
-Happy Birthday my love.
-Please call me.

She opts to ignore them. It's frustrating how, in her experience with men, they often come to recognize her actual value only after demonstrating their worst sides. Richie couldn't appreciate her value until she was no longer within his reach.

There's another text from Audrey, offering a birthday wish, along with an automated birthday text from her dentist. Birthday emojis from Landon pop up, which he must have sent right at midnight.

"Hey …"

She turns around, surprised to find Colin sitting up, his thick mop of hair a mess. She powers down her phone.

"What's wrong?" he asks, his morning voice cracking.

"Nothing. Just can't sleep. Maybe I should have taken the weed pen from Shay."

Colin snorts and pats the empty side of his bed, silently inviting her to join. She reluctantly yet curiously obliges.

Olive recognizes she's in the same boat as Colin, the spouse who was cheated on. Now they lie together in the same bed. Both are fully clothed in thin sweats. It is intimate in a nonsexual way. She reflects on the last time she felt this kind of closeness. Perhaps it was during the early days of motherhood, when she was so lonely and sleep-deprived. She had met Audrey in their neighborhood park, the two sharing all their desperate, tired thoughts. But like some relationships, over time, *something* had drifted them apart.

She had no inkling of the extent of Audrey's struggles with JJ, just as Audrey remained unaware of Olive's lingering pain and need for a friend to push past the barriers she had built. She realizes now, however, that by creating those barriers to keep out the dangers, she inadvertently shut out the good stuff too. It's a trade-off, really—safety at the expense of openness.

Then again, some say people enter our lives for a reason or a season. Maybe Audrey had been the season of young children and Colin's reason is yet to reveal itself. After all, she barely knew Colin a month ago.

And yet, here they were, sharing a bed. She felt safe with him, but it was marred by uncertainty. Colin might be using her to rattle Richie for his affair with Julie. Olive didn't entirely mind, though. Colin had pushed her to climb out of her emotional abyss. She didn't *need* his saving, but he was the cherry on top of her ice cream float.

They drift back to sleep until, at some point, it appears that the sun is ascending through the window of the old cabin. They now face each other, his eyes opening slightly, fluttering like a child's. She studies his soft lips and the freckles around his nose. He stares back at her, seemingly admiring the rarity of her vibrant green eye color. She licks her lips, and he glances at hers and she can no longer resist the urge. Leaning in, she kisses him gently. Her hand rests on the back of his neck, and he responds by pulling away slightly before instinctively leaning in for another kiss. This kiss is magnetic.

She knows it's wrong. Does this make them bad people? As if sensing her thoughts, Colin abruptly pulls away, pushing her hands down. "We can't do this," he says harshly.

Olive isn't sure how to respond. His words say no, but his body conveys an entirely different message. Her heart is racing, and she feels alive. She leans in towards him once more and he quickly gets out of bed, the morning light now brightly shining through.

"I'm going to shower. We have the sand dunes soon," he states before entering the bathroom and locking the door behind him. She feels rejected, but also turned on by his will and integrity.

A sudden vibration rattles a water bottle on the dresser, drawing Olive's eyes. It's Colin's phone, an alarm blaring across the screen. She reaches over to silence it just as a new notification lights up the display. A message preview hovers from a contact saved as *Wifey <3*.

Did you tell her everything yet?

Olive's breath catches. She hesitates, then swipes the screen, only to be met with the passcode lock. No access. No clues. Just that one tantalizing line. The shower stops. She quickly sets the phone back face down, her pulse drumming in her ears.

The mystery unsettles her as she hears him loudly jiggling the bathroom door, trying to open the old thing.

"Damn door!" Colin exclaims, finally emerging from the bathroom, towel wrapped around his chiseled waist, his skin still glistening from the shower. Olive resists the urge to dwell on his undeniable allure and forcefully reminds herself that her knowledge of Colin remains incomplete, despite their deepening connection.

CHAPTER 31

MONDAY 9 A.M.
JULY 3, 2023

The group arrives at Sleeping Bear Dunes National Park, an enchanting gem often touted as one of America's most stunning natural wonders. Olive hasn't been here since she was a kid, but it is exactly as she remembers. It is a tourist hotspot, with an undeniable allure.

As the bus traverses towards the parking lot, Olive ponders the memory of little Landon singing the Great Lakes song and reciting his dune knowledge, with Kate relaxing in her lap on the hammock. She recalled him saying the lakeshore was an impressive thirty-five-mile stretch, primarily designated for its remarkable dune formations. It saddens her that she can remember such trivia but remains unable to recall further details of that fateful night. But she has Goya's upcoming help to change that.

The group collectively walks along a pathway that offers panoramic views of Lake Michigan, its shimmering blue waters crashing against the shoreline. The expansive waters resemble those of the Atlantic Ocean, making it hard to believe they are just a lake. Olive and Colin walk side by side, their awkwardness mimicking their silence on the bus. They follow closely behind the park ranger and Dodge.

"If you look to your right, this particular dune is where the Sleeping Bear Dunes name originates." The ranger points behind a cluster of tall pine trees. Along the forest's edge, a massive dune vaguely resembling a sleeping bear can be seen.

"Locals call this dune the Mother Bear," the ranger continues. "The legend claims the mama bear awaits her lost cub."

"And you don't want to mess with a mama bear," Dodge

adds, chuckling to himself.

"Mama bear"—a term so endearing to describe the ferocity with which a mother would protect her child, Olive muses.

Below the colossal dune, Lake Michigan stretches out, seemingly infinite.

The group continues down the sandy path, taking in the awe-inspiring spectacle. Towering dunes stretch out before them, soaring to the sky, their golden sand reflecting the sun's rays to create a surreal and ethereal landscape.

The wind rustles through the dunes, producing a gentle, almost peaceful sound that eases Olive's mind. The weather is a perfect seventy-five degrees, sun shining, a slight breeze, and under different circumstances, she might have relished in the moment. But Julie's text message continues to nag at her, somewhat distracting her from the breathtaking surroundings. As she observes sweat trickling down Colin's strong forearms, she realizes she needs to confront her feelings and speak to him directly.

The group comes to a sudden halt as they reach a large sign that reads: "Warning: enjoy the view from here. Down is optional. Avoid getting stuck at the bottom! Lake levels are high. The only way out is up." The sign's message makes Olive feel small. The lake's vastness seems almost contagious, like her problems.

"I'm gonna have to urge everyone to stop here, take photos if you like, but please don't venture down," the ranger states matter-of-factly. "The sand is quick to pull you towards the water. Be careful, everyone."

Dodge nods in agreement, captivated by the spectacle. A bunch of callow teens races past them, descending the sandy cliffs with laughter. Colin steps back, accidentally bumping into Olive, and the two make eye contact for the first time since their intimate encounter earlier.

"Follow me," he whispers. Olive hesitates before trailing him down a nearby path. The rest of the group scatters, some taking photos, while others settle at a nearby picnic bench for a snack.

Colin leads her further through the dense trees in the opposite direction from the dunes. She notices a creek merging with a faster-flowing body of water further ahead.

"Here," Colin gestures to a fallen tree trunk by the river's edge for the two to sit on. "I think that's either the Platte or Crystal River there," he says, seemingly trying to diffuse the uncomfortable tension. Olive doesn't take the bait. They sit there for a moment, on the banks of the river. They observe a young couple in kayaks paddling through the crystal-clear waters that flow through the dunes.

"Can I tell you a secret?" Colin asks. Olive nods, hoping it is about the text. "I'm going to take toad venom here tonight, DMT," he reveals, looking at her expectantly.

She vaguely recalls him talking about the toad venom before, on the drive up. Apparently, Julie had done it in Mexico on a girls' trip, and it was the catalyst that led her to rehab.

"Julie said it completely changed her outlook on life. She's never experienced anything like it before. Will you do it with me?"

Olive can't help but smile at the image of Julie "licking" a toad in Mexico, even though she was well aware the substance was actually smoked. She can't fault Julie either for turning to unconventional means for healing. After all, the notion of Terrance seeking answers through hypnotherapy was equally unexpected. While she maintains her reservations about Ouija boards, a remnant from her Catholic upbringing that warned against dabbling with the supernatural, she holds no judgment towards those who dabble in specific drugs. Given her past entanglements with Schedule IV narcotics, it isn't her place. However, she is past seeking refuge in substances. Numbing herself is no longer an option she wants to entertain.

"I'll pass. No more numbing for me."

"It's not about numbing," he shoots back. "It's about seeing. Like, actual visions and clarity."

She arches a brow. "And you think that's safer? Should you even be messing with that stuff? Isn't it still illegal here?"

"Oh, come on," he urges, nudging her. "Do you want to spend years talking about your feelings with Dr. Everly, or do this *once* and potentially heal yourself completely? Julie said it was like ten years of therapy in fifteen minutes. It's not like mushrooms, where you're tripping for hours. It's a maximum of twenty minutes. You can even recover repressed memories from it, or so I've read."

Olive sits there, staring blankly at the river and creek. She feels like a rebellious teenager, hiding away in the woods from her real life. Is she genuinely considering using illegal drugs with a neighbor she has a schoolgirl crush on, all in the name of healing and uncovering the truth about her daughter's death?

"Haven't you heard that one quote? 'I went to the woods because I wanted to live deliberately.'" Colin grins at her with a goofy expression that Olive can't help but find endearing.

"Boy Scouts?" she asks with a chuckle.

"Henry David Thoreau, actually," he corrects, his tone steady. "He went to the woods for answers, to understand our place in the world and what nature can teach in its purest form," he recites, clearing his throat. "But hey, maybe you think all this is cheesy." His grin remains wide, his lips mirroring the wild pink daffodils swaying gently beside them.

"I'm not even sure I want to be sitting next to you right now, let alone take hallucinogens in the woods." Olive's voice sharpens slightly as she hopes Colin finally gets the message: it's time to come clean about whatever he's still hiding and stop with the metaphors.

He exhales deeply. "I'm sorry about this morning. It's not that I didn't want to … believe me, I did. It's just …"

"Julie," Olive interrupts.

"Yes, Julie. We're going to try to make this work. I'd be a hypocrite if I did the same thing she did to me. That's not getting even; it's hypocrisy at its finest. And there's something else." Colin bites his bottom lip, as if unsure how he should phrase what his heart needs to convey next. "Something I've still been keeping from you, something that might make you hate me for not telling you sooner."

Olive's heart now begins to race. No one is within earshot or eyesight. "It's why I brought all that paperwork with me. The actual reason," Colin confesses, his face now turning deep red. He struggles to articulate the words, and Olive's patience wears thin. She can no longer take it.

"Just say it!" she urges.

Tears begin to stream down his cheeks, his voice strained as he speaks. "Lucy is … she's not mine. Your husband is her biological father."

The declaration hits Olive right in the gut. It's not the secret she was expecting. She thought Colin was holding back on something he knew of *that* night. Maybe even that Julie was the one responsible for her spiked drink. This omission was a blindside. But as Dr. Everly said, secrets have a way of surfacing in due time.

Quickly doing the math, she realizes that Lucy is six years old, seven in October. Colin and Julie always had elaborate Halloween-themed parties for their next-door neighbors. She was likely conceived around the time of the party. The party will have happened seven years ago tomorrow—her unlucky number. It had been 2,519 days without Kate, and Colin has had Lucy for almost as long.

Olive stands up, the trees encompassing her, her head pounding. Her right leg feels slightly numb.

Colin grabs hold of her hand and pulls her back down gently. "I know you're seeing red. I'm a damn biology professor, and I didn't realize that my brown-eyed daughter wasn't mine. Did you know that it's very rare for two blue-eyed people to have a brown-eyed child?"

Olive looks over at him, and he seems to be in even greater despair than she is. "I always thought they were hazel," she responds. They both force a smile, and Olive is glad it lightens the mood.

"I figured it out just before Christmas break. I was reviewing Lucy's medical chart, confirming what we all hoped: that she was healed. Julie and I were both tested by Dr. Hernandez to see which one of us was a carrier for the genetic cancer. It was assumed one of us must be. It was only when I received the email saying neither of us was a carrier that I realized it. Lucy didn't just have any type of cancer. It was the exact same type that Kate had. That's why Julie turned to *him* for help."

Richie. She realizes it's too painful for Colin even to say the man's name, let alone learn that his only child was not biologically his. The timeline of events surrounding Christmas strikes a further chord, as she recalls Colin's outburst at work, which led to his being put on leave, and then his subsequent confrontation with Richie at home, to which Hannah was another witness. It occurs to her that perhaps this chain of events had pushed Julie towards rehab as well.

"And he knows? Richie knows he's her father?" Olive questions, still trying to piece the ever-changing puzzle pieces together. But she doesn't need Colin to respond to know the answer. Considering his access to Lucy's medical charts and his personal time with her, he must have suspected something. Richie was many things, but one thing he was not was oblivious.

How could he keep something so monumental from her? And how could she have been so far gone that she didn't notice? Any lingering hope of salvaging her marriage quickly evaporates within her, leaving her empty. No tears form. When she thinks of Richie now, she feels neither anger nor love—she feels nothing.

"He knows," Colin replies, his face displaying a visible expression of disdain.

"And the check? I saw it in your kitchen, from Richie," she questions lightly.

"Child support," Colin replies with a touch of sarcasm. "His hush money, a way to keep me from revealing his misdeeds when he saw you and me together. He knew I needed the money. But just so you know, I'm not cashing it. I just feel so much shame about all of this.

Olive's heart drops for him. "Shame isn't bad. It's proof you still have honor." She continues to mull over this flood of new information, her mind racing to process it all.

Then the words slip out. "I'll do it," she announces impulsively.

Colin turns towards her, the saline tracks still running from his rosy cheeks. An instinctive desire to sweep away his tears invades her. It's peculiar, she muses, how from a young age, we're coached to believe that erasing tears is a gesture steeped in love and comfort. But Olive understands it differently in this moment; it's merely a way to avoid and deflect. It's an impulse she must unlearn. Cognizant of this, she retracts her hand, allowing his tears to carve their paths unrestricted, allowing him to immerse himself in his vulnerability, to experience his emotions truly.

"I'll try the toad venom or DMT, whatever it is. We're in this together, right?" she asks.

Colin forces a smile and nods. The idea of experimenting with this substance feels desperate, but desperate people do desperate things. And Olive desperately needs the whole truth. She stares back at the creek and the river. She is no longer content to remain stationary like the creek. She's ready to plunge headfirst into healing and submerge herself in verity. No matter what unconventional form it came in.

CHAPTER 32
RICHIE

MONDAY 12 P.M.
JULY 3, 2023

"Well, they say when love isn't served to you on a silver platter, you learn to savor it from the sharpest of knives," Maxwell Conch remarks. The distant sound of a passing boat confirms my suspicion that he took our second phone interview while on vacation. He doesn't take me seriously, and he should. I may be a big fish in a little pond, but I did discover the cure for a devastating genetic cancer. I also desperately need this conversation to go better than the last. This article must serve as the true springboard for my career, to catapult it to new heights. It would also lead to more funding for my hospital—*it's always about the funding*. Concurrently, however, I'm also burdened by the desire to reclaim my former life, the one where my wife cherished me—the one where I was her world. Now, I've messed that up, or at least, Colin ensured that I did. It's come to my attention as a husband that wives aren't as forgiving as mothers.

"Anyway, that's the CliffsNotes version of my childhood. Thanks for indulging me, Doctor Wentworth. But let's hear more about yours—what led you down the twisted path of medicine—before we plunge into the intricacies of how you derived this cure," he probes.

My eyes drift to the office clock. It's almost noon, and I've yet to hear from my wife on her birthday. I know her well enough to understand she won't advertise it either, wherever she might be, this odd wellness retreat. How well can you cope with being surrounded by the unwell? In my book, medication works faster for healing. My heart sinks, longing to call her once more, but I know her phone remains stubbornly off.

"My childhood …" I begin to reply, but my attention veers towards Sheri Schmidt, the neighborhood's resident gossip, as she hauls her trash to the curb outside my bay window. She's oblivious to the fact that there won't be trash pickup tomorrow due to the holiday, and that a mob of raccoons will soon ransack her cans. I loathe raccoons.

"As I mentioned a little in our previous chat, my brother Wells also battled this cancer when we were younger. I suppose that's what drove me to become a doctor, that it could have saved him, even though it seemed like an impossible feat at the time." My voice trembles slightly, and I hope he senses the raw sincerity in my tone. It's all true, but I've omitted the grim conclusion of Wells' death.

"I understand. As you've mentioned, it's a genetic condition and, tragically, you passed it on to your daughter, who also met a tragic end," he says, likely enjoying a piña colada. Prick. As if I didn't already carry the burden of guilt for passing this cursed gene to my daughter—or daughters. It didn't take many sessions with Lucy to realize she was mine. The unmistakable dimple, her wisdom beyond her years, and her strikingly similar hair color to Kate's.

Acknowledging it would have shattered Olive, and I couldn't do that to her. Julie was a brief, reckless affair that started just before the Fourth of July bash, reigniting a connection from our days at Beaumont Hospital. I could sense it the moment I laid eyes on Julie; she was as broken as I was. After Kate, she was there for me in a physical sense, even though I knew it was wrong. I did a bad thing. Repeatedly. Our last rendezvous happened to be on Devil's night of that same year, the day before

Halloween. Maybe that makes me the devil in all of this.

Maxwell Conch taps his pen impatiently on the other end, transporting me back to our call.

"Returning to your earlier quote on childhood, Mr. Conch, we teach people how to treat us, and sometimes, people aren't shown how to treat others properly, even in a medical context. I witnessed that firsthand with my brother. He was often dismissed, written off as incurable. I wanted to be that change—an empathetic doctor who could truly make a difference, starting with my research approach," I reply, offering partial truths. We indeed teach people how to treat us, but in my case, our father treated us like dogs, and not the pampered lapdogs of wealthy older women kind.

"Excellent, Dr. Wentworth. I'm intrigued by your direction on this. Could you elaborate on your research process?"

I begin to lay out, in layman's terms, my process, my team, my tactics, all the while haunted by memories of my brother and the day he drew his final breath. It wasn't an accident, like my father told everyone afterward.

The three of us—my father, brother Wells, and I—were out on the ice in the dead center of Lake Superior. It wasn't a planned outing. My dad woke us up before dawn, tossed some rods in the trunk, and drove north without so much as a second thought. No coats. No real gear. No hut. Just a whim. I remember standing there, in the open wind, wondering why we weren't inside one of the two bright-orange fishing tents I could see off in the distance. Their sides flapped gently in the breeze, probably warmed from the inside by propane heaters and the smell of hot coffee. Meanwhile, I was shivering, my toes going numb, my teeth rattling like dice in a cup.

Dad stood over the hole we'd drilled with a borrowed auger, squinting like he expected a fish to leap out and volunteer itself. Despite the beauty of the winter landscape and the anticipation of a catch, I was left shivering without a coat. "You don't need a coat," he grunted when I'd asked for mine. "Toughens you up." Then, when the fish didn't bite fast enough for his liking, he blamed me, saying I was too loud, scaring them away. He stormed off across the ice toward the car, muttering about needing a smoke.

Wells turned to me. "You need this more than I do," he said, voice hoarse but steady. He shrugged off his thick navy coat—his cancer coat, Mom used to call it—and draped it over my shoulders. The lining still held some of his warmth. I couldn't speak, I only nodded thanks. Then came the splash. A tug on the line. "Grab it!" Wells shouted. "That one's yours!" I yanked the pole, reeling in a writhing little fish. Wells was beaming until it slipped from my gloves and flopped helplessly on the ice, slapping the surface in chaotic protest.

And then ... something moved. The sun was beginning its slow retreat, crawling beneath the edge of the earth, dragging the last of the light with it. Dusk draped long shadows across the ice, and somewhere in the brittle dark, the night creatures stirred. A lone raccoon emerged, creeping silently along the frozen lake. It paused, eyes locked on the flailing fish, then lunged. In a blink, it had its prize—fish clenched between its teeth, the creature's masked face oddly triumphant. It skidded across the ice, vanishing into the deepening gloom. Tears streamed down my rose-colored cheeks, and Wells noticed. Without hesitation, he chased after the raccoon, farther and farther across the lake, all for me, to reclaim my fish.

Suddenly, a deafening crack split the silence. I spun around to see my dad, standing outside his car, cigarette clenched between his teeth, a .44 magnum in one hand. He fired wildly, not even with aim, just letting loose into the open lake like it might solve something. The shots rang out, echoing across the flat white expanse. One clipped the raccoon's leg, sending it limping off into the dusk—the ice, thick and solid, held firm beneath the impact. But Wells, already far out and turning back toward me, didn't make it far. There was no warning, just a sharp crack, then another. His foot slipped, and a spiderweb of fractures laced beneath him. The next step gave way. "Wells!" I shouted. And then I heard a scream, faint and panicked, rising up across the lake before the plunge choked it off. He dropped through the surface like a stone. The lake went still again, flat and blank as if it hadn't just swallowed a boy whole.

Initially, I believed Wells had been the one to scream, his swan song. But as my father finally approached me, he was still screaming. He peered down at me, a mixture of bewilderment and disgust in his eyes. From a distance, he had mistaken me for Wells, wearing his jacket and the same jet-black hair.

His only words to me were, "I thought it was you." If words had the power to kill, those surely did. The searing glare he fired upon me that day remains etched in my memory. Ironically, the worst day of my life had not yet come, and it would involve another drowning.

"In summary, that's why I prefer to keep the majority of my research methods discreet and exceptionally comprehensive. People entrust me with the well-being of their loved ones. Every member of my team has signed a confidentiality agreement and has been with me from the beginning, starting with my daughter. When it concerns people's health, you can never be too discreet, to put it bluntly."

"Well, thank you, Dr. Wentworth. That provided valuable insight into your research methods. If you don't mind, I have an urgent call to return. Can we reconvene in an hour or so? My apologies for any inconvenience."

"Sure," I reply, my annoyance barely concealed. It appears Mr. Conch has more pressing matters to attend to; perhaps his vacation guests require his immediate attention.

CHAPTER 33

MONDAY 1 P.M.
JULY 3, 2023

Sitting in a tranquil spot amidst yoga mats, with the lake's glistening edge in view, Olive allows her mind to wander. A subtle unease gnaws at her gut. Any uncertainties she had regarding Colin have vanished. Her instinct tells her he is a reliable confidant. But how much does she truly know about Julie? Could she have harbored a hidden agenda seven years ago? A motive to remove Olive's daughter from the equation and, in return, secure a child with Richie? These questions hang in the air, a haunting echo of doubt, and various scenarios swirl. Goya now approaches from the wooded bend, temporarily pausing Olive's thoughts.

The woman's presence is a radiant blend of compassion and wisdom, her large brown eyes framed by intricate braids that fall gracefully down her back. Her handshake is gentle, and her skin is soft, but the strength under it is palpable. "Welcome. This is a safe space," she assures Olive with a warm smile. Olive winces inwardly at the word "safe" yet again, but she's here with an open mind. The two women settle on the yoga mats, facing each other.

"Our journey begins with deep breathing, then I'll perform craniosacral therapy focusing on your vagus nerve," Goya instructs, inhaling deeply as she raises her arms skyward.

"My what nerve?" Olive interrupts, eyebrows furrowed in puzzlement.

"The vagus nerve, Mrs. Wentworth." Goya points to the back of her head and elaborates. "It's referred to as the *wandering* nerve in Latin, and it's the longest cranial nerve in your body. It originates in the brainstem and it's key to regulating your nervous system—breathing, even your heartbeat." Olive's bewildered expression prompts Goya to explain, "In simple terms, it controls your nervous system, whether you're in 'fight or flight' mode."

Olive remains perplexed; this information is all new to her, even for being a medical school dropout. Goya's hands move to Olive's neck and throat as she hums a tuneless melody, instructing Olive to swallow, then exhale. "As I suspected," she announces, "your thyroid is imbalanced. I imagine you have migraines? Dizzy spells? Your adrenals and cortisol levels are likely a mess, too." She gestures for Olive to recline on the yoga mat, retaining her gentle hold on the back of Olive's neck, turning it side to side. "The body internalizes what the mind can't bear to acknowledge," Goya says softly, "often manifesting in physical illness. The sickest you feel is usually the moment your body is working its hardest to heal."

Olive contemplates these revelations. No doctor, including her husband, has ever told her this before. They were always quick to slap on a diagnosis, hand her a prescription, and send her on her way, as if that alone could fix everything. "But I've been diagnosed with depression, anxiety," Olive starts, but Goya interrupts her with a dismissive shake of the head.

"Many are misdiagnosed, typically as mentally unstable. The issue often lies deeper, within the body. Western medicine doesn't think to go beyond what it can't externally see. To find the root," Goya asserts, her warm hands shifting to Olive's temples. "You're just stuck in survival mode. Have you ever suffered an injury in this area? A car accident, a fall down the stairs?"

Olive's mind circles back to that night—her tumble down the steep hill, the haze of consciousness muddled with fireworks and shards of glass.

"Yes, I hit my head that night," Olive confesses, "the night I'm trying to piece together."

Goya nods knowingly. "We'll explore that evening. Just beware of false or inserted memories. Focus on what you truly experienced then," she advises, rising to her feet. "Now, I want you to remain lying down. Listen to my voice." She begins to hum, louder this time, yet Olive finds the sound almost hypnotically tranquil, like the gentle breeze tousling her hair. "We'll commence with gratitude, something we can control. In the spirit of heaviness, always put on a garment of praise. You're here, you're breathing. You're the person who could make your younger self feel safe. Tell yourself you are in a safe place now."

Olive does this silently as she exhales, her breath synchronizing with Goya's guidance. Goya next instructs Olive to tap her temples, jawline, and legs gently.

"You might sense a detachment from your thoughts, yes? That's because your brain has separated those memories to protect you. This may cause feelings of dissociation, leading to being easily overwhelmed or fatigued. I want you to defy that feeling and empower yourself, push through."

Goya resumes her seat beside Olive, her skilled fingers probing the tension points on her neck and ears, applying light pressure. She explains how Olive is holding quite a bit of tension in her hips, a common issue for women and mothers. With a precise touch, she applies pressure to a trigger point, facilitating the release of tension.

"Mrs. Wentworth, it's time. Place your right hand on your stomach and your left hand on your ribcage. Feel your inhalation traveling from your chest down and descending into your ribcage."

As Olive follows the guidance, something within her shifts—ever so slightly, yet profoundly. For the first time in what feels like an eternity, she senses that the key to unlocking her past, and thereby her future, lies not in a faraway, obscured reality, but within her. And she is ready to take the psychological plunge back to that haunting night.

Goya's fingers settle on her shoulders like an anchor, grounding her as she navigates the depths of her memories. Her pulse quickens, each beat a desperate plea for clarity.

The night plays back: her bright kitchen; Julie laughing across the counter with her purple mouth, a glass of sangria in hand. Colin had entered quickly, followed by Audrey, who handed out the pitcher. But was it Richie who poured the drinks? Beyond the window, the obstructed view of the kids near the water's edge, their sparklers creating fleeting, mesmerizing patterns in the twilight, along with the fireflies. She can barely make out her daughter near the voluminous willow tree, a silhouette against the vanishing daylight—Landon, JJ, and Hannah entrusted with watching over her. She now thinks she should beckon them up before the sky explodes in colors. They'll have a much better view from the deck.

Suddenly, she finds herself underneath the deck where the walkout basement holds more neighbors. There's sangria on her lips, not the Malbec she'd been sipping. The sangria was most likely Julie's. She drinks it anyway, her eyes meeting those of someone she thinks is one of Richie's co-workers. Her vision narrows. Her mental compass spins wildly.

Conversations are blurring, and her steps lead her toward the front of the house, past Mrs. Schmidt, who is replenishing her pie supply from her neighboring house. There is Julie again, and another vague figure behind her. Julie looks horrified when their eyes meet, so Olive puts her head down, fixating on Julie's navy flip-flops instead, her toenails adorned with the same shade. They become a still point in a tilting world. A distant clamor seizes her attention, but she can't quite place it. It draws her gaze toward a shape lurking down near the willow tree, concealed in the shrubs, near the dock. It's too small for an adult. Perhaps an animal? Something pulls her in that direction.

She makes brief eye contact with Audrey, who hurries by. Fireworks begin assaulting the heavens. Her feet then betray her, slowly sliding, collapsing. Then everything plunges into darkness.

When she comes to, her cheek stings, warm with a mix of blood and red wine. Her feet radiate pain. A blur of green floods her vision. Not grass. Rubber. The Slip 'N Slide? Boots? Did she fall? Slip on one of them? She knows Kate is near, submerged in the water, but she can't locate her. Her veins ignite with adrenaline; her heart hammers like a warning bell. She then swears she sees her daughter floating now, a firework bursting overhead. Fear grips her, immobilizing her completely. It's as if her mind has frozen the scene, holding the frame still, no matter how desperately she tries to press play.

Goya intervenes, sensing her internal struggle. "Don't drown in that moment, Mrs. Wentworth," Goya warns, sensing the quicksand of Olive's mind. "Whether your drink was spiked, or your body simply froze in terror, the outcome was beyond your control. Don't detach. Keep going, you are safe."

Another inhalation, another dive into the murky depths of memory. Richie is down there, on Colin's beach, gripping Terrance as if his life depends on it, locked in a struggle she can't decipher. The large willow tree blocks all of this from the guests above—blackness, then a flash: Kate, limp and heartbreakingly still now on the shore. Olive tries to scream for help from the bottom of the hill, but her voice betrays her as she lies face down in the lush green grass. Fireworks entrance the world, her guests' mesmerized faces turned away from her tragedy. Richie and Terrance appear closer. Richie frantically tries to administer CPR. A voice cuts through the haze. "Call someone," Terrance says.

Exerting every ounce of her strength, she claws her way up the hillside for help, her feet impaled by shards of broken glass, her soul heavy with a darkness she can't shake. When she reaches Landon and Hannah, their faces are masks of horror, reflecting an ugliness she can't fathom, while Trudy glares contemptuously. "She's dead," Olive states. Their gaze remains fixed on her, brows raised inquisitively. A few moments later, they hear Richie's distant voice ring out: "Call 911." Hannah then dials.

She's back by the lake. Not Duck Lake, but the retreat's Torch Lake. Goya's compassionate eyes lock onto hers.

"I can't piece it together," Olive stammers, tears trickling down her cheeks. "Something is altered, it's wrong. There are still too many gaps."

Goya's touch is gentle but unyielding. "What state would you say your nervous system is in now?" Olive knows it's a rhetorical question. "You know we get cues from those around us. Sometimes we need to change our environment if our nervous system doesn't feel secure. You can't truly heal in the same place that made you sick."

Goya pretends to hand over a bottle of pills. "It's not about the pills, the special diets; they're not your salvation. Your unconscious is haunted. That's your real chronic condition. And you, Mrs. Wentworth, have been hostage to this toxic state for far too long."

Goya pauses, allowing Olive's eyes to drift toward the tranquil lake outside, a cruel contrast to the storm inside her. "You're more resilient than you realize. There's a reason why women give birth: it embodies a duality for women—the physical pain intertwined with overwhelming emotion. It often leaves them teetering on the edge of their emotional capacity. Men then call us crazy and often claim dominion over pain and emotion but would most likely find themselves lost in the whirlwind that is childbirth and its emotional aftermath. It's a powerful testament to the strength and resilience inherent in women." Goya hesitates, then rests her hands on Olive's knees. Olive holds the belief that both men and women can possess strength in various aspects of life. Nonetheless, she recognizes that childbirth and the subsequent toll it takes on a woman's body demands a unique kind of strength.

"The great thing is that our brains are remarkable. And a *mother's* brain is even more remarkable. It forever changes the moment she is pregnant—the baby's DNA remains in its mother's brain for a lifetime. *She* will always be a part of you, permanently etched into the fabric of your being, Mrs. Wentworth, always."

Olive listens, the weight of seven years lifting ever so slightly.

The lost memories she'd unearthed with Goya tangle like vines. She'd drunk from the wrong glass, hadn't she? Audrey *was* still present during the fireworks, despite rumors of her illness and early departure. Then there was Julie, skulking around the house's periphery. Richie and Terrance were in some kind of altercation down by the water. The pieces weren't fitting together. Michigan may be the lighthouse capital of America, but today, it offers her no guidance, no illuminating flash of precise truth. The jigsaw puzzle is still unfinished, but she dares to hope that the final picture might somehow, someday soon, make sense.

And, amid the wreckage of her life, she discovers a glimmer of something she believed had been lost forever: *faith* that the universe will reveal the secrets it has been earnestly trying to communicate.

After her session with Goya, Olive sits alone on a rustic dock, accompanied only by the silhouettes of two imposing, green canoes. As she peers into the water, a realization dawns on her: today marks the first instance in a considerable stretch of time that her body permitted her to release tears. The desire had been a silent wish, yet release had eluded her for so long. She had felt drained, void of the comfort that tears could bring. But Goya had succeeded in liberating a floodgate. It seemed that the somatic massage might have unlocked long-trapped emotions and traumas within her, giving way to a cascade of tears she didn't know she could shed.

A throaty roar of a car starting snarls behind her. Doctor Everly's car was fleeing the retreat grounds. Odd, considering their appointment was scheduled in five minutes. Raindrops, small at first, begin to pelt her, erasing the lake's tranquil surface. She registers the clamor of Rita and Dodge covering the firepit, then scurrying to their secure cabins. Thunderclaps sound in the distance, as if God might be applauding her for trying something new.

Out of nowhere, Colin materializes, his chest heaving. "What are you doing out here?" He grabs her hand and pulls her to her feet. Rain batters them as they stagger back to the cabin, both drenched to the core.

Inside the cabin, warmth greets their soaked bodies. Olive's wet hair clings to her neck, cold trickling down her spine. Colin strips off his soaked shirt, revealing a sculpted chest. He hands her a towel, his blue eyes darker, diminished. Their silence is thick with unspoken emotions. She can't seem to shake that something in Colin's pupils that hints at a new, deep hurt. She can tell that they have both reckoned with trauma today, as they inch towards one another.

"Is everything alright?" Olive questions, locking her eyes on his.

He moves closer, the air between them still charged. She yields to his touch as he wraps his arms around her, something in her uncoiling after a lifetime of tension. He holds her close. "I don't want to talk about my session. I want to be here with you." They meet in a slow embrace as she wraps her arms around him. Colin eases back a bit, his fingers delicately tracing the contours of Olive's face before their lips meet. The kiss, carrying the essence of rain, transforms into a fiery intensity. It was unlike anything Olive had felt in years—authentic, genuine, unhurried. With Richie, love had always felt like a transaction, and his fleeting affections stung, but here with Colin, her walls crumble. His touch breaks through her armored shell like a knife. Her fingers tangle in his wet, curly hair as their passion ignites, urgent and profound.

As they shed the barriers of fabric between them, Colin lifts her effortlessly onto the bed. The sheets are a cold shock against her flushed skin, but as Colin covers her with his body, all she feels is fire. It had been over a decade since she allowed herself such abandon. Her nails cut into his flesh—it had been twenty years since she dug her nails into another man's back.

Outside, the tempest roars, but in their confined space, another storm peaks—ferocious and healing all at once. When it's over, Colin's gaze meets hers, no longer dim but fervent and hopeful. He kisses her once more gently, and in that simple act, she finds sanctuary. She knew two wrongs didn't make a right, but it did feel good. And it was her birthday, after all.

CHAPTER 34
RICHIE

MONDAY 1 P.M.
JULY 3, 2023

I find myself drawn to the windowpane, gazing out in mute contemplation, still staring at Mrs. Schmidt's trash can. I'm in an uneasy limbo, awaiting Maxwell Conch's return call. He's probably basking poolside, the sun beaming down on him. This waiting game reminds me, oddly enough, of brain MRIs—not just the waiting per se, but the neurological differences between men and women, especially in that specific region of the brain that processes consequences. It's dimmer in men.

Could that be why I never weighed the risks when it came to Julie, or why spiking what I thought was Colin's drink for alone time with her at the Fourth of July bash seemed like a good idea? In turn, it somehow affected my wife instead. Or even staging my own horrific car accident, spurred on by my mother's dire warnings about Olive discovering her blood results. The self-inflicted injuries were agonizing, but the sympathy from Olive seemed well worth the price. I've seen the power of sympathy at the hospital; families willing to absolve all sins for another day with a loved one.

It all makes me reflect on the correlation between a traumatic upbringing and exceptional achievement. Lawyers, doctors, high fliers—they often have intriguing pasts. Those who've suffered just enough to fuel their ambition but not let it be derailed by destructive habits.

Those are the people who never stop striving. Not because they're innately wired for it, but because of their past. They have something to prove. Blame it all on my upbringing, perhaps on my father.

I glance at my silenced phone; still no call from Conch. But an anonymous text catches my eye: "She knows Lucy is yours."

Fuck. Colin. Damn him. Anger boils through me, tinged with the chilling fear that I could lose Olive—and my reputation—forever. My greatest fear about Olive attending the retreat, aside from the possibility of her transformation—I cherish her just the way she is, desolate and oblivious—was the potential secrets Colin might divulge during their private moments. I didn't think he'd have it in him. Why couldn't he take the money and keep quiet? A surge of revenge now pulses within me. In a rash move, I dial Julie's number, leveling an ultimatum as soon as she answers:

"Sever ties with Colin or face a legal battle for joint custody of Lucy. He's gone too far this time," I declare, my words fueled by anger. I understand that the latter would shatter Colin, utterly devastate him. His golden retriever-level devotion to Julie was exactly why I resorted to drastic measures, attempting to drug him in the first place that night.

"Slow down. This is part of the process for us to all heal. Olive can't be the only one in the dark," Julie replies calmly, driving me even more mad.

"Enough of this Kumbaya bullshit. This ends today, or I'll be taking Christmas as my holiday this year with Lucy," I counter, the grim reality of a protracted custody fight simmering over Julie. She doesn't know I'm bluffing. I would never consider formally filing for custody of Lucy, as that would create a damning record and a whirlwind of talk among my peers. Especially at St. Thomas, Laura would have the entire congregation against me in twenty-four hours. And while I do appreciate Lucy's company,

I have no intention of assuming responsibility for her care. Faced with the harsh ultimatum of possibly losing her daughter, Julie reluctantly but inevitably agrees to make the call to Colin.

Next, I dial the retreat's contact number, the digits displayed on a pamphlet that lay on our kitchen counter. A woman named Rita picks up. I explain the urgency. I need to speak with my wife. She promises a prompt callback. I'm banking on hearing Olive's voice on the other end, but instead, it's a different one—a Dr. Everly. By now, my desperation has already set a series of events in motion. And when circumstances turn dire, desperate measures become inevitable. Doctor Everly informs me that I shouldn't speak with Olive until she leaves the retreat, as if she were some kind of captive.

Restraining my mounting agitation, I confess my affair, my existential despair, and even hint at suicidal thoughts. It's a gamble, but Dr. Everly's hesitant agreement suggests it's paying off, though she mentions she has to report my suicidal intentions to another professional. No matter, I'll chalk it up to a gross misunderstanding when the time comes.

I hang up, a dismal temporary satisfaction settling over me. Olive will return. I've seen to that.

My phone rings again.

"Hello, Mr. Conch."

"Apologies for the delay, Dr. Wentworth," he responds, now noticeably more attentive. "Where were we? Ah, your treatment methodology. Do you incorporate any alternative forms of therapies?"

"Absolutely not," I snap. "I adhere strictly to empirical pure science, tried and true."

A tense silence follows. "Interesting. And Lisa Hernandez, how does she fit into this picture? She wasn't listed among the members of your research team, but she had quite a lot to say about your methods just now."

For the third time today, I curse inwardly. Things are

unraveling faster than I can weave them back together. And I may have to reap what I've sown.

CHAPTER 35

MONDAY 5 P.M.
JULY 3, 2023

Entangled in Colin's arms as if clinging to life itself, Olive finds comfort in sleep's embrace.

A duck's quack from the lake outside stirs Olive from her peaceful slumber. She inhales Colin's scent, a fragrance that had evolved into a comforting, familiar anchor. He lies next to her, so still he could almost be mistaken for lifelessness. In his vulnerability, she finds a strange kind of allure, his chest a haven where her thoughts come to rest.

Yet, the mind can be a slippery slope, skewing one's moral compass; had Julie nudged Colin onto this course? She wonders if their recent intimacy was Colin's lifeboat in a storm, and she was merely the nearest buoy he could grasp. In the throes of drowning, desperation fuels instinct, causing one to latch onto any lifeline.

Is that all she is to Colin … a lifeline? A mere oxygen mask he reached for in his asphyxiated state?

But it was Colin who had pulled her from the depths. She hadn't felt that alive in years. She now examines her own betrayal through a softer lens, one shaded in gray. From afar, Colin and Julie's relationship always seemed healthy; the grass always seemed greener. She supposed the same could be said for what outsiders observed of her and Richie.

Her thoughts scatter as a knock on the cabin door interrupts the room's stillness. She springs from the bed, dons a pair of sweatpants from the floor, and hastily pulls her hair into a bun.

Opening the door slightly, she greets, "Dr. Everly, what a surprise," forcing a smile onto her face.

"I apologize for missing our earlier meeting. An emergency came to my attention, then with the storm, it took me a while to get back to the grounds," Dr. Everly explains, her eyes wandering past Olive into the dimly lit room. Olive takes care to leave the door only slightly ajar, ensuring she doesn't expose Colin in bed behind her.

"No worries. How about we reschedule for tomorrow morning before I leave?" Olive begins to shut the door, hoping for a quick agreement.

"Why not now? I have something important to discuss," Dr. Everly insists, her tone tinged with concern. Olive hesitates, careful not to betray her own indiscretions or divulge her and Colin's hallucinogenic evening plans.

"I'm just not really feeling up for it today. Goya was great, but that journey was draining."

"I completely understand. It's just your husband called and is insisting on speaking with you. In fact, he was almost demanding it. He didn't sound okay."

Olive lets out a sigh. It's hardly shocking that Richie would go to such lengths to interfere with her healing. She is well aware of his gift for persuasion, and she anticipates that he'll remain perfectly composed until her return home tomorrow evening. "Thanks for letting me know."

"Well, get some rest. If you're hungry, Dodge is making gumbo tonight. No more intense healing exercises, I promise," Dr. Everly assures, lifting two fingers as if taking a scout's oath.

Just as Olive starts to close the door, the doctor halts it with her palm once more. "And Olive, when you see Colin, could you give him this?" She hands over a business card that features her assistant's details, including the title "marriage counselor" at the bottom. She can tell by the look Dr. Everly is displaying that Colin's session did not go well.

With a nod, Olive takes the card, closing the door as the doctor retreats towards the woods. She debates whether to wake Colin. Her indecision is interrupted by his groan.

"Hey … who was that?"

Sitting back down on the bed, Olive becomes aware she's

wearing Colin's sweats. She passes him the business card. He exhales heavily, eyes lingering on the card. "Was this a mistake?" she blurts, her words stumbling over each other.

Straightening up, Colin grabs a water bottle from the nightstand and takes a long sip. "No, it wasn't a mistake. It's been a while since I truly connected with someone who was fully present with me. It was different. Nice."

Olive doesn't know if she should be flattered or offended. Nice. She would have chosen words like "passionate" or "intense." Anything but *nice*. Clearly, Julie didn't specialize in bedroom *nice*.

"Julie called me earlier. Let's say the other shoe fell," he continues, laying the card on his lap. "She thinks we should separate, spend some time working on ourselves individually, then maybe try marriage counseling down the road. Oh, and she confessed to another affair. So, there's that. Guess you were right."

"I'm sorry," Olive says, her fingers tentatively touching his wrist. Her empathy isn't feigned. She's always been sensitive to others' pain since she was a small child. She could feel it and see it in her own mother even before her ALS diagnosis.

"She's toxic," Colin mumbles. "Doctor Carillo said as much. She makes me feel like I don't exist, like I'm not good enough. I got so caught up in trying to fix her that I lost myself. She stole the very essence of who I was. Even being a dad—"

Olive doesn't need him to finish. She knows he's saying Julie even stole his role as a father. "I get it," she reassures him, sliding closer.

"Do you? Because I think we share something. We can't separate how we feel about someone from how they make us feel."

"Meaning?"

"Julie might be sexy, smart, and fun, but she makes me feel alone and worthless. That's my reality. You can think Richie is a God, but if he makes you feel like you're nothing, that's your reality."

Olive leans against Colin, feeling his heartbeat and his words, but remains silent.

"Anyway, yesterday's worries are tomorrow's afterthoughts,"

he continues as if reassuring himself.

"Did you make that up?" she asks, lifting her face closer to his.

"Could be Boy Scouts of America. Could be Phil Collins," he quips. His phone chimes and he briefly glances over at it.

"Okay, let's talk about good stuff," Colin says, changing the subject. "Are you ready to try DMT tonight? Make this a plant-based retreat, yeah?" he questions, dead serious, then grins once more.

She removes herself from his chest and instinctively folds her arms. "Yeah, no. I mean, I want to, but is it risky?" Olive's inner concern lingers, especially after unlocking only a few new memories with Goya's assistance. She ponders whether this drug can truly facilitate a deeper exploration of her mind.

"No," he says, "it's a tool for healing past traumas. We're getting it from a reputable source, a professor I know who's bringing it from the Ontario border with a legit shaman. We will be fine."

The very word "border" gives Olive an involuntary shudder. In her mind, the Ambassador Bridge connecting Detroit and Windsor holds too many shady dealings. Even as a college student—going through customs without so much as a speck of contraband—she felt uneasy. All she had been back then was a nineteen-year-old looking to enjoy a legal drink in Windsor with friends.

"They won't make it through the Ambassador Bridge. That's why people jet off to Peru or the jungles of South America for this stuff," she counters, her voice tinged with maternal concern.

"No, no. They didn't use the Ambassador Bridge. They crossed via the International Bridge in the Upper Peninsula," Colin reassures her, pausing to gauge her apprehension. "We're meeting them in a few hours. But you don't have to do this. I think it would be healing for both of us, though. Trust me?"

She hesitates. Trust is a precarious thing these days. "I'm not sure about anything right now. My session with Goya gave me more questions than answers. I thought I saw Julie on the side of the house, not just in the kitchen, and I was convinced Audrey left before the fireworks went off, way before we found Kate."

Colin clenches his fist subtly. "If you saw Julie on the side of the house, then that was accurate. That's where I found her *with* Richie. And are you sure you saw Audrey leave, or was it just mentioned to you? Memories can be implanted by mere suggestion."

As she mulls over his words, Colin leans in, his lips brushing the curve of her neck. "You're quite cute when you're in deep thought," he whispers. She rolls her eyes at him. "Look, this could give you clarity, or closure at least. I've been researching it," he declares, lifting his hands as though accepting an academic accolade. "I've even discussed it with researchers at Johns Hopkins. The results are revolutionary."

"In what way?" she challenges.

"DMT, otherwise known as the 'God Molecule,' is made in the pineal gland and offers clarity equal to years of therapy. It's baffling, it's illegal while alcohol and nicotine aren't," he states earnestly.

Curious, Olive pulls out her phone, turns it on, and starts researching. In Canada, DMT isn't broadly approved, but under Health Canada's Special Access Program, doctors can apply for its use in psychedelic-assisted therapy when conventional treatments have failed. Still, it's far from mainstream. She also notes that in the U.S., it's listed as a Schedule I substance, with possession carrying the weight of a potential ten-year prison sentence. She wonders how Colin managed to convince these people to bring it across the border.

"Trust me, one puff, and you're going to gain so many new insights. Mike Tyson and Joe Rogan swear by it," he offers.

"My heroes," Olive retorts, her voice dripping with irony.

"Listen, you've already tried every other medication under the sun, and none of them worked. Think of your body like a pop can. If you keep shaking it without releasing the pressure, eventually it will violently explode."

Olive gives him a wry smile. "Careful, Professor. You're starting to sound like Bill Nye the Science Guy."

"I'm serious! This could help you face your demons at their

very source—within you," he insists.

"I know. I'm just scared," Olive confides.

"What you're afraid of is likely what will benefit you the most," Colin responds, his tone resembling that of a philosopher rather than a biology professor.

Maybe he's right. Maybe it's time to dive into the unknown.

CHAPTER 36

MONDAY 8 P.M.
JULY 3, 2023

Olive and Colin stand by a crackling fire. They are close to where the sand dunes lie, but in the darkness of the night, it's difficult to determine their exact location within the dense forest. The grass has begun to dry from the rain, and the sound of crickets and other nocturnal creatures fills the night air. She and Colin are here for answers, healing, and venturing into the unknown with experimental psychedelics. She had never anticipated trying something like this. Yet, her conventional methods hadn't been yielding the answers she so desperately sought.

Across from them are two other people—Ophelia and Norman. Ophelia is a professor friend that Colin 'goes way back with.' Olive assumed the professor would be a male, which was sexist of her; she had to admit. She also feels more at ease having another woman present. Ophelia is in her mid-fifties, robed in a flowing white dress that resembles a poncho, adorned with a matching headband piece rich in beaded ornamentation. A leading figure in the University of Toronto's research on therapeutic uses of DMT for PTSD in veterans, she brings an air of scholarly wisdom with her.

Beside her stands Norman, the shaman tasked with leading their psychedelic journey. Before coming here, she'd turned to the internet to demystify the term "Shaman." She discovered it referred to someone with the ability to navigate between the realms of good and evil, to diagnose and heal ailments, and to communicate with profound clarity. Norman, towering and pale-skinned, appears to be in his late sixties. His physique is impressively lean, marked by sinuous forearms and a mane of unruly grey hair. Dressed entirely in white, he seems to radiate an unexplained energy.

Surveying the scene, Olive's eyes fixate on the two small cots spread across the forest floor and a lone bucket set beside them.

"Sapito?" Norman enquires.

"Yes, toad," Colin confirms, revealing a surprising grasp of Spanish.

Norman slowly walks toward them, extending his arms as if feeling the air around them. He closes his eyes momentarily. A quizzical look from Colin prompts Ophelia to whisper, "He's reading your energies."

When Norman stands before Olive, he shakes his head. "No sapito. Ayahuasca for you," he declares, his statement laced with a French-Canadian cadence. Olive turns to Ophelia, her expression a wordless plea for translation.

"Ayahuasca is another form of DMT, consumed as a brewed tea," Ophelia elucidates. "It involves two plants, one containing the DMT, and the other, the ayahuasca vine. It's often used for deeper emotional work. Typically, someone does this when they find themselves at a crossroads seeking answers. Are you seeking revelations from your past? An epiphany, perhaps?"

Colin seems to hang on Olive's answer as well. "Yes, I am," she finally responds. While the term "ayahuasca" isn't entirely foreign to her, she had only heard about it in passing, as something celebrities indulged in for enlightenment or ended up vomiting through the night. The buckets now made sense.

Yet, for some, it promised a transformative experience, a gateway to the recesses of the self. As Olive recalled from one of her many college psychology courses, Freud had once called dreams the "royal road to the unconscious."

But was she truly prepared to dive into the suppressed corridors of her mind? The hidden recesses might hold paradigms and scars she'd been holding back from herself for years. The idea of a bad trip loomed like eternal hell, even if Colin assured her the effects would last less than an hour. Then again, they say ayahuasca chooses you, not the other way around. If celebrities like Megan Fox and Chelsea Handler could muster the courage, perhaps she could too.

"Alright, so it's settled. Sapito for me, Ayahuasca for her," Colin announces. A rush of heat flushes through Olive's ears, and her stomach churns, preemptively queasy before even partaking.

"Is this … safe?" she asks, glancing at Norman, who gives her another once over.

"The medicine is safe. It's humans who are the danger," he replies, pulling various items from his bag. "No one dies from a snake bite; it's the poison that kills."

"What do you consider … poison?" Colin chimes in.

"Anything beyond what we need. Because the answers are already within you."

For a heartbeat, Olive contemplates fleeing this mystical-looking scene in the woods. Now that night has fallen, she realizes she's never been surrounded by such darkness. Yet, something within her fortifies her to stay. *I came to the woods.* She is ready.

Norman begins mixing elements in a bowl. Ophelia hands them each a notepad, then states, "Write your intentions so you can be clear on what you wish to achieve tonight. I've noticed that humans are unique in often falling short of their intentions, undermining themselves. However, in the natural world, you won't find a beaver building a bridge; its sole focus is on constructing dams."

Olive turns to Colin, both experiencing a dose of déjà vu. "What did you write down last night at the bonfire to release?" she probes.

"Too many things. Anger, resentment, DNA results." He laughs, trying to keep the mood light. "But tonight, I intend to find happiness."

Norman clears his throat and stares up at the moon. "The Summer Buck Moon is upon us, when male deer shed their antlers. It symbolizes renewal. Your goal is not to find happiness, which is external and temporary, but to find purpose. Once you find purpose, you'll find joy, which is internal and lasting."

Colin's eyes light up. It's some real shaman life advice. He looks over at Olive. "What did you write last night?"

Olive pauses. "*Myself.* I wanted to release myself."

"And now?"

"Truth," she writes down, feeling more certain.

Norman nods approvingly. "You'll find your answers."

Olive watches as Norman prepares a glass pipe with a concoction made from toad secretion and sets it beside the fire, then returns to his bag.

"Professor Baker," Ophelia announces, "you will smoke as soon as Olive drinks. Yours will kick in immediately, and it will heighten your level of consciousness right away. You will be physically incapacitated for about twenty-five minutes."

Colin and Olive lock eyes once more. "You will drink first, Olive. It will take around twenty minutes for your body to relax and purge." Ophelia motions to the bucket.

"Better out than in," Colin adds. Ophelia places her hand lightly on Olive's small frame.

"You need to purge. It will feel cathartic and assist you in letting go of any anxiety, fears, ego—anything holding you back from your true self—so you can dig deep into your subconscious."

"Will I get back my memories then?" Olive asks.

"Norman will assist with that. He will chant and circulate smoke to stimulate visions. But remember, your experience is your own. Don't fight it. Resistance will be your psychological downfall. You have to succumb to Mother Ayahuasca for it to work."

At this point, Olive's uncertainty evolves into full-fledged anxiety. Her palms are clammy as she stares at the stars above.

Colin squeezes her hand three times. "You're okay. Just drink and let it purge your system. Then you can receive what you need."

Norman appears beside her, offering the concoction. Suppressing a grimace, she gulps down the bitter liquid, which tastes like a liquified jungle floor, miles away from the Jägerbomb shots in Windsor.

Norman gestures for her to sit, encircling her with smoke. She watches as Colin takes a deep inhale from his pipe and instantly collapses into a trancelike state. Norman picks up a wooden rattle and starts chanting.

"This helps the medicine work," Ophelia whispers, handing Olive the bucket. As soon as she does, Olive feels her insides purging, a guttural force. It is everything all at once, expelled in a violent rush. Then, complete and utter silence settles around her.

Everything falls still. It's a quietness that seems to echo in her heart, a deafening tranquility that presses in heavily. Never has Olive felt silence this profound before. Reclining on the mat, she observes Norman's soft chanting and Colin's gentle breathing. Though he appears lifeless, she can see that he's very much alive. The aroma of incense swirls in the air as the medicine courses through her.

Her consciousness begins to drift slowly, pulling her into an expansive and vivid voyage through the maze of her memories. A kaleidoscope of geometric squares and radiant colors surrounds her. For a moment, it's as if she's transcended to another realm within her own mind, a world where time ceases to exist. There's animal imagery parading around her in surreal forms. What do these creatures have to do with the truth? Soon, a powerful feminine presence materializes beside her, appearing as a luminous white dove. It beckons her to follow. This must be Mother Ayahuasca.

The beautiful dove draws her to a series of radiant windows in the tapestry of her memories—she instinctually knows these squares contain key moments from her life. Olive steps into one that glows brighter than the rest, similar to selecting an app on her phone. She finds herself frolicking through tall grass with her cousins from Indiana, lost in a landscape of youthful laughter and flying corn kernels, a tableau of idyllic innocence that she wishes she could inhabit forever. But the scene evaporates as quickly as it appeared.

Gripping the tail of a tiger, she is whisked away through cornfields as the dove glides steadily overhead. She's in her childhood home, still in child form, peering down from a staircase at her parents. Her father berates her mother, a glass of alcohol in hand. This version of her father is new to her. She had believed his drinking had escalated only after her mother's death. A painful clarity strikes Olive: her method of coping with conflict imitates her mother's passive acceptance of intolerable treatment. She always thought keeping quiet, like her mother, kept the peace. Now she realizes whose peace it was truly keeping. She wonders how accurate the saying "kids are resilient" is, when simple interactions and experiences from one's childhood can shape their whole personality. Maybe it was a comforting myth for adults to use to justify their failings, *the resilience of children.* Kids shouldn't have to be resilient. After all, a child's greatest fear is losing a parent. The second is not being loved by one. Olive had lived through both, and that ache stayed with her—a quiet, lifelong effort to win the love of a parent who never gave it freely.

She now spots a young bear and follows it to the front door of her grandmother's house in the Upper Peninsula. Her mother pulls her inside and over to the piano, where her little fingers dance on the piano keys alongside her mother. They perform a duet of "Heart & Soul," a treasured memory. It's supposed to be a duet, so when played alone, it can be not easy. The memory quickly dissolves once more, replaced by the gaping maw of a whale that swallows her whole.

Inside the whale, a cascade of love envelops her as she gazes down at Landon as a baby. He will never know the countless times he has saved her, both literally and metaphorically. She was just a young adult, a twenty-four-year-old med school dropout, but her maternal love was fierce, unfiltered, and unwavering. She'd do *anything* to protect him.

Rabbits race by her, and Olive now finds herself on her eleventh birthday, sipping imaginary tea with her father, the day after her mother's devastating diagnosis took a turn for the worse. She wasn't allowed to cry, but he tried to cheer her up with a delicate porcelain tea set and new painting brushes. For once, he didn't nudge her toward the woods or insist on target practice. Instead, he seemed to recognize—if only briefly—what she actually loved. In his own unique way, he loved her the best he knew how.

Abruptly, a procession of ants draws her eyes, leading her to another memory—her college years. Striding along the banks of the Cedar River in Lansing, she's suddenly aware of a potent masculine presence, almost like a paternal figure. It's so comforting and compelling that she can't shake it off. Standing at the fork of a path, flanked by the dove still overhead, Olive finds herself at a crossroads in a valley. Trust in herself and her own reality wavers. She doesn't know which way to choose and something seems to be closing in on her from behind. She opens her eyes.

Norman, the shaman, sits beside her, grounding her back in the tangible world.

"No, no, keep your eyes shut. Let your guard down," he urges her. "Think of yourself as an artist, painting the canvas of your life. Don't search for logic or others' interpretation of it—good or bad. Just let yourself experience it. Your answers will come."

Her eyelids close once more, and Olive finds herself back at the fork in the valley. Both paths before her seem dark and foreboding. Her limbs go cold. Tears well up in her eyes, but the fatherly presence takes her hand, casting a radiant light to illuminate one of the paths. Together they walk it. The surroundings look ominous, but her fear dissipates. She senses that life is full of darkness, but also light, and just a sliver of light can conquer the dark. They arrive at a cul-de-sac in the path. Olive looks up to the motherly dove for her final question, the reason why she is doing all of this. "Where's Kate?"

The scene then shifts. She's in her own backyard on Duck Lake. A thunderous noise, equivalent to a gunshot, shatters the air. It's a firecracker, scaring Lulu, her riot of bright feathers scurrying down the lawn towards the willow tree. Kate is chasing closely after her. This must be why her daughter ventured down by the dock. Olive's eyes shift to Richie and Julie by the side of the house, wrapped up in each other. Julie meets Olive's gaze briefly before Richie kisses her neck, his arms circling her waist. Landon and Hannah crouch behind the Jacuzzi, as if hiding. As she refocuses, Kate is perilously close to walking onto the dock, where Lulu has taken up residence. Olive tries to move closer to her down the hill, but her legs are unresponsive, wobbly like Jell-O.

In the distance, she hears Colin yelling at Richie, accompanied by loud music— "Down by the Bay"—the tune her children played incessantly. As she attempts to get closer and closer to Kate, the landscape changes drastically; the plush grass turns coarse, and Olive is covered knee deep in toads. "Back to my home, I dare not go." The song continues to repeat as the sound of the amphibians croaking louder and louder, the willow tree appearing closer.

The moment she reaches the first step of the dock, her body freezes. A boy rushes by in a blur, neon shades reflecting off his green boots.

"Ready or not, here I come!" he shouts. Kate is oblivious and kneeling, looking for Lulu, who is hiding under the dock. She realizes the boy is JJ. He careens into Kate, pushing her with such force that it resembles an offensive lineman coming at a quarterback. "You're it!"

Olive watches, immobile, as Kate tumbles headfirst into the rock seawall, constructed to counter the lake's erosion by the boats. JJ looks down at Kate's half-submerged body being slowly pulled into the water's current.

The young boy then runs right past Olive, towards his mother atop the hill. Audrey *was* still there. She looks at him, bewildered, then retches into a flower bed before grabbing his arm and quickly departing.

As the noises of the celebration of America's independence continue, her neighbors and guests, enamored with the illuminating sky, Olive focuses on reaching the water. She stumbles far this time, falling face-first, her legs giving out from underneath. Below, she feels the slickness of the Slip 'N Slide. She mentally wills herself forward, stumbling over a pair of green boots before plunging into Duck Lake's rippling waters. Reaching for Kate, she finds her father in her arms instead, his form frozen like a statue, reminiscent of how she had envisioned the police discovering his body near Commerce Lake.

Lifting her gaze, she recognizes a dim figure: Terrance near the willow tree. His broad frame is unmistakable, slowly inching toward Colin's dock. She cries out, voice raw and desperate. But he doesn't move. Doesn't flinch. Just stares through her like she's made of mist, like she isn't really there at all.

Another entity disrupts her focus, a towering figure cloaked in a mask that mimics the form of an owl. But the eyes behind the mask lack the luminous quality of an owl's; they are flat and void of light. The figure abruptly thrusts Olive back under the water, holding her down. She struggles against its force, gasping for the air she cannot reach. She feels herself touching the bottom of the lake, frantically searching for a way up and out.

Then, a calm envelops her. She feels her body relax and cease to resist the owl-like figure and the penetrating waves. Instead, she allows the current to sweep her further from the shore as the water itself seems to shift, the lunar pull drawing her deeper into its depths. Above her, the silhouette of a graceful deer glides across the moonlit sky. It's said that water holds memory, and it feels as if the lake is trying to give that night back to her, as if the lake is returning a stolen moment. Kate now appears by her side, placing her tiny hand in hers.

A wave of clarity and purpose floods through Olive, washing away residual grief and guilt. She no longer seeks mere survival; she yearns for life lived meaningfully. A profound peace now settles over her. Grief is just love without a place to go. She understands Kate's place in the universe and feels awestruck by her own mortality and the gift of transcending time and space. The motherly dove enfolds her in its wings and tells her that she already possesses everything she needs and wants for a full life; all that remains is to find herself. In doing so, she will achieve utter clarity. She will be complete. She will be at peace.

Revitalized, her spirit finally unburdened, Olive feels as if she's undergoing a rebirth. A deep, life-affirming breath fills not just her lungs but her very essence. She senses one identity departing, making room for another. She has received all she has wished for, all she has needed; they are one and the same. Time, she reflects, is both an ally and a foe. It can be a plunderer, stealing moments and people before you realize their worth. But that very impermanence makes life precious, she now understands. Time, in its enigmatic flow, also carries the curative power of healing.

Olive blinks and opens her eyes, finding herself back on the cot in the forest clearing. Across the shuddering firelight, she sees Colin seated cross-legged, offering her a warm smile. As she takes in an inhalation of the fragrant smoke that Norman wafts through the air, a newfound lightness fills her. She is truly awash in warmth and happiness.

Ophelia kneels beside her, gently wiping the tears that have streamed down her face. The emotional journey has been at once painful, exhilarating, and liberating—a cathartic release of all she's kept suppressed for far too long.

"The visions you've had may not make immediate sense," Ophelia advises softly, still beside her. "Most people have a greater reawakening the morning after, where additional pieces begin to fall together."

Olive nods and attempts to stand, but quickly returns to her seated position on the cot, feeling as if she's on a bobbing vessel. Colin stumbles over to her, still appearing somewhat dazed himself, sweat beads running freely down his face.

"You both need to recharge," Ophelia says, as Norman's chants diminish to nearly a whisper level.

"Like, a Gatorade?" Colin suggests.

Ophelia chuckles. "No, you need to recharge your electrons. The planet provides everything right beneath your feet—food, medicine, trees, grass, animals. Look around, everything living is an electron donor."

"What about the river?" Olive asks, finally noticing the moonlit water coursing through the trees.

"Yes, flowing water is alive, a giver of energy."

With Colin's assistance, Olive manages to rise, feeling as wobbly as a former mermaid venturing onto dry land for the first time. They make their way to where the river bends into a lake.

Stepping into the water slowly, Olive experiences an unprecedented tranquility, as if years of accumulated doubts and hypotheticals have been cleansed from her. She reflects on the significance of the choices she's made, the turns and bends in the road. It was a hellish path that eventually brought her to this heaven. She now understands the value of what she's had all along, like the lake she's lived beside but never fully appreciated until this moment. It is probably the same for most things in her life.

Clutching onto Colin, her arms wrapped around his neck, they both drift weightlessly, with her blush-colored dress gently swaying in tune with the water's gentle current. She feels rehydrated, both physically and spiritually—a baptism of sorts. She makes a mental promise never to allow herself to become parched again, in any sense. Colin leans against her and plants a wet kiss on her lips, his hands holding her waist firmly. They both look up; the sky is much more visible now, as if the darkness itself has thinned. The Northern Lights stretch across the horizon, their luminescent ribbons of green and purple weaving and twisting like glowing silk against the inky sky. Faint streaks of pink ripple through the edges, flickering softly, as though the heavens are breathing. The aurora borealis, a rare summer sight, seems to hum with quiet energy, casting an ethereal glow over everything below.

Norman's voice inches closer, his words carried by the still air as he softly advises, "Be good." And for the first time in a long while, Olive genuinely believes that being good—to herself and to the world—lies well within her reach. There's just one final soul she must come to terms with.

PART THREE

CHAPTER 37

TUESDAY 8 A.M.
JULY 4, 2023

Olive stirs awake, her clothes heavy with dampness, too exhausted to even change from the prior evening's life-changing events. Her eyes meet Colin's in a mutual, unspoken understanding that they are no longer the same today as they were yesterday. Today, they are strong and unbroken. Olive is no longer a hollowed-out reflection of herself. It's a feeling entirely detached from her previous life.

While some questions surrounding the night of her daughter's death still linger, they don't torment her like before—the weight of it all has lightened. Still, she wonders, did someone meddle with her drink, or had she picked up the wrong one meant for another unfortunate soul? What was the confrontation between Terrance and Richie by the water really about?

She ruminates on the most difficult revelation from last night: JJ's unintended role in Kate's passing. He was just a child at the time, a detail that leaves Olive wrestling with the ethics of blaming him for something so accidental. Yet her thoughts keep returning to Audrey. As the adult present during that pivotal juncture, why hadn't she stepped in when Joey told her? Why hadn't she raised her voice?

Getting to her feet, Olive turns away from Colin to shed her soaked dress. Through the open window of the cabin, the soft coo of a mourning dove filters in. Colin clears his throat. "Did you know that the frequency of a mourning dove's coo syncs with the brain's delta waves, soothing the nervous system? Bees have a similar effect; they vibrate at healing frequencies too."

Slipping into an oversized hoodie, Olive returns to sit beside him. She threads her fingers through his tousled, blond curls. In that moment, she becomes acutely aware of her own hunger for touch and authentic connection, how starved she had truly let herself become.

"You're like a walking encyclopedia," she observes while smiling. "How are you feeling today?"

"I feel like everything is going to be good. I'm always going to be 'Dad' to Lucy. Do you feel like you died last night? And now, can you live again somehow? It was like … a brief moment in eternity. Is that even a thing?" he asks while grimacing.

Olive takes in his question, mulling over the death of her own marriage. Leaving hadn't been a foreign thought to her after learning about Lucy's paternity or with her newfound intimacy with Colin. Yet the prospect of putting the final nail in her marriage's coffin after seventeen years still leaves her disquieted, as if her entire reality and identity are shattering into pieces.

"It's a thing. And I'm just relieved I didn't die on my birthday. Or get kidnapped and smuggled over the border or something," she finally responds.

Colin looks at her, confused. "Wait, yesterday was your birthday? Why didn't you tell me?"

Olive shrugs, throwing her hands up.

Colin pulls her into his chest and holds her a moment. "My dad used to say that every woman needs four hugs a day. Consider this a minute-long birthday hug."

She pushes away slightly, the statement reminding her of Landon. "Actually, we *all* need four hugs a day just for survival. Eight for maintenance and twelve for growth."

Their conversation is cut short by a knock on the door. Colin rises and creaks it open to find Dodge.

"Lookin' like you slept in a ditch last night, my man."

Colin looks down at his dirty, wrinkled T-shirt.

"We need two more for a morning euchre game. You in?"

Colin glances back at Olive, who mouths "no." He turns back to Dodge. "Count us in. I'll bring the birthday girl."

Dodge's voice fills the room with a boisterous "Happy birthday!" as Colin closes the door and catches the pillow Olive flings at him.

"What's wrong with you? I'm still on DMT, I'm not up for playing an intense game of euchre." It was a competitive card game that could only be played with four people, no fewer, no more.

No one could deny that euchre could get heated. In fact, Olive's own father didn't speak to his brother for ten years over a euchre game gone awry.

"Relax, I'm the world's best euchre partner," Colin counters while laughing as he heads to start the shower. "And that stuff is already out of your system. Today is officially your new birthday."

Olive ponders the idea of sharing the shower with him, a practical way to conserve water. But, as she nears her suitcase, her eyes fall on Ophelia's notepad. It's opened to a page where she'd penned her intention word: "truth." Underneath it, in her own script, are lines she doesn't remember writing:

Paint me as the one to blame, frame me for the crime you claim.

Accuse me as the guilty one, indict me for the deeds you've done.

Make me question every word you said, creating doubts within my head.

Sow the seeds of doubt so deep, turning certainty to something cheap.

The words strike her, and she knows what she must do next. She needs to talk to Audrey.

Olive quickly finds herself at the mercy of whatever cards she is dealt—the unpredictable waters of euchre, a game she hasn't played in years. She recalls that Jacks are the crown jewels of the deck, worth even more than Aces. She had tried reaching Audrey on the walk over, without success, but the fates favor her now with a red Jack. As she locks eyes with Colin, who sits across the table, his grin gives away too much. He either has the matching bower or a handful of hearts.

Dodge passes, and Olive instructs Colin to pick up the King of Hearts in the center. Card games have a way of reviving forgotten rules, first slowly, then all at once. The same seems true for social interactions. Her guard lowers as she exchanges laughter with Rita and Dodge.

Studying Rita's lined face and warm eyes, Olive surmises that the woman must have faced her own share of trials, losing a child of her own, yet in turn, she founded such an enriching retreat. Rita has turned her wounds into wisdom, her past into purpose.

"Ope, got you, dear," Rita chimes, laying down a card that effectively blocks their play. Colin groans, competitively frustrated.

"I had the best hand! Dodge, you're letting Rita carry your entire team."

"In that case, I could go for a Faygo right about now," Dodge muses, rising. "Colin, help me grab some ice and drinks." The two men head toward the main cabin.

"So, birthday girl, why the secrecy?" Rita nudges Olive.

"I'm not big on birthdays," Olive confesses.

"You sound like my niece. I always tell her to celebrate the little victories from the last year and embrace the new year like a fresh chapter."

That niece must be Dr. Everly, Olive presumes. "Oh, I actually have an appointment with Dr. Everly this morning," she exclaims.

"Go on, then. Happy birthday. Remember, our greatest growth comes from our greatest struggles," Rita imparts, clearing the cards from the table.

For a reason she can't articulate, Olive feels glued to her seat.

Rita pauses her actions and catches her eye. "I wanted to tell you there is a peace about you today. It's our deepest desire as humans to be honest. Peace is what calms our fears and clears our minds … I see peace in you today. And you'll feel it within your bones when you're fully healed."

On impulse, Olive leans in and hugs Rita, a spontaneous act she hasn't allowed herself in ages.

"There's more good than evil in the world, just remember that. People tend to hold onto the bad longer," Rita whispers as they part. "It's within our trials that we find our deepest peace."

For perhaps the first time, Olive genuinely believes her.

CHAPTER 38

TUESDAY 10 A.M.
JULY 4, 2023

Olive settles back into the modest wooden chair in Dr. Everly's makeshift consultation space. The woman's heavy black glasses are perched atop her nose; her eyes, however, look weary today, as if they've witnessed something unsettling. Olive recalls her mentioning an emergency that pulled her away the day before, and that Richie had called.

"So, is everything okay … on your end?" Olive ventures, striving for professionalism despite the awkward intertwining of their social circles.

"I'm fine. How about you? Happy birthday, by the way," Dr. Everly replies, shifting back to the papers on her desk as she nudges her glasses back up the bridge of her nose.

"Thank you. I'm good," Olive replies, meaning it. Yet she notices that Dr. Everly's eyes still betray a lingering apprehension, as if she's bracing herself to speak.

"We should discuss your upbringing. It's safe to say the reason you're here, at this Al-Anon retreat, is because of your father. I'm sure you would agree that you carry some unresolved traumas from your past?"

Olive is confused by the sudden mention of her father, but she complies and nods.

"Are you familiar with the idea that we often choose a known hell over an unfamiliar heaven? It explains why we stick with jobs we hate or relationships that harm us. We find comfort in familiarity, even if it's painful."

"Sure, better the devil you know than the devil you don't," Olive replies.

Setting her notebook aside, Dr. Everly removes her glasses. "Allow me to be candid with you for a moment. I once dated someone who seemed wonderful in the beginning. Slowly, I began to see troubling signs. He became controlling, isolating, and seemed incapable of simple empathy. It took me a while to realize how much this was dysregulating me. So, let me ask you, does your husband lift you or weigh you down?"

Instantly, heat rushes to Olive's face, warming her ears—she's on guard. Her husband, flawed as he might be, had nothing to do with her troubled upbringing or the heartache surrounding Kate. They were both adrift in the same boat of sorrow, and if anything, they grieved together so they both didn't sink. She wonders if word has spread about her husband's affair. Could it have been Laura? She could spread gossip throughout the church like wildfire.

"I guess what I'm trying to ask you is how your marriage is? Because sometimes people can appear to be lovely on the surface, but underneath, they are desperate, dark-intentioned people."

Olive's stomach now flips, teetering on the edge of nausea. She fights the impulse to bolt from the room, choosing to stand her ground instead. Maybe she really *had* changed, she thinks quietly.

"Listen, Dr. Everly, if this is about Richie's infidelity, that's a private matter. I will handle it when I'm ready. No one's faultless here. I've been medicated for seven years. I'm no cakewalk to live with either, rather a burden actually," Olive says, her own words resounding in her head with her father's timbre.

"I see. And who medicated you?" There is a long pause. "Who prescribed you the medications? You're hard to control when you're healthy, Olive. You're even harder to manipulate when you're clear-headed. And you're possible to lose when you're at peace."

Just as Olive had thought she'd found her peace, it starts to unravel. Or could it be lingering effects of the ayahuasca? Perhaps Richie had never genuinely wished for her to heal, but rather to remain numb, confined at home, dependent on him.

"I find relationships rooted in mutual suffering to be particularly dangerous because the moment one person begins to heal, the cracks in your compatibility start to show. You may even realize that the other person is stunting your growth … perhaps intentionally so."

Olive senses Dr. Everly's words resonating in her heart, even though the rational part of her mind urges her to resist. "But Richie helps people. He's a good doctor," Olive mutters, almost to herself. She had thought she'd touched heaven last night, and now she's grappling with her own personal hell sitting here.

"His profession isn't the point. I don't doubt his intelligence. I doubt his motives. He's trapped you into thinking you're the problem, but that is not true. You're an empath, and empaths become easy targets to narcissists." Doctor Everly pauses to give Olive a moment to let her words sink in. "Your inconsistent childhood love has made the inconsistent affection from him addictive. It literally rewires the brain—distorts your reality."

Doctor Everly's words puncture Olive's consciousness. She had found it curious that during her journey last night, there were no visible damning visions of her husband, leading to a lingering doubt about whether her connection with Colin was wrong, even in the face of her husband's own indiscretions.

"One of the greatest signs of childhood trauma is trying to make those who hurt us love us, rather than walking away. I don't doubt you needed some of these medications after the incident. But for seven years? And that amount? What's really causing your health issues is your emotional state. It's control, it's anger, it's fear, it's anxiety, it's hopelessness. They're all normal states of consciousness in response to your *current* environment," Dr. Everly adds.

"So, I should for sure walk away?" Olive enquires, her vision clearing.

"I'm not telling you to walk, I'm telling you to run." Doctor Everly leans in, her hand gently brushing Olive's wrist before retreating. "The most dangerous person you can be with is someone who refuses to love you properly, yet refuses to let you go. And tread carefully. Unmasking a narcissist can be dangerous,"

Dr. Everly warns.

At the mention of the word "mask," Olive feels a surge of recognition, like a lightning bolt shooting through her. "Unmasking?" she questions.

"It's metaphorical. He will fear being exposed. Beneath that grand exterior lies a frightened child plagued by shame. They wear a mask to keep their true selves hidden."

The conversation rakes at the edges of Olive's self-assuredness, igniting a series of unsettling thoughts. She instantly conjures the image of the tall figure wearing an owl mask, the one who had been submerging her underwater in her vision.

A chilling realization swells through her, a veil lifted: The man concealed behind the owl mask was *him*. She'd wasted countless hours justifying his actions to the jury in her mind. The clues had been there all along, masked by his charisma. But no more. She won't let him silence her again. The mask has cracked, and the darkness it hid is spilling out. Still, one question claws at her:

What else has he buried?

Olive's phone buzzes. It is Audrey.

CHAPTER 39

TUESDAY 1 P.M.
JULY 4, 2023

"Thanks for meeting me on such short notice. This place is charming," Olive remarks, artfully skirting the actual reason she's persuaded Audrey to join her for this rendezvous. They had chosen Fishtown in Leland as a convenient midpoint, and Colin graciously agreed to wait in the car before they embarked on their three-hour drive back home. Olive hadn't disclosed to him the specifics for the meetup or what she'd seen in her vision—especially not the unsettling details concerning JJ. Nor had she ventured to discuss the delicate issue of where she and Colin now stood after their newfound closeness and crumbling marriages. All of that could wait. For now, she sits across from Audrey, whose oversized Gucci sunglasses glimmer from the sun's reflection.

"Of course, anything for a friend. It's been a chaotic week," Audrey replies, her eyes lingering on the rustic fishing shanties that line the Leland River. Built of aged wood and chipped paint, the structures evoke a quaint nostalgia. A server arrives, breaking the momentary silence.

"Shall we toast belatedly to your birthday?" Audrey suggests, focusing on Olive.

"I have to drive later, so a pop will do," Olive answers. Audrey doesn't press the issue and nods in agreement. If she was in the mood to celebrate, it wasn't showing today.

"Make it two Diet Pepsis. And your fantastic fish dip, please," Audrey adds. The server nods and retreats, leaving behind the aroma of freshwater and fish in her wake, a lingering testament to the local fishermen's daily labor. Seagulls caw and swoop, eager for any neglected scraps, while the distant rumble of boat engines serves as an ambient backdrop, like a low drumbeat.

"I almost forgot, here …" Audrey says, pulling a small package from her purse and sliding it across to Olive. Olive unwraps it to reveal a beautiful Petoskey stone necklace. She forces a smile, remembering the ones she and Audrey had made with the boys many summers ago.

"Happy Birthday. I picked it up in Elk Lake; it reminded me of you," Audrey adds softly.

Olive thanks her, fastening the necklace around her neck before finally addressing the subject that's been lingering in her thoughts.

"How's JJ?" Olive inquires, noting a slight twitch in the vein on Audrey's forehead after she asks.

Audrey removes her sunglasses, revealing her tear-brimmed auburn eyes. "Motherhood's a double-edged sword, isn't it? The ceaseless worrying combined with the little moments," Audrey's voice quivers, her eyes tracing a seagull as it makes off with a scrap of fish from a midair catch. "Do you remember the day we first met at the park?"

Olive smiles nostalgically. "Of course. Joey tumbled down the slide onto Landon, and then they became inseparable. Mario and Luigi costumes for three straight Halloweens."

"Yes, but do you remember when *we* met? I was struggling, Olive. Looking back, I definitely had postpartum depression, but nobody really talked about it then. Joe wanted to problem-solve, but you … you just listened. You were my lifeline."

Olive feels a sharp pang at Audrey's revelation. She had always seen Audrey as an endless well of energy—cheerful, social, and perpetually smiling. Sure, little Joey had been a handful as a child, but most kids are. The thought that Audrey had been battling her own demons catches Olive off guard. Maybe Audrey's bright, blooming roses were just a way to distract others from the tangled, venomous weeds in her own garden.

It strikes Olive then: on the surface, everyone looks untouched and unscathed, but when you dig deeper, the darker stories emerge. Perhaps they're all navigating the same turbulent waters, just in different boats—some tugboats, others luxury vessels—but all fishing for the same elusive sense of peace. Here, in Fishtown, the docked boats seem as mismatched as the lives they symbolize, yet beneath it all, they're more alike than they appear.

"And I failed you, when you needed me the most," Audrey continues, her voice catching.

"Your fish dip and pops," the server interjects, setting the items down a tad too abruptly. Sensing the heavy atmosphere, she withdraws as quickly as she arrived. A pause stretches between them.

"I suspected something was off with Joey from the beginning. Our hearts can deceive us, and our minds can lie—either to protect or to warn. But our gut instinct? It never lies. I knew something was wrong, and I couldn't place it … why was he so aggressive all the time? Doctors wanted to medicate him. I wanted to avoid him. Joe wanted another baby, so along came Ava. And Joey? He just spiraled further into anger," Audrey says, sipping her Diet Pepsi and staring distastefully at the bowl of pale pink, creamy fish dip as if it were a physical manifestation of her internal turmoil. She appears genuinely unwell.

"What happened to JJ? Where is he now?" Olive's words emerge as a hushed undertone, heavy with concern.

Audrey hesitates, as if she's navigating a minefield in her own head. "JJ was sent to a juvenile facility, mandated by a judge. He was tried as a minor since he's not eighteen until the fall, thank goodness," Audrey starts, her voice tight. Olive already knows about the DUI and the altercation with the police officer, per Laura, but she feigns surprise as Audrey continues.

"Yesterday, he was involved in a horrific fight with a group of boys there. He was hit multiple times in the head and had to be airlifted to the hospital. The emergency MRI scan and subsequent surgery revealed a cyst, the size of a golf ball, in his left temporal lobe. The surgeons managed to drain it and he appears stable as of now."

Audrey's hands tremble as she attempts to spoon some of the creamy fish dip onto a cracker.

"My God, Audrey, that's awful. Can you visit him?" Olive responds, shocked.

Audrey shakes her head. "No visitors until tomorrow. He's being held at a hospital in Grand Rapids, so we'll head down then. We wouldn't have driven all the way up to the cottage had we known ahead of time." She takes a sip of pop and swallows hard. "My main point is, we now have our answer, our 'why.' I called Richie immediately for advice. He told me that violent tendencies can be linked to that particular area of the brain. Joey likely had this since he was young. Meanwhile, I've been blaming him for not handling his emotions, when I can hardly manage mine." She takes another bite of the dip. "The doctors said he'll never be the same. We're actually hoping that's true."

Audrey now appears somewhat relieved, leaving Olive to grapple with whether or not to voice her haunting suspicions. But is there any point? After all, the past is an unalterable tapestry of intentions and consequences. It's sealed, immutable. Joey never intended to harm Kate, just as Audrey hadn't meant to shield a potential wrongdoer, only to safeguard her son—actions any mother might understand. Yet Olive can't shake the ethical tug-of-war inside her. How far should a mother go in protecting her own child when it might lead to harm to another? *Another's death.*

Gathering her courage, she finally breaks the silence, as if giving an admission of her own. "I did ayahuasca in the woods last night to help me seek clarity about Kate's death … to heal. During the ceremony, or experience I should say, I had a vision. Joey, or at least his green boots, was by the dock with her. I can't be certain of what I saw; maybe he pushed her, but I felt I had to share with you. To ask you …" Olive's words trail off, her voice tinged with vulnerability.

Audrey lowers her head, re-placing her sunglasses, just as the sun begins to loom directly overhead. Their table catches reflections from the variety of boats all gently bobbing in the lake's ever-present breeze.

"You deserve to know your 'why' too, Olive. JJ was playing a game with Kate. He came to me right when the fireworks started. He said he accidentally hurt her. I asked if she was alright, frustrated with yet another incident. He assured me she was fine; he said she was by the dock watching for ducks. I told him to send Landon or Hannah to get her. I was worried you might be irritated. After that, my memory blurs. I was inebriated, threw up on some hibiscus or roses. Joe came to assist and carried me to the car. I mean, we were all half in the bag that night. We all could have kept better tabs on the kids …"

Tears flow freely down Audrey's cheeks as she resumes her tale. "The next morning, when I heard … about Kate, I was nauseated. I knew it was because of JJ. I should have told you. Instead, I pushed you away and advised JJ to keep silent, which likely exacerbated his emotional torment. Joe is still oblivious to this day about that night. Then I became pregnant with Ava. I threw myself into her, as if I could erase that night."

Olive grips the edge of the table, knuckles pale, her breath shallow and sharp. She feels a painful sense of liberation. Her eyes sting and a dull ache settles in her chest, bittersweet and strangely steadying. She exhales slowly, like letting go of something she hadn't realized she'd been gripping for years. The knot inside her begins to unravel. She's found her "why."

"The thought of losing a child is every parent's worst nightmare, but I think deep down, so is raising a bad human … it's another nightmare altogether. A human who could take a life," Audrey says softly.

The two women lock eyes, tears streaming down their faces. No words are exchanged. Olive reaches across the table, her hand clasping her old friend's with a comforting squeeze. She hopes Audrey, like Rita, will one day share her story of resilience, offering it as a lifeline to someone else navigating turbulent waters. The age-old adage comes to her mind as the colorful boats of Fishtown surround the two women: ships are safest in the harbor, but that's not what they're built for.

They embrace once more, Audrey softly whispering, "Watch out for deer, now." The two then part ways, each carrying the weight of their own long-standing pain, yet lighter for having shared it.

CHAPTER 40
RICHIE

TUESDAY 2 P.M.
JULY 4, 2023

Regret is a heavy chain I often find myself wrapped in, though another voice in my head points fingers elsewhere. They say the heaviest heartache of the dying is the realization of never having become the person they aspired to be. Having spent ample time around those at life's threshold, I can vouch for the truth in that sentiment. Given my conversations with Mr. Conch, that emotion resonates even deeper. We're spoon-fed a narrative: secure a spot at the top university, earn trophies, find the ideal partner, settle in a coveted neighborhood, and voila—you've made it. Yet, often, after studiously ticking off each accomplishment, you're hit with a stark realization: perhaps you've been chasing the wrong ideals. At least, that's how I feel about my journey.

"And Lisa Hernandez, how does she fit into this picture?" The question, seemingly simple, feels like a leaden weight in my stomach. Quick-witted responses are my forté. Years in the medical field have honed my instincts. Life and death decisions were routine for me. But in this instance, the unyielding pressure from Audrey Assyrian's continuous calls has distracted me.

"She's not in the equation anymore," I state firmly. "She was part of the team, but the board deemed her erratic."

Maxwell Conch lets out a hum, reminiscent of a mockingbird's song, only this time, it's laced with skepticism. "She claims to be the true discoverer of the cure. She accuses you of blackmail, alleging threats against her family if she didn't relinquish full credit to you. Pretty heavy stuff."

"That's an overstatement," I retort, my voice tinged with frustration. *Semantics.*

While truth forms the basis of many tales, it's often stretched to fit personal narratives. In this scenario, I hadn't threatened her family. I'd merely shed light on their shady dealings. Investigations had revealed her husband's dubious activities related to his upscale restaurant in Grosse Pointe. Misusing pandemic aid meant for his staff and evading tax norms had put him in my crosshairs. How could Lisa dare accuse me of unethical conduct, especially when she piggybacked on my decade-long research for her recent breakthrough? The accolade belonged to me. This cure was the culmination of my life's dedication—a tribute to my brother and daughter.

"She has proper documentation and evidence, Dr. Wentworth. She's ready to tarnish her family's reputation for what she believes you stole from her."

I swallow hard, realizing the gravity of her sacrifice. She's willing to gamble everything for recognition, not dissimilar to me. I have to acknowledge Lisa's audacity. Most often, women are conditioned to suppress their instincts, fearing being labeled as difficult, aggressive, a bitch. Lisa obviously had no such reservations.

"Look, Mr. Conch, Lisa and I have a tangled history. Her perceptions may be skewed," I try to reason, hoping he grasps the subtext. I can't let Lisa threaten my legacy. It's not just about me. Every decision I've made has been to honor my precious Kate.

When I first held my newborn daughter, an overwhelming rush of love and a primal urge to protect her surged within me. In her trusting eyes, I was more than just a father; I was her beacon, her superman. And after her devastating diagnosis, she was mine for the saving. It was the first time I felt compelled to place someone else's needs above my own. I embraced the daunting responsibility of healing her, my darling daughter.

Maxwell interrupts my thoughts, "If I find substance in her allegations, not only will this interview be terminated, but I'll also expose any misconduct and report it."

The conversation ends there. I dial Audrey back, reassuring her that JJ will be fine. As I hang up, my thoughts wander. Men's accomplishments are often measured by their achievements. With everything hanging in the balance, a haunting proposition surfaces. What's the point of achieving everything if you end up losing your very essence along the way? Your wife. Your children. Your lakeside home.

CHAPTER 41

TUESDAY 4 P.M.
JULY 4, 2023

In the confined space of Colin's car, Olive observes him, a soft hum accompanying the tune on the radio. With a nonchalant air, he runs his fingers through his hair, this time with ease. Every time she witnesses him do this, an unexpected allure sparks within her, similar to the simple joys of inhaling the scent of a puppy or feeling the sand beneath her bare feet.

Thoughts of life without Richie then clouded her mind.

"Isn't it peculiar how the company we keep shapes our perceived value?" she poses to Colin.

He detects her discomfort and lowers the radio's volume. "I'd agree with that. It really depends on how much influence you allow someone to have and what truly holds significance."

She senses Colin's penetrating sight fixed on her from her peripheral vision before he eventually enquires, "Is everything alright?"

"I think I'm just tired. Gonna rest a bit." She leans into the comforting warmth of the window, letting her eyes close, though her thoughts keep spinning. A familiar song plays softly from Colin's car speakers, "The Wreck of the Edmund Fitzgerald." Olive recalls Richie once telling her that music helps reactivate areas of the brain associated with memory, and as the lyrics drift over her, an unsettling realization emerges. Her vision of drowning beneath Richie's force feels like a deeper truth; a reflection of his stifling influence. He had held her back from healing, without her even knowing it.

As sleep overtakes her, she feels herself slipping back into the imagery from the night before. The sensation of being thrust into the lake returns, the cold abyss swallowing her whole.

Below, obscured by the murky depths, are medical files, their ownership unclear. An icy caress on her neck jerks her abruptly back to the waking world.

"Shit!" Olive gasps, recoiling from Colin's reach. Glancing around, she finds them parked at an isolated gas station.

"Sorry, didn't mean to startle you," Colin says. "Thought you might want something from inside, or a restroom break. We're about halfway home."

Groggy and slightly disoriented, likely remnants of the DMT and the post-experience repercussions she'd been cautioned about, Olive manages, "No, I'm okay."

As Colin begins to shut the door, she stops him. "Actually, cold water sounds good. Thanks." He acknowledges with a nod and signals to her to lock the car before departing. Olive clicks it, then recalls the last image from her dream. Baffled by her visions of medical records, Olive's attention is drawn to the back seat, where Lucy's files protrude from Colin's bag. Next to the file containing Lucy's documents is a bulkier one labeled Katherine Wentworth. Richie or this other assisting doctor must have given them to Colin for reference, since Lucy had the same condition.

Handling the file with reverence, Olive skims through the records labeled "confidential"—blood results, doctors' notes. Everything indicated improvement, that is, until she reached the end of the folder, records dated May 6, 2016. An icy shudder crawls down her spine. She vividly recalls that last Mother's Day weekend with both her children. Richie was irritable, almost to the point of indifference, not even acknowledging the holiday.

The results from May 6, highlighted in glaring red, revealed that the *candidate had rejected serum x*. Kate's white blood cell count had plummeted. Olive continues, flipping to June's records. Kate's last full month alive. Something catches her eye. Another test and injection were done in late June; a procedure Olive wasn't privy to. It reads: *additional test conducted; patient's levels failed to stabilize*. Those numbers were horrifyingly off the charts, another adverse reaction to the serum. Kate did seem more fatigued than usual that month, but Olive had dismissed it, blaming the unusually hot summer humidity.

Yet the final page of the file held the most disturbing discovery—an email thread involving Dr. Richard Wentworth, with his assistant, Dr. Lisa Hernandez, BCC'd, corresponding with their superiors. The discussion centered around their plan to showcase evidence indicating that Kate had successfully endured the treatments for nearly a year. Richie had provided confirmation. The culmination of the conversation was a request for the most recent bloodwork to be presented to the board of directors by the end of August.

It was a nauseating revelation. Richie had never actually possessed a dependable cure, despite his insinuation of successful testing over the course of a year. Such a false statement, if unfulfilled, would damage his reputation, especially if Kate wasn't entirely cured by the presentation date. Although she understood that it hadn't been finalized and presented due to Kate's drowning, the newfound realization that Kate's body had been resisting the remedy for months beforehand was a jolting shock.

As Colin's knuckles rap lightly against the window, Olive's startled fingers instinctively hit the unlock button. "What are you looking at?" he asks, setting aside his Vernors and offering Olive a bottle of water.

She hurriedly slides the incriminating files toward him.

"Have you read through these in their entirety?" she questions with an assertive tone. "Where did you get these files from? Kate's file."

"I mean, I glanced at them briefly—not really Kate's documents. They were Lucy's, from her other doctor, Lisa Hernandez, the one I met with the other night. She handed them all to me and mentioned it was for safekeeping. I didn't pry, but I trust her. I've always preferred dealing with Dr. Hernandez over Richie at appointments," he explains.

Before he can elaborate further, Olive abruptly interposes, thrusting her hand toward the May 6 document. "He didn't have a real solution for Kate. He was slated for a major presentation in August, with no real evidence that the serum was working long-term. But all that fell through when Kate … drowned." Olive's voice trails off, her eyes clouded with emotion. Then she catches herself dwelling on that name: Lisa Hernandez. This must have been some of the leverage she had over Richie, something that began seven years ago with Kate. Something that would prompt her husband to hire a private investigator to dig up Dr. Hernandez's own secrets in return.

Scanning the research, Colin tries to make sense of the data. "But he did find the cure eventually, Olive. Look at Lucy. She's healthy now. We've monitored her levels for over a year."

She takes a moment, digesting the new insight, then says, "He found the cure eventually, seven years later. Back then, he wasn't nearly as advanced in his research as he portrayed. Time was of the essence, and he was running out. Kate wouldn't have been saved in time."

Colin fixes his gaze on Olive once more.

"What are you getting at? I mean, Richie's a piece of work, but …" He trails off, waiting for Olive to fill in the blanks. She meets his face squarely. "You're not suggesting he had a hand in Kate's death? I was grilling him about Julie on the side of the house mere moments before it happened. The guy couldn't have juggled an affair and a murder on the same night."

The gravity of their conversation lingers in the vehicle, thickening the atmosphere. To even entertain the thought that Richie played a role in Kate's demise feels like trying to swallow a stone, and Olive had faced her share of bitter pills in her lifetime. Colin's logic is sound. The pieces don't quite fit. With Audrey's haunting admission, JJ was the likelier and more plausible culprit. All the evidence pointed in that direction, yet something within Olive resists that neatly wrapped conclusion. The timing was too suspect. How opportune for Richie, she muses, that his secret never got out.

Olive recalls Dr. Everly's words: accusations from someone with a superiority complex often symbolize their own guilt. Richie had been pointing fingers at her over Kate's death for years. Might it have been simpler to endure the premature loss of a child than face the reality of failed corporate promises and shattered dreams?

"Just because he's a philandering narcissist doesn't mean he's capable of murder," Colin asserts.

"Every Dateline episode begs to differ. It's always the spouse. And invariably, there's infidelity involved." Olive turns sharply, tucking the file securely away. Her eyes catch a familiar tint in a water bottle adjacent to the briefcase. She seizes it. "Is that what I think it is?" she probes.

Firing up the engine, Colin looks at Olive, caution in his eyes. "Be careful with that. What you're holding is the residual ayahuasca. Didn't want to let it go to waste," Colin says, eyes downcast. It makes Olive question if the remnants were initially meant for Julie.

Accelerating out of the gas station, Colin leaves behind a trail of thoughts in Olive's mind. Still grasping the bottle, Olive ponders her next step. If the adage is true that two wrongs don't make a right, but two lefts lead you forward, then her strategy had to be one from left field. Richie wasn't one to be easily probed or questioned. But Olive recognized her temporal advantage. Not only was it her birthday, but Richie was also in the doghouse. That leverage might be sufficient to persuade him to partake in the ayahuasca experience, loosening his tongue, prompting him to reveal any further hidden truths.

Olive holds the bottle closely, looking to Colin for approval. "I want to take this with me. Is that alright?"

His eyebrows knit together in concern. "I'm not sure that's a good idea. Given your size and the potency of that batch, it's best not taken alone."

"It's not for me," she retorts.

Colin's scans between the brown liquid and Olive's earnest green eyes. "Absolutely not," he says, grabbing the bottle. "We don't know how it might affect Richie. It affects everyone differently. What if he becomes aggressive or something? Besides, your current home setting is far from ideal."

He isn't wrong. The last piece of advice Dr. Everly imparted to her as they exited that makeshift office in the woods was a stark warning. If she stayed living in her lakefront home with Richie, it would be the equivalent of residing in a chemical plant, inhaling toxins daily. It would be a slow but lethal process. She thought of her mom upon hearing Dr. Everly's words.

"But consider this," Olive presses on. "The serenity of the lake could provide a safe space and you'll be right next door if I need you. And I won't force it on him. If I can get him to partake willingly, maybe, just maybe, this might offer a rare glimpse into Richie's true self, compelling him to be honest … for once."

Colin grips the steering wheel harder, refusing to meet Olive's eyes.

"Colin, please, I'm desperate. I need to know if he did anything to Kate. I won't be able to find peace until I have that answer," she pleads. "Do you trust me?" she asks, repeating his own words from when he convinced her to try the alternative therapy.

He hesitates for a moment, then hands the bottle back to her. This *could* be the key to unlocking the truth within Richie. But, she's still keenly aware of the volatile nature of mixing objects and elements that were never meant to meet, like an oil tanker splitting open at sea—thick, black slick spreading fast across once-clear waters. One contaminates, the other tries to stay pure. However, the damage is instant and irreversible. No matter how much water surrounds it, the oil always rises … staining everything it touches.

Colin's voice pierces through her thoughts. "I honestly just wonder why we stayed for so long," he reflects.

She hears his words but realizes that leaving is never linear or straightforward. It's easy to stand from the comfort of the shoreline, swearing you'd never wade so deeply into treacherous waters. Yet, when you find yourself immersed in the thick of it, with no memory of how you ventured so far out in the first place, the choices seem scarcer, the decisions become murkier.

The question wasn't why she or Colin stayed; the more profound question was why would anyone deliberately inflict such pain on someone they claimed to love?

"But it seems to me, some of the worst endings could make great beginnings." He shoots her a reassuring smile, taking another sip of his Vernors. Olive feels suspended, neither in heaven nor hell—just limbo.

As Colin's car eases into his garage, a knot of anxiety tightens in Olive's chest. Their prolonged journey home, extended by detours and holiday traffic, might have been a factor, but the real source of her trepidation is clearer. Exiting the comforting cocoon of Colin's car means she will soon have to face Richie. The idea of not just confronting but persuading a master manipulator to partake in an ancient and powerful psychedelic is instantly overwhelming. The audacity he possessed to push her to such lengths stirs deep resentment within her.

Olive had long believed that Richie, in his sporadic moments of kindness, was her salvation. But the truth was more sinister. Those moments of apparent refuge were also moments of erasure, moments where her identity, her humanity, was being subtly taken away. On good days, Richie's love felt like sunlight breaking through storm clouds, intensifying the contrast and confusion. But on stormy days, his emotions were tempestuous, making her wonder if she'd ever see the sun again. That's the insidious nature of manipulation; it is what makes their bond so difficult to sever.

Colin turns to face Olive, eyes tinted a shade of red, perhaps from the drifting cottonwood of the July breeze or possibly from the weight of heavy contemplation. In that silent exchange, an unspoken understanding passes between them—the recognition that their past decisions had been made, unchangeable and beyond reproach.

"Welp," Colin announces, patting his thighs in a gesture all too familiar to Olive. It was the classic Midwestern nudge, a gentle hint that it was time for departure.

"Are you sure about heading back there?" He jerks his chin towards her home, his question drenched in genuine concern.

Olive gives a small, deliberate nod. "Are you sure about heading back in there?" she asks, gesturing toward Colin's door.

"Julie and Lucy aren't home yet; they're at some birthday party for another hour or so. After that, we'll see where my night goes. I'll probably end up on the couch, or she'll head to her mom's." He exhales, then lets a faint smile break through. "On the bright side, the Woodward Dream Cruise is coming up. I'm finally pulling my dad's '63 Mustang out of storage. You're welcome to join me." A soft, strained chuckle escapes his rosy lips.

As Olive stares at him, she delicately plucks an eyelash that rests on his freckle-strewn cheek, holding it up for him to see.

"Maybe I will. Now, make a wish." She extends her finger, prompting him to blow the eyelash away with a fleeting grin.

"Haven't done that in ages. I wished for your happiness, I mean, joy. Definitely joy."

Olive lightly swats at him playfully. "You know you're not supposed to reveal your wishes, right?"

"I was manifesting it," he replies. In a spontaneous gesture of affection, he leans over, pressing a gentle kiss to the spot where her cheek meets her ear, a touch reminiscent of bygone childlike days, filled with pure warmth. It was endearing and *nice.*

CHAPTER 42

TUESDAY 7 P.M.
JULY 4, 2023

Olive carefully nestles the ayahuasca beside Kate's folder in her bag, her slender fingers quivering slightly. She mentally girds herself, resolving to focus solely on uncovering the truth about Kate first before addressing the paternity matter regarding Lucy. Richie wasn't a man you could confront head-on. He was more like a wild horse—skittish, proud, unpredictable. You didn't charge at a creature like that. You waited. Watched. Let him circle close, thinking it was his idea all along.

Opening the door slowly, she's greeted with an unusual scene: her husband cooking. She'd been away for a transformative three days, the longest she has ever been apart from him since giving birth to Landon. She never could have predicted coming home to this sight. Pausing at the doorway, she observes him, unnoticed. Her eyes wander over to the polished white cabinetry and newly installed, sparkling, grey quartz countertops paired with elaborate golden knobs. His concentration is distinct as he checks the recipe, adjusting the settings on the sleek stainless-steel stove. The aroma wafting from the oven isn't the only enticing thing in the room. As much as she loathes acknowledging it, Richie looks strikingly handsome. When she felt that immediate pull, that spark, many years ago, fleeing should have been her first response; however, it was the naïve, hopeful part of her, her inner child, lured by his deceptive charm. And the attributes that captivate someone initially in a relationship can, in the end, be the very factors that lead to its demise. Richie seemed too ideal, too flawless—simply too good to be true. *And he is.* A painful truth she has come to learn.

Catching her presence, Richie offers a surprised smile and ambles over on his crutches.

"Hey. I missed you. I cooked you a belated birthday dinner." In an awkward maneuver, he envelops her in a hug. "And I apologize, Olive. I'm sorry you felt that I jeopardized our relationship by keeping the Julie issue from you. As I've mentioned, it will never ever happen again. Let me know if there's anything else I can do on my end to fix this," he pleads.

He waits, allowing Olive to make the next move, to possibly reveal what else she knows, so he can sweep that under the rug, too.

Inhaling intensely, Olive says firmly, "Richie, we need to talk."

"I couldn't agree more. I've been trying to speak with you for three days." Producing his phone, he displays all his attempted calls to her. "Here's a ludicrous thought. If you want to talk to someone, turn your phone on. But never mind that, let's talk over dinner." He gestures her toward the kitchen table, his eyes steadfastly locked with Olive's, patiently waiting for her to settle in. The table has been repositioned to look over the enchanting sight of the willow tree, swaying rhythmically under the caress of the lake breeze. The lavish new granite island surface gleams, bouncing the ambient light around the room as she takes her seat.

Pushing a luxurious hunter green Birkin bag toward her, Richie beams from ear to ear. "Happy Birthday. The saleslady claimed it's the last of its kind in the country. Almost lost it to some woman from Orchard Lake." His smirk feels self-congratulatory. He has never understood, in nearly two decades together, that gifts do not serve as her love language. He could buy her whatever she wanted, really, but he could never look her square in the eye. He is deceiving in his sincerity; always telling the truth, even when he lies. If he truly understood her, he would realize that her love language is quality time. Yet time was something Richie wasn't inclined to give away willingly or freely.

"Feeling better after your little adventure?" he asks, sarcasm heavy in his voice as he neatly tucks a napkin into his crisp Ted Baker shirt. He follows it up by pouring himself a generous glass of red wine.

"It was very … enlightening," she replies tersely. She looks down at her untouched meal —a sumptuous baked salmon, a fresh salad, and something that resembles mashed potatoes. Of course, he would exert some form of effort to regain his control over her and reel her back under his sway. But this display is surprising, even by his standards.

"Good." As he begins to cut into his salmon, he abruptly jumps up, using his crutch for support. "I almost forgot your favorite, homemade cream of mushroom soup. And I'm not going to lie; it was quite difficult to make." With precision, he ladles the soup into a bowl, adding a sprinkling of chives and parsley, before limping back over to her. "Enjoy," he mumbles, placing the bowl before her, steam wafting up.

She meets his stare evenly. "Not particularly hungry right now. I'd rather we just talk," she asserts. Every fiber of her being brims with emotion, though she miraculously maintains her poise. Typically, standing her ground feels like a struggle, but today, she's too close to the flames. One wrong move, one careless word, and she'll be burned. "I brought you back something."

Curiously, Richie watches as she retrieves the ayahuasca from her bag, placing it on the table. "What is that?" he asks, taking another mouthful of salmon.

"Ayahuasca. I experienced it last night. It's transformative, really. We could try it together?"

Richie dismisses her with a shake of his head. "No interest. Not into that stuff. I like being in control of my own body. And can you please try the soup?" He gestures pointedly with his knife toward the steaming bowl. Olive realizes she might need to provoke Richie a bit to get him on board. She stands up abruptly and starts to move away.

"Heading somewhere?" he questions.

She turns around, smirking. "Colin wasn't afraid to try it with me. Understandable if it intimidates you. I'll be back after I freshen up; it was a long car ride, and we both got a little sweaty." She's aware that she has effectively poked the bear when Richie's fork clatters against the hardwood floor.

"You can't keep acting erratically. This is why you need medication. Look at this dinner, and you're throwing it back in my face. Just try the damn soup."

Traditionally, Richie's voice would have caused her to withdraw, to retreat within herself like a turtle recoiling into its shell. But tonight, she moves towards him with the precision and intent of a lioness. She positions herself on his lap, confiscates his wine, and indulges in a generous sip. It's been seven years since she's let a drop of alcohol pass her lips. Richie's face initially registers anger, but it quickly morphs into a look of fascination as intrigue flares in his eyes.

"You want me to taste your soup?" she whispers, feeling his nods. Leaning down, she kisses him, biting his lip gently. "You want forgiveness?" she questions further.

He swallows hard and nods once more.

"Then try the ayahuasca."

Richie pauses for a moment, as if savoring the gentle illumination of the sunset that frames Olive's face. "Fine. I actually just read a new medical report on the benefits of *some* alternative medicines. However, I want it known that I'm a licensed doctor choosing to take this. No one tells me what to do," he asserts, pointing his finger at her before reluctantly reaching for the bottle.

Olive prepares the brew, handing it to him. He chugs it down, grimacing. "That tastes vile," he grumbles, reaching for a swig of water.

"It does wonders for the soul," she counters, obliging him with a spoonful of the still-too-hot soup. The heat singes her mouth, forcing her to spit a portion into her water glass for relief.

"Good soup," she remarks, though feeling unsure of what to expect next. Despite their continued small talk and her prodding at the overdone salmon, Richie seems unaffected by the ayahuasca. *He's resistant*, she thinks. Excusing herself, she heads to the bathroom. When she returns, Richie's demeanor has drastically shifted; his face is contorted in evident distress.

"Are you okay?"

"No, I feel different. You poison me with that stuff or something? My throat's burning and my head feels like it's being split open," Richie rasps out, clutching the back of his head.

"It's getting the spiritual toxins out. Why don't we sit in the basement? The calmer environment might help." She extends her hand, trying to guide him, knowing this is part of the process.

They descend into the cool sanctuary of the basement. Olive unfurls her yoga mat, gently settling Richie down onto it. "What's next?" he mutters, discomfort evident in his eyes.

"Do you feel like you might throw up?"

"No, just … woozy." He reclines, letting his eyelids fall.

"That's it, just relax and inhale," she directs him, invoking her own inner shaman.

Olive's focus shifts to the sliding glass doors of the walkout basement. Beyond them, the night is dark, illuminated sporadically by neighbors setting off fireworks over the lake. Her attention is then drawn to the long-neglected piano in the corner, its protective white sheet discarded on the ground. It's been ages since her fingers have caressed its keys. She feels drawn to it, taking a step in its direction, but is immediately yanked back, losing her balance.

"What did you make me drink?!" Richie's grip is vice-like on her arm.

"Let go! Stop fighting it. It's medicine." She pushes his grip away and stumbles a few steps back.

"Screw this. I'm getting some hydrogen peroxide. I'll puke this shit back up." Richie pushes himself up, intent on getting to the stairs. Olive, realizing the urgency of the situation, lunges for her bag that lies near the stairway, extracting Kate's folder and thrusting it towards Richie. It's now or never.

"What the hell is this?" He thumbs through it, scanning the contents. His face blanches as he reaches the last email. He discards the folder as if it burned him.

"Why don't you tell me about our daughter's last few months, Richie?" Although she feels small as she stands in front of him and the stairway leading back upstairs, she stands her ground, determination radiating from her. In the dim light of the basement, Richie's eyes appear almost predatory.

"I'm not doing this. I'm not reliving the past. Move!" he growls.

"Not until you tell me. You say you want to fix our marriage? Tell me the truth."

She crosses her arms, standing defiantly, daring him to push by her.

Richie's voice drops an octave. "The truth would haunt you. Is that what you want?"

Olive, without wavering, ascends a step, bringing them eye to eye. "That's exactly what I want."

"Fine. Fuck it." Richie's pacing quickens, sweat dotting his forehead, his arms quivering. His pale face contrasts starkly with the dark basement, giving him an almost ghostly appearance. "Her condition was worsening. She didn't handle the last few rounds well. I know you can read that shit. You're smart." Richie winces, as if begrudgingly admitting her intellect harms him. "I was going to suggest halting the project. Or at least requesting an extension, but then ..."

"Then our daughter conveniently and mysteriously drowns one month before the presentation," Olive interjects, her voice dripping with skepticism.

His façade is rapidly disintegrating like a sandcastle overwhelmed by high tide.

"You dare insinuate I had a hand in it? That I wanted that?" Richie advances, his face mere inches from hers. They stand in a tense face-off, Richie's eyes eventually shutting as the weight of the situation and the ayahuasca bear down on him. His breaths become labored as he presses his palms against his forehead. He begins to mumble to himself, as if in a trance.

"No. It wasn't like that, Terrance."

Olive surveys her surroundings, perplexed. He appears tortured, as if undergoing a visible exorcism, if such a thing exists. He's having similar visions to the ones she experienced of that night from taking the ayahuasca.

"Terrance, stop. Let her go! I'm not giving CPR to someone

who's going to be dead in six weeks."

Olive, reacting instinctively, pushes Richie, disrupting his trance. She senses her blood retreating from her limbs, making her feel faint as anger surges to the forefront of her being—fury replacing her confusion.

"You denied our daughter CPR?" Olive's voice trembles with anger, her pulse elevating. Not only was she subject to Richie's manipulation, but she had also exposed her children to his toxicity. How ironic and appropriate that Richie was the one who cured cancer but also could cause such pain and suffering. What once seemed like a mere twist of fate, or an act of God, was clear as day, a calculated choice made by one bad soul.

Richie, disoriented, narrows his grey eyes at Olive. "You can't fathom the pressure I was under. I didn't want to watch her suffer again. She was *my* daughter."

"She was also mine!" Olive exclaims, her hands clasping the top of her head. "So you played the hero, the savior, pretending to rescue her? Not just once, but twice!" Her voice elevates, extenuating her agony. Her mind replays Dr. Eisenberg's words when he told her the story of the Oakland County child killer. "It's never a boogeyman. It's always someone you know."

Richie's glare intensifies, emanating a sort of intoxicated wrath. His vision validates what she had already internally suspected. He had extinguished a part of her before her time; he stole something that wasn't his to steal. He was a false God. He is also inescapable.

"I … I didn't mean for you to take *his* drink," Richie says. "Maybe if you didn't drink it, you would have watched her better."

His drink. A spiked drink meant for someone else by *her* own husband. A drink that rendered her useless. A desire to wound him as he had wounded her takes over.

"Colin is not only a better man than you, but a better lover too."

He lunges for her as she flees up the stairs. She secures herself within the bathroom, firmly locking the door behind her. There is no planned course of action, only adrenaline and primal instinct fueling her. For a split second, she considers fleeing the house entirely, vanishing into the night. But she doesn't. Maybe it's panic. Maybe defiance. Maybe the deep, cold truth is that if she leaves now, Richie wins.

Footsteps hammer up the stairs. Olive holds her breath as he passes, heavy and fast, before veering into his den. A sinking feeling grips her when the distinct sound of the safe's door indicates it's being opened. Is he fetching a weapon? The possibility freezes her in place, like a deer caught in headlights. Tears threaten to spill.

In moments, Richie has forced the bathroom door open. His arm sling loosened a bit, he grips her and drags her into the living room, pushing her to her knees. The cold, hard barrel of a .44 magnum revolver is pressed against her forehead. Olive recognizes the weapon as an inheritance from Richie's father.

She remains paralyzed, terror anchoring her in place as the demons within Richie are unleashed. But she also doesn't beg. Sometimes, silence is the most powerful response. The memories and thoughts of her daughter are weapons more potent than the gun itself. When she lifts her eyes to his, she sees his shame and profound guilt and suffering laid bare. His true self—mask off.

"Go ahead. But a .44 magnum is one of the loudest guns you could have chosen. Not very discreet if you're planning to murder your wife on the exact anniversary of our daughter's death at the very same location. Quite the coincidence." Olive's voice is firm.

Richie's face twists. Olive's reference to preserving appearances is a sharp reminder of his obsession with his reputation. His eyes dart to the den.

"Your other options aren't any quieter, Richie. Shotguns, a Desert Eagle—they'll echo across the lake." She hopes that under his current influence, he won't realize that it's the Fourth of July and fireworks are about to go off, which would muffle the sound of the gunshots. And if she learned one thing from her father, it was about guns. It might not be the typical father-daughter bonding, but in Olive's case, it could be her salvation tonight.

Richie's eyes depict a storm of emotions as he winces in pain, the gun lowering slightly. He seems to grapple with his next move. Olive remains still, her composure and spirit unbroken. He paces to and fro, then his observation locks onto something through the back window. A wild, desperate look infiltrates his features, and he bolts towards the lake, firearm still clutched in his good hand. Olive observes every move, her heart lodged in her throat, as Richie stumbles down the deck, then the hill without his crutches—resonant of both Terrance's and her own painful descent from years ago. He regains his footing, mounts the boat, and whisks away into the lake's embrace. Given Duck Lake's confined dimensions, she ponders where he could be venturing to.

With nerves still frayed, Olive cautiously moves towards the kitchen. Instead of reaching for her lifeline—the cellphone—she chooses a dinner roll and takes a bite, seeking a fragment of normalcy in the chaos. In her current state, the idea of summoning help doesn't even cross through her mind as she moves to the deck and drops herself into a patio chair beside the Jacuzzi. Across the way, Colin's house glows softly. She spots him through the screened-in porch, watching the fireworks with Lucy. The sky erupts again in a cascade of noise and color. Olive turns just as Colin rises and catches her gaze. She lifts a hand to signal she's okay. He gives a brief nod, then turns back to his daughter—both returning to their small pocket of calm amid the chaos.

CHAPTER 43
RICHIE

TUESDAY 9 P.M.
JULY 4, 2023

Adrift on Duck Lake, I sway like a discarded object. Overhead, fireworks erupt, each burst echoing the tumult within me, while a persistent dull pain gnaws at my foot and shoulder.

What secrets had I laid bare to Mr. Conch, Olive, or even to the recesses of my own mind? The distinction between right and wrong in my head isn't black and white or clear-cut; it dwells in the shadows, reminiscent of twilight on the lake.

I thought that, tonight, I'd finally be able to restore the proper dynamics of our marriage. But then Olive offered that tainted burning drink, which in turn forced me to confront my cruelest memories. My defenses shattered, I had to relive the night I've suppressed for seven years.

I remember Colin shoving me against the side of my own home. He had spotted Julie and me together. Terrance came to my rescue. I then spotted Lulu down by the dock and figured out that Kate must have trailed her down to the waterside. I then remember Terrance standing in front of me, holding Kate on the beach. He had stumbled upon her, adrift near Colin's dock, after relieving himself by the willow tree. He pulled her to the shoreline, pleading with me to perform CPR—she still had a weak pulse. At that moment, I pondered if this situation was the best outcome for Kate and me. I had to consider the humane course of action—whether to revive her to a life of agony and an inevitable death within a few short months.

Terrance's following words resonated within me, reverberating through every fiber—"Salvation never comes without a cost to someone." To this day, I still don't know how much of that night Terrance remembered or how much he'd buried. He never brought it up again. Maybe that's why I kept writing him those prescriptions for all those years, to stay on his good side.

For me, the following nights after her death were sleepless, filled with the soft strains of her poached lullabies. The nocturnal breeze carried the haunting whispers, the tunes weaving tales of forsaken aspirations and dreams. Was I a thief, a plunderer of hopes? Or was I her savior, her Superman—saving her from suffering any further?

On the boat, I survey the vastness of my current surroundings. The stillness is unnerving; the dark, flat water seems to threaten to consume me. In the distance, I can distinguish a few boats, fireworks intermittently illuminating the night, marking what feels like my personal day of liberation. I see my house, my castle, seemingly disintegrating. The darkness is overwhelming. It's eager to swallow every glint of light. In the pale glow of the moon, I confront my true reflection. It's as if the surface of the water has become a mirror, and my reflection is all too familiar: it's my father staring back at me. In being somewhat responsible for causing the death of my own child, I had transformed into the entity I dreaded the most, *him.* The cruel irony: children don't grow to embody your expectations; they grow to mirror who you are. And mirrors—when placed face to face—don't shatter. They echo endlessly, multiplying every flaw, every truth.

Does that mean Landon will become a reflection of me, destined to inherit my flaws and scars? "Heal the boy and the man will appear." This phrase resonates profoundly with me, especially in my profession as a doctor.

But what if the man is not someone you want to be? What if Colin was right last Christmas when he shouted that I treat people like objects—to be used, experimented on, and manipulated for my own amusement?

A movement in the corner of the boat interrupts my reverie, revealing a sight I detest. A damn raccoon. Here, on my boat, in the middle of Duck Lake. It's rummaging through a discarded bag of trash from the boys' wakeboarding festivities a few days ago—evidence of the carelessness of Landon.

Given the holiday festivities, the raccoons are likely prowling everywhere like predators beneath the gleaming full moon, desperate for scraps. I level my gun at the damn thing, mimicking the actions of my father years ago. It bares its teeth, intent on attacking, and then it lunges at me. Before my finger can squeeze the trigger, its sharp claws latch onto my shoulder sling. It dangles there, emitting sharp hisses. It's just a juvenile, and I attempt to shake it off. Where could its mother be?

An agonizing snap resonates through my intact foot, sending a searing pain up my leg, causing it to buckle as I totter towards the rim of the boat. I cast a glance below, meeting the glowing, irate eyes of the mother raccoon. The boat sways due to an unexpected wave and, in the blink of an eye, my firearm discharges.

The sound of the gunshot is deafening, rippling through every fiber of my being as I submerge into the midnight blue water. My head burns as I thrash in the water; the revelation then strikes that if I die, it's likely to be construed as a suicide. Doctor Everly, no doubt, will confirm the threats I professed the day prior.

I perceive no actual pain as I attempt to scream for help, my voice likely lost, a mere whisper amidst the symphony of exploding fireworks. There's nothing to cling to as I descend, my cast pulling me like a heavy anchor, the sling tightening around my neck like a noose. For a fleeting moment, there's a brief illusion, almost as if unseen hands are yanking me further, deeper.

They say clarity's in death. I see that now. Perhaps I sought to validate myself in the eyes of others, like my father, rather than validating myself for my own sake. I could have proven him wrong by merely being a good person—to my wife and children.

I didn't embark on this journey with the intent to harm anyone, but that's the tricky thing about intentions: they often get twisted. I was too proud, and pride is one of the seven deadly sins. So is greed. I never cherished moderation or what I had until I was submerged in excess.

Drowning is deceivingly quiet from the outside, as it takes hold of you swiftly and gradually drags you into the darkening depths of the abyss. But on the inside, it's chaos. My chest seizes, lungs locking up, a raw panic clawing its way up my throat. I kick, my body desperate to find the surface, to trade water for breath. But it's gone. I've sunk too deep—my nose floods. I gag, cough, and swallow nothing but cold. The water scorches as it fills me, burning down my throat like acid. My limbs convulse, instinct overriding reason. I can't see. Can't think. I suck in again—reflex, not choice—and fire explodes in my chest. Then … the fight fades. My arms drift beside me like they belong to someone else. The burn recedes. My thoughts come untethered, floating just out of reach.

It's peaceful now.

CHAPTER 44

TUESDAY 9 P.M.
JULY 4, 2023

Olive had gone back to the kitchen, seizing the remainder of Richie's wine along with another dinner roll, before making her way down to the dock. She observes the boat's steadfast presence in the heart of the lake, her curiosity piqued as to how this will play out. As of now, she feels vindicated in how she extracted the whole truth from Richie through her unconventional approach.

There are only a handful of other boats on the water, spread far apart, their occupants immersed in the aerial spectacle of fireworks. She reasons that the low attendance may be due to the primary fireworks show on the lake having been held on July first this summer. Most of her neighbors probably headed up north, preferring a different scene.

She sits in solitude, feet immersed in the water, a proverb pulsing in her mind. Perhaps Rita or Laura's influence had finally permeated her thoughts, that *pride comes before the fall.* Then, in the distance, a distinctive sound pierces the celebratory cacophony of fireworks—that of a .44 magnum firing. The sound is likely lost to most over the reverberation of the explosions, but not to Olive. She lifts the wine to her lips, taking a long, deliberate sip, and immediate relief flows through her. She realizes this was the best-case scenario for her and Richie. A newfound light permeates her being, as if balance has been restored to her spirit.

Now comes the process of healing, of slowly reclaiming the lost morsels of herself. She didn't lose the war over her soul.

In the distance, rumblings signal the imminent arrival of another summer tempest. Many choose to merely bide their time, waiting for the storm to pass, but Olive has gained the understanding that life isn't about avoiding hardship or storms. It's about pushing through, gaining understanding, and reemerging from the other side stronger, more fortified. The storm's eye is often the most serene part, offering a moment for introspection and growth.

She glances downward to find Lulu and two other golden ducklings fluttering their tiny tails. Lulu appears exhausted, a feeling Olive knows well. She tears a piece of her dinner roll, crumbling it for the little family to savor. Then, submerging the remainder of the roll in the wine, she takes a bite—her unique rendition of communion—a symbol of rejuvenation.

She observes as a body gradually drifts away from the back of her lavish boat. For an instant, she believes she perceives another splash, reminiscent of a raccoon with glowing eyes adjacent to Richie's body, but she's well acquainted with her mind's deceptive antics. She depletes her wine, then reenters her home through the walkout basement door, approaching the cherished piano. The sole legacy from her parents. Her fingers touch the keys, a smile unfolding on her lips as memories of her daughter and mother warm her heart. She then muses on the enduring nature of grief. It never entirely dissipates, but heaves more like fluctuating waves. Some waves are overwhelming, seemingly ready to drag you into profound depths, while others are merely subtle ripples, barely whispering before they drift away. Some require a dedicated moment of contemplation. Yet, each one is a reminder of love that once was, a love that continues to persist.

A recurring glimmer of fluctuating red lights begins to bathe the basement in familiar hues; it's either the sparkle of fireworks or the steady glow of police cars. Olive's fingers begin to dance over the keys, weaving a tale of two tunes, starting with the playful notes of "Down by the Bay" and effortlessly shifting into "Heart and Soul." A tune typically performed by a pair, she manages it herself seamlessly as a feeling of joy sneaks in amongst the muddled melancholy —she allows it.

Should anyone have proclaimed her a figure of resilience and strength just a few days prior, she would have dismissed it with a laugh, one that she could almost hear being shared with her father. Surely, she wasn't "Ford tough" or built with grit and might. But now, she sees it clearly: the strength within her, a quiet force that has been there all along, waiting to be recognized.

As her fingers dance along the keys, she contemplates whether it is an inevitable reality that those burdened with pain end up inflicting it upon others. No, she would like to think that while some might succumb to this relentless spiral, others manage to transcend it. It's not our wounds that dictate our actions but how we react to them. Every soul on this earth has experienced pain, and from this, some propagate it, but others choose to heal, to love, to value, and to embrace others with kindness.

She concludes the song, letting the last resonant note fill the air, lingering in the tranquil dimness of the basement. Her eyes soften on the lake beyond, the place that has caused her so much pain and so much joy. It's peaceful now.

a laugh, one that she could almost hear being shared with her father. Surely, she wasn't "Ford tough" or built with grit and might. But now, she sees it clearly: the strength within her, a quiet force that has been there all along, waiting to be recognized.

As her fingers dance along the keys, she contemplates whether it is an inevitable reality that those burdened with pain end up inflicting it upon others. No, she would like to think that while some might succumb to this relentless spiral, others manage to transcend it. It's not our wounds that dictate our actions but how we react to them. Every soul on this earth has experienced pain, and from this, some propagate it, but others choose to heal, to love, to value, and to embrace others with kindness.

She concludes the song, letting the last resonant note fill the air, lingering in the tranquil dimness of the basement. Her eyes soften on the lake beyond, the place that has caused her so much pain and so much joy. It's peaceful now.

EPILOGUE

SATURDAY 3 P.M.
JULY 22, 2023

"Forgive me, father, for I have sinned." I can't help but wonder if he can see my eyes through the little slots in the old-school confession box. People tend to get stuck on my eyes, and I've been to enough Masses here that he'd surely recognize them. Father Paul sits there in silence on the other side of the screen, waiting for me to continue.

"It's been seven years since my last confession." Since I last spilled my guts in one of these boxes, I think to myself. My mind flashes back to the day I found Kate by the dock, looking like a sleeping fairy-tale princess. Everyone kept saying it wasn't anyone's fault, but deep down in the pit of my stomach, I knew it was mine. I was the one who didn't run for help. I was the one who pushed her back in. But I was just a kid then. And I didn't see myself as a selfish person, making a selfish choice. Not that anyone bothered to ask. No one ever really asks "why," except children.

Kids, they're always popping up with the "why" question, even when it's the least relevant question for survival. Parents must lose their minds over the number of "whys" kids can drop in one day. But what parents don't understand is that unquestioned obedience isn't a sign of goodness. Questioning "why" is a sign of intelligence. We need our whys—we need to know why we're here. Our "why" is essential. For me, my "why" was my mom. And if it's a mother's job to bring up a baby to be a boy, it's on the father to guide a boy into being a man. Or so I was taught.

"Continue, my child," coughs Father Paul, hacking into his handkerchief. Up until now, I was starting to think the old guy was snoozing through my confession.

I roll into the usual roster of sins—dirty thoughts, dropping the F-bomb too often, the standard stuff. I stare at Father Paul's blue eyes through the little slats as I continue my rambling. I wonder if he's always been good and holy, or if he was a disobedient kid and that led him here, somehow. It's odd to envision that a priest was once a child, too.

A quote by Alden Nowlan begins bouncing around in my head. I love a good read and have a photographic memory. It went something like this: the moment a kid sees the cracks in the adults around him, he grows up a little. When he stops blaming them, he becomes one. And when he stops blaming himself, that's when wisdom begins. I'm standing at the threshold, ready to step into wisdom, ready to let go of the guilt for what I did to Kate. It was immediately after my own father's funeral that I realized I needed to see Father Paul. I had to unburden myself and get this off my chest. I could never admit any of this to Dr. Everly back in the day; I'm not stupid. Still, her grieving tactics did help me move on since then.

"I failed someone back when I was just a kid, and they died because of it," I blurt out to Father Paul, my final sin. Then it's just silence. Just a thick, heavy silence. Since my dad died, I've been trying to get used to that silence, trying to live with it. I had to face up to my own screwed-up moral compass, to deal with it before I end up exactly like him: the same doom. And like my favorite animals, amphibians, their ability to survive and thrive depends on their ability to adapt to an ever-changing external environment. My environment has changed, as I'm now officially fatherless.

Though to me, my old man was gone long before he actually kicked the bucket. Sometimes, when something is already dead, you have to amputate it from your life … especially when all it does is cause you pain. I always felt like more of a bloodstain he couldn't bleach off his pristine doctor's coat than a son.

We used to have this thing—watching sci-fi movies together,

especially Star Wars. I always saw him as the wise guide, the Obi-Wan to my Luke. But that fantasy shattered fast. It turns out he was more like the Emperor pulling the strings behind the curtain, or maybe I was the misled Anakin. It's ironic how those stories preach about light and dark, good and evil, yet both sides seem equally rigid, caught up in their own sense of righteousness—no room for anything in between.

Life, however, offers no clear-cut absolute platforms. It's not some epic battle of good versus evil. We all navigate the same dark waters, sometimes crossing lines we shouldn't. But, hey, maybe my perspective's a bit skewed 'cause anyone can justify pretty much anything as long as it sits right in their own moral grey area.

Father Paul appears to have dozed off, and I can see his eyes are shut. A moist hack then comes shooting out. I'm not sure if I should wake him or offer him some hot Vernors. I'll give him a minute.

But, as I said, everyone carries their own interpretation of the truth, one where they emerge as the hero. I wanted to be that for my mom. When I overheard my dad whispering on the phone in his office with some woman, a Linda or a Lisa, I got a glimpse of the harsh, grim reality of Kate's condition. That's when I understood. My dad's priorities were not with Kate but with the cure. His obsession lay with the looming presentation date. Even at the age of ten, I could see the devastating toll my sister's fluctuating yo-yo-like condition was taking on my mother. Most of her attention and care went to my sister at that point.

Something had to give. It all started with Joey. Unbeknownst to him, he set things in motion. He pointed me to where he had left her, told me that she was hurt, while Dad was preoccupied with another woman, who wasn't my mother, and Hannah was keeping watchful eyes on them. Then Joey left with his family.

I found myself by the dock, wearing Joey's green boots he had left behind, to keep my feet dry and free of sand. I peered down at her, my emotions a swirl of love and resentment. It seemed Joey had pushed her from the dock, and she had landed on the large rocks that served as the seabed for the wakeboard boats below. I jumped down beside her, hesitating, unsure if she was even alive. In hindsight, she was probably unconscious, but who can really know? Then, I made the decision—I cast her tiny body into the lakebed. All those years in Catholic school had been pretty clear about what was right and wrong. But does a kid, any kid, really get how final, how irreversible death is, and the ripples it sends? But I did it for her. No one wants to see someone else suffer. When my mom told me she saw Kate—before anyone else did—I was terrified she knew it was me who pushed her in. That fear has always lingered in the back of my mind. But since my father's recent passing, I see her starting to live again. She doesn't place the blame on herself anymore, or even on me; it's him she casts as responsible.

"Jesus said, 'Father, forgive them; for they do not know what they are doing.'"

I shift slightly at Father Paul's words as he comes to. I suspect his advanced age might have confused him, having him believe he is leading a Mass service.

"Okay." My response flows more in the form of a question than an acknowledgement.

Images flare in my mind, echoes of my dad uttering that he couldn't resuscitate Kate. It was, ironically, one thing he managed to do correctly. My response had been a simple "okay," to which he just stared at me, perhaps expecting more. Looking back, I suspect it was intentional; he didn't honestly want to attempt to resuscitate her.

"Has there been any other incident of such nature, my child?" he prods, his voice threading the silence.

I'm seized by thoughts of Terrance now, guilt quickly coloring my feelings. He had posed a threat, attempting to separate me from Hannah after he delved into the realm of hypnosis. He had discovered that Hannah and I had rekindled our relationship, leading him to confront me with allegations about Kate, claims he must have extracted through his hypnosis sessions. I also felt like someone was watching me that night I submerged Kate. It wasn't my mother; it was Terrance. He instructed me to steer clear of his daughter. I suggested a meetup, a man-to-man conversation, which he agreed to. Once at his home, I consented reluctantly to keep my distance from his daughter. When our paths diverged that evening, he was living, breathing—I would lay my hand on the holy Bible and swear to it.

The only other soul I crossed paths with that night was Mr. Schmidt, roaming doorstep to doorstep, clipboard in hand, assembling signatures for his recurrent petition against wakeboard boats. There was something odd about it, given that Harold Schmidt didn't reside in the neighborhood anymore, not since Mrs. Schmidt threw him out. He always seemed like a nice guy, but how well do we really know our neighbors? But speculating malice from Mr. Schmidt towards Terrance seems far-fetched. Discussing it would only ensnare me in a web of self-incrimination and unwarranted complications.

"No, nothing like that," I reply quietly.

Father Paul releases another phlegm-filled cough. I brace myself, anticipating a request for a monetary offering as atonement, but, surprisingly, it doesn't come. Instead, he assures me that repentance will lead me to forgiveness.

"And until you have fulfilled your penance through seven Hail Marys and an act of service to others, absolution remains pending," he concludes, leaving the compact, wood-enclosed space, I assume, to take a nap.

Penance. To right my wrong, a path to correct my misdeeds. I remain engulfed in the ensuing silence. A shade of relief might have brushed my soul for a moment, but I think of what my father and I did ... how the consequences can't be washed away with any amount of prayer. The question isn't "why" anymore; it's "who." Who is the true villain in this narrative? Because every one of us is capable of good, but also capable of some evil. That duality defines human nature, and it's as inescapable as the shadows that follow us.

ACKNOWLEDGMENTS

This story is deeply personal to me. I hope anyone reading it connects with someone struggling with addiction—it truly holds no bias over who it affects or the people it touches. And as for grief, I think it's something that connects us all as human beings. When I started writing this book, I was going through a hard time with my health. My autoimmune conditions had flared, and I wasn't feeling my best. Writing became my outlet, my medicine, really. Like Olive, I was searching for any kind of healing. Somewhere in that space, Objects in Lakes was born.

Writing a book starts as a quiet, lonely, lovely thing. It's just you and a blank page, or a blinking cursor, and a head full of scenes you're trying to catch before they disappear. But once that first draft is done, it's no longer just yours. You have to let other people in. People you trust to read those early words you think are brilliant (but are probably pretty average).

To both my sister-in-laws, Lindsay and Keely: thank you for reading one of the very first drafts (back when only one person was involved in Kate's drowning, not three!) and for encouraging me to keep going.

To Jenna and Karen: you were the next to read it, and I'll never forget how you both said you could see Michigan so clearly. You've told me you still think about this story all the time, and that means the world to me. You two will forever be my go-to, first-round beta readers and hype girl queens.

A huge thank-you to Alex Brown for taking a chance on a debut author and bringing Objects in Lakes into the real (publishing) world, and to Tina Beier for editing it so thoughtfully and making it even better. Alex, thank you for seeing the vision of this book from the very beginning—for understanding its threads of addiction, grief, and healing, and recognizing how important (and sometimes heavy) stories like this are to tell. And thank you, too, for knowing exactly when to switch gears and debrief the latest Real Housewives scandal, proof that balance is everything.

To Abby Sharp: thank you for being on my team. I could not have done this process without your grace and guidance. You truly are such a lovely person.

To my wonderful parents: thank you for always encouraging my creativity, even when it looked like making Blair Witch Project-style movies in the woods. Because of you both, I've never doubted my worth or that I'm loved.

To my brother, Eric: thank you for designing the beautiful cover of this novel and for being my lifelong creative partner and best friend.

To my mother-in-law: the avid reader who told me this book ruined other mysteries for her, I can't think of a better compliment.

To my father-in-law: your beautiful lake is where this story was born. To me, Sherwood Lake will always be the true Duck Lake.

To my husband, Kevin: for supporting me through all the ups and downs of being a creative person. For the middle-of-the-night wakeups when I had a "good idea." For knowing the twenty-year-old version of me and growing with me into the thirty-eight-year-old version. Thank you for building this beautiful life with me, and for being the most amazing partner and father to our two incredible children.

And to the readers: thank you for spending time in this world, for sitting with these characters through their moments of loss and hope. Even if you're not from the Midwest, I hope you still felt that Michigan vibe—the stillness of the water, the ache of distance, the beauty tucked inside the quiet. Stories, like lakes, hold reflections of who we are and what we've endured. If this one found you at the right time, I'm grateful.

May its ripples stay with you.

ABOUT THE AUTHOR

Rachael Ramas is an American author, producer, and Michigan native who writes gripping thrillers rooted in emotional truth and moral complexity. A member of Mystery Writers of America and International Thriller Writers, she co-owns a law firm with her husband in Boca Raton, Florida, where the legal world offers endless story inspiration. Living with a rare autoimmune disease and partial hearing loss, Ramas advocates for authentic disability representation in literature. *Objects in Lakes* is her debut novel. Her sophmore novel, *Meanwhile in Florida,* is releasing Spring 2027.

DISCUSSION QUESTIONS

AUTHOR'S NOTE:

When I wrote *Objects in Lakes*, I wanted to explore how grief distorts memory, how love can twist into obsession, and how a seemingly peaceful place can hide unimaginable secrets. Olive's search for truth is messy, painful, and deeply human, and so are the people around her. Every character in Duck Lake carries guilt, shame, and a story they're afraid to tell. I hope these questions spark reflection and honest discussion about the choices we make ... and the ones that haunt us.

— Rachael Ramas

1. Olive's life is shaped by the loss of her daughter. How does her grief influence her perception of the truth? Can grief distort memory or clarify it?

2. How do Olive and Richie's coping mechanisms differ, and what do they reveal about the nature of shared versus solitary grief?

3. Do you think Olive's search for the truth is driven by love, guilt, obsession, or something else?

4. When Olive begins to suspect that her daughter's death wasn't an accident, what changes in her, emotionally and morally?

5. Addiction touches several characters in different ways. Who do you think is most affected, and how does it shape their choices?

6. Trauma can leave both emotional and physical scars. How does Olive's body carry her pain throughout the story?

7. Olive steps far outside her comfort zone, she even turns to psychedelics in the woods in her desperate search for answers. How far would you go to uncover the truth about a loved one's death?

8. All the characters in Objects in Lakes are flawed, their moral compasses slightly skewed. How does this moral grayness make the story more believable—or more unsettling?

9. Did the final revelation change how you viewed the earlier chapters, and why do you think Landon chose to confess only at the very end of the novel?

10. Who do you believe bears the greatest responsibility for Kate's death: Richie, Landon, or JJ? Why?

11. What role does the town itself play in keeping the truth hidden? Could the tragedy have been prevented if people had spoken up sooner?

12. In Duck Lake, the truth never stays buried. "Secrets always have a way of resurfacing." What does that line mean to you by the end of the story?

SNEAK PEEK OF RACHAEL'S

MEANWHILE IN FLORIDA

RELEASING SPRING 2027

PROLOGUE

The last thing I think about as I lie here dying is flamingos. It's not what I expected. I expected my life to flash before my eyes. And it's not because I'm lying on the hard travertine pool deck staring up at an inflatable pool toy shaped like a flamingo bobbing towards me. No, it's because I imagine myself as one. My once white shirt soaks up my blood, taking on the lurid pink hue of those fluorescent pool lights.

I think of how terrible I'll look when somebody stumbles upon my body in the light of the morning sun. Surely, I'll look as drained as I feel—worn out from motherhood and from the tireless cycle of thoughts. Perhaps the mortician can soften the edges, make me look nicer. Like a loving mom, doting wife, kind friend. Is it superficial to think about how your body will look to others when you're dead? At least my hair will look good. I just washed and blew it out.

The poor, tormented pool toy now edges nearer, half deflated. Is it odd that I wish I could inflate it a little before my demise? Possibly tidy up my house before the police and medics arrive? Maybe this is why I'm so exhausted. My mother once told me that flamingos are so tired after they give birth that they lose their vibrant pink color. They turn ghostly white, like my own pallor must look, as I bleed out. But, as flamingos navigate the chaos of raising their young and feeding on extra pink shrimp, they eventually recover their color. And I was slowly getting my vibrancy back the day I met *her.* Until betrayal left its sharp sting in my belly. The irony in all of this is that the words that preceded the betrayal sliced deeper than any blade could.

My mother also used to say, "'No' is a complete sentence."

If only I hadn't wanted a friend so badly. If only I had refused the original plan that led to my own brutal undoing.

I hear frogs and other nocturnal amphibians; their sounds carry heavily in the Florida humidity. Whispers of a reassuring, "Mommy's okay" linger. But that can't be? Surely, I'm not okay. I have a kitchen knife lodged in my stomach—the one that filets fish, to be exact. Perks of being a Floridian.

The inflatable flamingo drifts nearer, its movements taunting, caught in the whims of the breeze, a mockery of my predicament. The pool lights still illuminate the palm branches, and the water grows neon blue now. Florida is full of bodies of water. Those very waters also contain actual bodies. I wonder if mine will end up in one. Footsteps approach. They must be back to finish the job.

Everyone flocks to Florida to escape their previous lives. But once you're here, there's nowhere left to run, no escape from regret and past misdeeds.

LOOKING TO ADD TO YOUR TBR?

CHECK OUT MORE OF RISING ACTION'S UPCOMING THRILLERS!

Beylynn never meant to join a cult—at least not the kind without incense or scripture. This one comes wrapped in pastel branding, protein shakes, and the promise of a Skinny, Happy Life™. As the rising star of the SHL Lifestyle MLM, she's cashing in while teaching other women that joy comes with a shrinking number on the scale.

But everything changes when Beylynn vanishes during an exclusive incentive trip.

Her disappearance is the company's worst nightmare: their glossy, influencer "boss babe" has either been murdered… or she's finally had enough and escaped. Either way, it's a PR disaster waiting to explode.

Behind the filtered photos and motivational mantras lies a world steeped in obsession—social media manipulation, dangerous ambition, illicit affairs, and money powerful enough to make people kill. SHL isn't a sisterhood; it's a cult built on control.

And if Beylynn wants to survive, she'll have to find a way out before the perfect life she sold becomes the one that destroys her.

Some love is lost in the fire; some love is forged with flame.

Blooms from the ocotillo cactus make Javelina, Arizona, look like paradise, but Claire Wilson is all too aware of the barbs hidden beneath its beauty. Recently placed in the witness protection program as a cashier at the local market, she looks forward to seeing one man, Armando Vega, whose rugged beard and chiseled muscles could be on display on aisle three.
Emotional attachments aren't an option for her if she wants to return home to her life in New Jersey. When her cover is blown, Claire must stay one step ahead of the people who want her dead. Unsure of whether the demons of her former life have found her, or if a new threat lurks in Claire's recent history, she begs Vega to become her bodyguard.

Medically retired from the Marines, Vega is too busy drowning his mental scars in whisky to babysit Claire, even though he's fascinated with her strength and determination to survive. But then Vega's best friend is framed for murder, and the mystery surrounding Claire Wilson is the key to solving the crime. Once his heart becomes involved, Vega stops at nothing to keep Claire alive

Truth hides where the past refuses to stay buried.

Recently fired and adrift, Charlotte Boyd agrees to oversee renovations on her parents' small-town summer home that holds a tragic past. After discovering an enthralling diary hidden amidst junk the previous owners left behind, Charlotte connects with the author—a troubled teen named Lark Peters who died by suicide at the house sixteen years ago.

When an unsettling incident forces Charlotte to seek refuge at the local pub, regulars, including the police, warn her of Lark's older brother, Darryl, who has become a recluse since Lark's death, and may know more than he's letting on. But Charlotte sees a side of Darryl others don't, being an outsider herself.

In a search to uncover the truth, Charlotte must question those closest to Lark and reconcile her own past trauma. Because if Lark was actually murdered, then whoever is responsible might be lurking in Charlotte's own backyard.

Detective Ryan Boone thought the simple jewelry heist was an open and shut case. That is until he discovers an unknown drug, and this minor crime he was investigating may be tied to a string of seemingly unconnected murders.

Meanwhile, Mel Parker, unscrupulous leader of a less-than-legal high-end escort service, stumbles across the same pills. On top of protecting her "investment," she has her own reasons for attempting to unravel the mystery behind the medication.

Ryan knows someone has the answers he seeks, and Mel can't come forward. To complicate things further, five other women are implicated in the murders despite most having never met.

As the trail turns up as many mysteries as resolutions, Ryan and Mel must discover the twisted connection before someone else ends up dead.